The Cornish Dukes

Born to inherit, destined for love!

Vennor, Eaton, Cassian and Inigo grew up together on the coasts of Cornwall, knowing that one day they would inherit their fathers' weighty titles and the responsibility that comes with being a duke.

When Vennor's father is shockingly murdered, that day comes sooner than expected. All four heirs are forced to acknowledge that their lives are changing. But the one change these powerful men might not be expecting? Love!

Enjoy this tension-filled new quartet by Bronwyn Scott

Read Eaton's story in *The Secrets of Lord Lynford*

Read Cassian's story in *The Passions of Lord Trevethow*

Read Inigo's story in *The Temptations of Lord Tintagel*

Read Vennor's story in *The Confessions of the Duke of Newlyn*

Author Note

Readers, it was so much fun bringing you Vennor's story. His story deals with the masks people wear, both metaphorically and literally, as well as the things we use the masks to hide. I think his story has special relevance in the age of social media, where platforms show an outer glimpse of people's lives but not necessarily the interior. In this book, it's not only Vennor who wears a mask but Marianne and the villain as well. Both Marianne and Vennor struggle with the costs of keeping the mask on as well as the costs of taking the mask off. Will people still accept them if they aren't who people thought they were? Certainly, a timeless issue for us all.

I hope you've enjoyed the Cornish Dukes and each of their journeys to find love.

BRONWYN SCOTT

The Confessions of the Duke of Newlyn

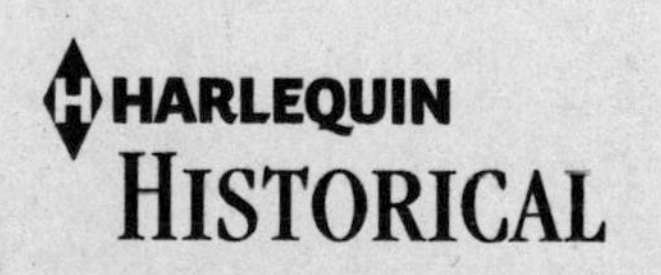

HARLEQUIN®
HISTORICAL™

Recycling programs for this product may not exist in your area.

ISBN-13: 978-1-335-50576-7

The Confessions of the Duke of Newlyn

This edition published by arrangement with Harlequin Books S.A.

For questions and comments about the quality of this book, please contact us at CustomerService@Harlequin.com.

Harlequin Enterprises ULC
22 Adelaide St. West, 40th Floor
Toronto, Ontario M5H 4E3, Canada
www.Harlequin.com

Printed in U.S.A.

Bronwyn Scott is a communications instructor at Pierce College and the proud mother of three wonderful children—one boy and two girls. When she's not teaching or writing, she enjoys playing the piano, traveling—especially to Florence, Italy—and studying history and foreign languages. Readers can stay in touch via Facebook at Facebook.com/bronwynwrites, or on her blog, bronwynswriting.blogspot.com. She loves to hear from readers.

Books by Bronwyn Scott

Harlequin Historical

Scandal at the Midsummer Ball
"The Debutante's Awakening"
Scandal at the Christmas Ball
"Dancing with the Duke's Heir"

The Cornish Dukes

The Secrets of Lord Lynford
The Passions of Lord Trevethow
The Temptations of Lord Tintagel
The Confessions of the Duke of Newlyn

Allied at the Altar

A Marriage Deal with the Viscount
One Night with the Major
Tempted by His Secret Cinderella
Captivated by Her Convenient Husband

Visit the Author Profile page
at Harlequin.com for more titles.

For B, who says I never dedicate any books to her. This one is for you. Just you. And here's your mom's best advice: always be you. Being you is enough. Thanks for helping me get through this book. You were there to do everything I needed when the going got tough on this one and I thought it would break me. I won't forget it. You are incredible. —Love, Mom.

Chapter One

London—May 1826

The Vigilante's work was done for the night. Vennor Penlerick tucked the black silk mask inside his coat pocket the moment he stepped foot into Mayfair. In these environs he wore a different identity—the Duke of Newlyn. It was only out there, in the bustle of common London amid the masses, that he was the Vigilante: a fighter of crime and vice who stood against the evil that roamed dark London streets, preying on the unsuspecting and undeserving. It was out there where he could be a man who stood for those who could not stand for themselves, where he had a calling, something that offered direction for his life.

Perhaps it was for those reasons that it had begun to feel as if the mask was more often wearing him than that he was wearing the mask. These days, he was more Vigilante than he was Newlyn, admittedly by choice, although it came with consequences. The chasm between the two was widening: the Vigilante had a purpose of his own while the Duke had only the inherited purposes left over from his father's life, but none that were completely his own. When he was the Vigilante, he knew what he was about. He could not say the same for being the Duke. Although, he supposed in reality there was little difference between the two despite the chasm. Titles. Masks. Both were designed to obscure the man who bore them. But not the cause. They had that in common.

Vennor turned up the street towards Portland Square and the Newlyn town house, doing his best to hide a slight limp as his leg began to ache from an earlier scuffle, his eyes and ears habitually on alert for potential trouble, but the Mayfair evening was uneventful. It was early yet, by society's standards. Give it a few hours, he thought grimly, and that tone might change. Over the past three years as the Vigilante, he'd learned no place was immune to crime. Originally, when he'd donned the Vigilante's mask it had been to further his efforts to find his parents' killers. In the early days following their deaths, the Duke he had become could order investigations and could throw the weight of his title behind those commands. When those investigations failed, Bow Street and the Watch deciding there was nothing more they could do, it had become clear even a duke's reach had its limitations. But a masked man with no identity did not. The Vigilante could go where dukes dared not tread.

Dukes could certainly not go barging around the

stews and expect to get answers. What they could expect was to be a target. While he doubted anyone would risk killing a peer, a duke in the stews stood out. He was deprived of stealth and concealment. If he stepped a foot into the slums, the criminal underground would know. Anyone he might want to find would flee. But the Vigilante might be discreetly approached, a hint dropped here and there. The Vigilante might even uncover clues of his own overlooked by Bow Street.

Vennor winced as he took the steps leading up to Newlyn House, a shooting pain running up his thigh. The Vigilante had paid for that identity tonight. The Covent Garden bullies who'd been harassing the flower girl must have done more than nick him, after all. Still, it was far better that the bullies turn their attentions on him, a man who could stand up to blades, than a defenceless flower girl who would have no choice but to submit.

His front door opened on cue and Vennor stepped into the well-appointed but austere hall with a grin to the butler. 'Honeycutt, I'm home.'

'I can see that, Your Grace,' Honeycutt's tones were clipped with exacting precision and disapproval. 'You're hurt. Again.' His sharp eyes missed nothing despite his age. Honeycutt had served three generations of Newlyn Dukes and had known him since birth. Vennor had long since stopped trying to hide anything from him.

''Tis nothing but a scratch,' Vennor assured him,

but the injury was beyond disguising as he ascended the steps. 'Nothing a hot bath can't fix.'

Honeycutt followed behind, concern smoothed away by years of practised aplomb as if dukes came home limping every day of the week. 'Very good, Your Grace. Your bath is waiting for you and I've laid out your evening clothes. I'll send for some whisky and bandages, none the less. One can't be too careful with ruffians' blades.'

The whisky Vennor agreed with. 'I don't need bandages.'

Honeycutt would wrap him in cotton wool if left to his own devices.

'Scratches can fester as easily as deep wounds. We can't risk it,' Honeycutt argued with a sternness that bordered on censorious. If the man hadn't served the family for generations, his behaviour would be considered insubordinate. As it was, Vennor knew exactly the risk Honeycutt referred to—the risk of the dukedom expiring before he did. No butler worth his salt wanted to outlive his childless employer.

Honeycutt's concern was not the idle worry of an old man. As long as Vennor remained unmarried and insistent on playing the Vigilante, there was a real possibility he could die without issue. Vennor's grandfather had died at sixty-one and Vennor's father in his fifties, both deaths unanticipated, and neither of them had possessed the luck of siring a bounty of sons. The threat to the succession was legitimate, but it would have to wait until the larger threat was dealt with.

Vennor had no time for romance at present, which was both a blessing and a curse. It wasn't that he didn't want a family. He did. But how could he take on the responsibility of a wife and children while this task weighed on him? There was always next year. Things might be different then. Anything was possible. He'd promised himself he would marry, just as soon as the killers were caught. He knew his duty and he would do it. At least in this way he would not fail his parents, even if he'd failed them in others. 'It *is* just a scratch,' Vennor said again, offering assurance for them both that he was young, invincible and had time.

Vennor reached his room, a haven of warmth and privacy. The tub was set before the fire, steaming in welcome. Ah, this was pure bliss. For a few moments he could be a man, not a mask, not a title. He didn't have to worry about purposes and progeny, matchmaking mamas and elusive murderers. He stripped out of his clothes, already eyeing the evening attire on the bed with distaste. He gingerly lowered himself into the tub, hissing when the hot water met his scratch. He felt like staying in with his bath and his whisky and playing the recluse. He could get away with it. He had made a habit of limiting his social obligations since coming out of mourning. Everyone knew he kept his appearances to a minimum these days. Deciding not to show up would surprise no one.

'Miss Marianne is expecting you at the Fordhams'.' Honeycutt divined the direction of his thoughts. 'Shall I send word you'll have to cancel?' It only *sounded* like a question. Honeycutt's disapproval of such tactics was evident in his tone and Honeycutt was right. Staying in was the coward's way and, whatever else he was, Vennor Penlerick did not consider himself a coward.

Vennor leaned his head back against the copper rim of the tub as Honeycutt put a glass in his hand. He'd have to rejoin society in full force at some point. He couldn't hide behind the excuse of mourning for ever. Best to attend on a night when he had Marianne's company to help him through. 'No, don't cancel. I just need a few minutes.' He closed his eyes. The evening wouldn't be an entire waste if he got to see Marianne.

The Trelevens were old friends from home, near Porth Karrek in Cornwall. Marianne had made her come out the year his parents had been killed and Vennor had always felt illogically guilty for their deaths having put a blight on her first Season. He'd made up for it during her second Season, though, as soon as he'd been decently able to set aside mourning. He'd squired her whenever he went out—not that she'd needed it. While he'd been in mourning, she'd become the toast of that Season and the next. She claimed being on the arm of a duke made her more interesting. He thought she'd demonstrated rather aptly that she was interesting enough on her own.

Now, he squired her about because he wanted to. There was enjoyment in the company of someone from home, someone who knew *him* and had no designs on his title. It was a practical arrangement, too.

Her companionship kept the matchmaking mamas at bay. Marianne was his shield, as he suspected he was hers. They both had secrets to protect and neither was in a hurry to marry. Between them, they'd built an effective defence. Few dared to gainsay a duke's attentions and Marianne could be selective.

Vennor finished off his drink and emerged from the tub with some relief. The heat had made his leg feel better for the time being. Honeycutt stood by with salve and a towel, a huge, swathing, soft luxury of cloth, the last of his peace before he had to face society. He had a valet, but on nights when he was out as the Vigilante, Honeycutt waited on him. The fewer people who knew the better. Secrecy was everything, even at home. It wasn't only in London stews that dukes couldn't wander alone, hunting killers. They were subject to scrutiny in their homes as well. Servants talked. Gossip spread everywhere. Who knew what dark corners it might land in, or whose ears it might reach? He didn't want the Vigilante unmasked—it would be akin to losing part of himself, the only part of himself that seemed to have any meaning.

'How was the Garden tonight?' Honeycutt enquired with a brisk professionalism that didn't fool Vennor. The dear old soul was worried and was masking it for his sake. Honeycutt didn't want to add to his troubles. Vennor appreciated it as much as he appreciated the very concern it hid.

'The usual.' Vennor tossed the towel aside. 'Pickpockets and whores. It's not nearly as dangerous as the docks or Seven Dials.' He gave a confident smile. 'The Garden is the safest of the rotation.' He split his efforts between different dark spots in London. At least crime in the Garden was predictable. On the docks and in Seven Dials, the crimes were downright dastardly, things that would curdle a man's blood.

'That's what I am most afraid of, Your Grace. Even on a "safe" night something can go wrong and tonight it did.' Honeycutt smeared a healthy dollop of salve on his thigh, the single sentence a reminder of several previous conversations. After years of turning up no new clues regarding his parents' murders, Honeycutt wanted him to give up the Vigilante, wanted him married and living like a duke, safe behind town house walls and phalanxes of servants.

Vennor shook his head, spraying droplets of water from his blond hair with his insistence. 'I can't give up. We never know when a clue might come to light.' Of course, at times, he shared Honeycutt's frustration. It was like running a race blindfolded and not knowing how close to the finish line he was.

'I'd hate to stop just steps from completion.' But there were other reasons he didn't want to stop. If he stopped being the Vigilante, who would he be? He'd be the very thing his father had despised most in this life: a person of privilege with no purpose. He'd have failed his parents and all that the Cornish Dukes stood for on the grandest scale possible.

'Very well, Your Grace.' Honeycutt cleared his throat. 'Now, let's see about turning you back into a duke. We don't want to keep Miss Marianne waiting.'

Chapter Two

Vennor spied her the moment he stepped foot inside the Fordhams' ballroom. It was hard not to notice her. Marianne drew the eye naturally with her deep, rich auburn hair. The stark brilliance of her snow-white sequined silk gown merely enhanced her attraction. Vennor was of the opinion that no one in recent years had worn white quite as well as Marianne Treleven and tonight was no exception. She was a brilliant beacon amid the quieter, subtler pastel gowns populating the Fordham ballroom.

Tonight, Marianne held court near a column wrapped in spring greens and white roses, a wide circle of eligible bachelors and smiling debutantes gathered about her. The crowd was a testimony not only to how well liked she was, but also to her kindness. Marianne was gracious with her popularity, using it to include others. Marianne favoured him with a smile as he approached and the circle expanded to incorporate him, albeit somewhat nervously. People weren't always sure how to be with him now that he'd inherited. Dukes by nature were intimidating. But not to Marianne. To her, he was still just Vennor. 'Your Grace, you've decided to join us at last,' Marianne teased. 'It's eleven and I was beginning to wonder.'

Vennor grinned, falling into the usual routine. They'd grown used to one another during her Seasons in Town, their friendship deepening over the years as three of her sisters finished their Seasons and married, as had his three friends, leaving them both alone and unwed. She'd always been a good friend, but these days he counted her among his closest friends.

He took her hand and lifted her gloved knuckles to his lips for a kiss. 'I trust I'm not too late to take you in to supper?' He reached for the little dance card at her wrist and pencilled his name in the usual place. She always saved the dinner dance for him on account of not wanting to risk being stuck with a bore for a whole hour. And, of course, it saved him from the matchmaking mamas as well. It was an arrangement that had suited them both in Seasons past. But tonight, he sensed an undercurrent of discontent in her court at his arrival. Someone wasn't pleased with his appearance.

Vennor's gaze moved to her right, meeting the steely grey eyes of Viscount Hayes before returning to Marianne. 'I hope the arrangement meets with your approval, Miss Treleven? Forgive me if I've been too bold.' It rather obviously did not meet with Hayes's approval. The man was fairly bristling at his presumption, but he wasn't asking for Hayes's permission. He was asking for Marianne's and Hayes was far too well bred to do more than glare at him. Still, the action was duly noted.

'There is nothing to forgive.' Marianne nodded to him and turned her smile on Hayes, quick to smooth things over. 'My lord, I believe this our dance.'

Vennor watched from the sidelines as Hayes and Marianne took to the floor, her crystal sequins shimmering beneath the chandeliers as they danced. So that was the lay of the land this Season. It confirmed the gossip floating around the clubs. Hayes meant to declare himself. How interesting. How inevitable. Something inside him sank.

He should not be surprised. Hayes was newly returned from a two-year Grand Tour of the Continent, apparently ready to wed and it was a given that Marianne would marry well. She was a beautiful young woman who'd acquired a certain polish in the years since her debut. Intelligent and sophisticated, imbued with a respectable dowry, she'd managed to rise above her father's station as a Cornish baronet to catch the eyes of men much higher up on that ladder. A glittering, confident woman had replaced the tangle-haired tomboy who'd once begged to be taken along on fishing expeditions and truffle hunts. Time had not stood still nor had Marianne while he'd mourned. Viscount Hayes had noticed and he'd taken advantage.

Vennor reached for a glass of champagne from a passing tray and swallowed thoughtfully. Marianne was an ambitious girl in ways that did not limit themselves to matrimony. She would not settle for an idle life. What would Hayes say if he knew those ambitions? He might be in for a surprise. And so might Marianne if she wasn't careful.

His own reaction to that pairing was worth examining. Was he envious of Marianne's good fortune? Jealousy seemed too cruel a word for his feelings. He only wanted the best for her. Frien-vy, perhaps? He tried the made-up word out and gave a wry smile. He liked it.

The dance ended and Hayes and Marianne returned to her court. She was slightly breathless, her cheeks flushed. 'Our supper dance is next.' She looked vibrant and happy as she took his arm. Why shouldn't she be? There were no shadows in her world, no death, no loss, no failures to mock her in the darkness of sleepless nights. Marianne seized the world by the horns and made it dance to her tune. He was surprised such a trait appealed to the strait-laced Hayes. The man was something of a puritan. But Marianne had other traits that no doubt offset that. Vennor could guess what Hayes saw in Marianne, but he wondered what she saw in Hayes.

Vennor led her out to the floor easily. They'd waltzed together often enough. Even before she'd come out, he'd spent afternoons pressed into practice at the Trelevens', partnering the Treleven sisters as they learned their steps. But tonight, he was more conscious than usual of his hand at her waist, of her hand in his, the way her body matched his in the steps, how the merest press of his hand at the small of her back was met with an instant response. She knew him and he knew her in even the smallest of ways, and he might lose her. When she married, he would lose Marianne's friendship. There would be no more supper dances, no more witty conversations, no more good company.

As much as he was determined to savour the dance, by the turn at the top of the ballroom, Vennor knew he'd overplayed his hand. Walking on his sore leg was one thing, dancing was another. Despite Honeycutt's salve and the hot bath, his thigh ached. The exertion of a waltz was simply too much.

'What is it?' Marianne's dark eyes searched his face with concern as he slowed their pace.

'Would you mind terribly if we stepped outside? I don't feel like dancing tonight,' Vennor confessed.

Marianne slanted him a curious look. 'Of course. I could do with some fresh air myself.' The dance sent them past glass doors leading to the gardens beyond the ballroom and Vennor took the opportunity to guide them outside. The ache in his leg eased as they slowed to a stroll along with the other couples. He wished he could say the same for the ache that had taken up residence in his heart. His parents' killers remained at large and Marianne was considering Hayes. Everything he cared for was slipping away.

Vennor had slipped a little further away from her tonight, that urbane mask he'd acquired when he'd inherited sliding further into place. Some day, she feared she might lose her friend altogether. 'Are you going to tell me what's on your mind or do I have to guess?' Marianne queried gently. It wouldn't be hard to guess. The same thing—person—was on her mind as well.

'Hayes wasn't pleased to see me tonight. He seems to think I am infringing on his territory. Am I?'

'I'd rather not think of myself as territory to be conquered or owned,' Marianne snapped and immediately apologised. Vennor was not responsible for her anxious state of mind. She ought not treat him as if he was.

Vennor lowered his voice confidentially. 'He means to offer for you from what I've heard. Do you want him to?'

The disclosure was not surprising. She'd suspected as much. Hayes had made no secret of his intentions. Her own intentions were less clear. 'I'm not sure,' Marianne confessed. That was the question she'd been debating since the Season opened and Hayes had taken up residence in her court. *Was* she seriously contemplating him? Or, more to the point, was she seriously contemplating marriage at all? It was nearly the end of May and she was no closer to an answer. She had time. He would not ask until the Season was nearly over.

'Is Viscount Hayes not adventurous enough for you?' They approached a fountain with a wide basin and stopped to sit at its edge, the burble of water lending their conversation privacy.

'I think that's the problem. He should be enough for me.' Marianne trailed her hand in the water and offered a little laugh. 'I will outrank all my sisters.'

But the humour fell flat. They both knew she had never put much stock in titles. 'He's very proper, highly respected. He doesn't appear to be riddled with vices. I could hope for no better in a man, yet I resist.' Vennor was the only one to whom she'd confessed those worries. She'd not even articulated them to her mother or in letters to her sisters. 'I fear I might disappoint him.' Their gazes locked and a frisson of understanding borne of long friendship passed between them. *You know why*, her gaze whispered to his.

'He does not know about your ambition,' Vennor answered out loud. 'You feel he would not approve.' Sometimes it was nice to have a friend who could read your mind. It saved having to put complicated feelings into words.

She nodded. There was a modicum of relief in knowing at least one other person understood. She could always count on Vennor for that. 'Can *you* see him tolerating Viscountess Hayes being a columnist—and for a *gentleman's* magazine no less?' Not that Hayes's approval would make her like him more. It wouldn't. Still, telling him in hopes of earning that approval was out of the question. She couldn't even imagine her parents approving of it, which was why she'd never told them. It would be one eccentricity too far for them.

'Perhaps you could continue to do it in secret?' Vennor suggested. 'If no one knows, why should that change?'

She speared him with an incredulous smile. 'I can't believe you'd propose such a thing, a wife keeping secrets from her husband? What sort of marriage would that be? Not one that I would want, *if* I married at all. I'd be lying to him. Besides, writing in secret is fine for now, but that's not my intention, as you well know.' Her ambitions went beyond an anonymous social column. She wanted to be a journalist who changed the world with her words, who didn't have to hide behind the pseudonym M.R. Mannering.

She gave the water a slap, her frustration mounting and not all of it due to Lord Hayes's persistence. 'There's little chance of that, though, when all I do is cover the opera and who wore what. Nobody will ever care about that.' She rolled her eyes. 'That's not serious journalism. Anyone can do that. I want to cover real events, solve a mystery, something meaningful people would want to still know about years from now.'

'The present is important, too. I think you do yourself a disservice in thinking your column doesn't matter. People need to be entertained and M.R. Mannering does a fine job of it.' He gave her a winning smile. 'For instance, I need to know what I missed with my late arrival.'

She couldn't help but smile back. She could always rely on Vennor to cajole her out of the blue devils. 'The Vigilante. Of course. He was out early tonight. There were rumours of him in Covent Garden defending a flower girl. He's quite the hero these days, having lasted so long. I would have thought the novelty would have worn off by now, but it is just the opposite. It intensifies the longer he goes unknown.

I think every woman in London is dying of love for him. Angeline Mercer even went driving in the stews in hopes of needing rescue just to meet him.'

'Did it work?' Vennor chuckled.

'No.' Marianne laughed, her mood lighter now that they'd moved away from serious topics. 'But I don't blame her for trying. I wouldn't mind meeting such a paragon of a man.' She gave him an impish smile and leaned a little closer, taking advantage of the fountain's burble for secrecy. This was the perfect chance to tell him of her latest plans. 'I have an idea for having a little adventure of my own *and* taking my reporting to the next level. I've been thinking maybe I should unmask the Vigilante. *That* would certainly get me a byline. He is all anyone talks about.' She waited for his smile, for his face to light up in commendation, perhaps even ask to join her in the adventure. She got none of those.

'Are you insane? You could very well end up dead.' Vennor's voice was a growl of disbelief. 'You can't possibly mean to go into Seven Dials, or the East Docks.'

She returned his stare, as surprised by his rejection as he apparently was by her suggestion. 'I was expecting your support,' she scolded.

'Absolutely not, Marianne. It's too dangerous. That man deals with real criminals, real violence. You could be hurt, or worse.'

'I'd be careful,' Marianne argued. 'I know how to shoot. I could carry a gun.'

He reached for her hands and gripped them with

an intensity that mirrored his words, his eyes holding hers, sending her pulse skittering again in that new way. 'Promise me that you will not attempt such a thing. You could never be careful enough. You don't know that world and what it's like. I need your word, Marianne.' His voice was low and imbued with seriousness. His grip on her hands tightened, a sure sign he would not leave the garden without her word.

This was her friend speaking, but also someone else, someone she didn't recognise. It was thrilling and unsteadying. Their eyes locked, and it seemed the air between them was charged, the atmosphere surrounding them changing. *They* were changing. A new awareness of the other hung between them. For the first time, she was mindful of losing him, to marriage, to the dukedom. The friendship they'd taken for granted over the years had suddenly become precious and fragile.

When she spoke, her words were quiet, hushed, out of reverence, perhaps, for that awareness. 'All right, Vennor. I promise. I will do nothing rash.'

Chapter Three

Damn, he was stiff—and not in the usual morning sort of way. Vennor nearly fell out of bed, a feat he hadn't managed since he was six years old. Back then, he would merely spring to his feet and carry on. This morning, however, he could barely walk. Honeycutt would say it was a sign he should give up his masked crusade, that one of these days he might be more than sore.

Vennor made his way to the washbasin with tentative steps and splashed water on his face. Lord, he was tired. Tired of late nights, tired of too little sleep, tired of it all amounting to so little. The man looking back at him in the mirror was tired, too. His eyes sported purple smudges beneath them and the beginnings of puffiness.

He'd like to go back to bed, but there was too much to do: bills to read from Parliament, a speech to prepare in support of his latest piece of legislation, the last of his father's special projects, and estate reports to review from land stewards on the various ducal properties—properties he had put off visiting since his father's death.

There was the Vigilante's work as well: baskets to send, supplies to distribute to those in need and arrangements to be made for apprentices and cabin boys, all in the hopes that his efforts would make a difference, that they were not a drop in the never-ending ocean of the London slums. He could not rescue them all, but perhaps he would make a difference in the lives of those he could. He raked a hand through his hair. He'd make no difference if he didn't get started.

His father had spent each morning from nine until one taking care of his responsibilities with a work ethic that had impressed itself on Vennor growing up. It had been a natural model to fall into when he'd assumed the dukedom, although many of his fellow peers didn't rise until after noon. He could at least do this much right, even if it was just pushing paper.

An hour later and only one letter answered, Vennor was rethinking that assumption. He wasn't doing this right or even at all. He pushed back from the desk in the office and rubbed at his brow. This morning, it was impossible to keep his mind on his work when it insisted on straying back to thoughts of Marianne. Marianne was considering Hayes. Marianne was considering unmasking the Vigilante. Marianne was considering gallivanting around the slums with a pistol in her pocket. Sweet heavens, just the thought of it in broad daylight caused him to break out in a sweat. Marianne with a gun would think herself invincible. She would be fearless and that would be her undoing, as would her stubbornness.

Vennor set aside his correspondence and walked to the long window overlooking the street, using the opportunity to stretch his leg. Her stubbornness worried him. He'd seen that look in her eye last night when she'd outlined her plans. She *meant* to find the Vigilante. He'd seen that same tenacity the day she'd told him she meant to answer the ad in *Gentlemen's Weekly* for a columnist even though it had asked explicitly for a male applicant. She'd triumphed against those odds. She was sure she'd triumph against these odds as well.

He'd disappointed her last night when he'd not offered encouragement. She'd been counting on him to support her latest endeavour, this next step in achieving her dream, and he'd shot her down. Guilt for that gnawed at him this morning. He was her friend, her confidant, the only one she talked with about her ambition, and he'd failed her—he was very good at that, failing people. But short of revealing himself to her, what was he to do? For both their sakes, he needed to talk her out of this.

He reached for the window and pulled back the curtain. Outside, the day was sunny and bright. The street looked peaceful from up here, so orderly, unlike his life. What was he to do about Marianne? Did he let her go off into danger hunting the Vigilante, knowing she'd never find him? Or tell her his secret in order to keep her safe at home? He wouldn't be safe, of course. Marianne might just shoot *him* when she discovered he'd been holding out on her. She'd entrusted him with her biggest secret and he'd not reciprocated.

Guilt dug at him, no longer merely gnawing, but chewing hard. He'd not behaved as a friend ought last night. The code of the Cornish Dukes insisted that one always had the backs of his friends. Whatever else he owed Marianne, he at least owed her an apology. He dropped the curtain and glanced at the clock. It was still early by town time, but Treleven House was one place he could call without standing on ceremony.

Downstairs in the pristine hall, with its immaculate black-and-white-tiled floor and dust-free consoles, Vennor shrugged into a coat and gave his cravat a cursory straightening in the mirror, a large, impressive rococo piece trimmed in pounds of gilt. Good lord, his entrance hall felt like a museum, quiet, stately, tasteful, but not lived in. He might as well be a guest passing through for all the blandness the place possessed. He looked about, seeing the hall in a new light. Clean and pristine was not enough to give a home personality, to give it character. His mother's home had always had that. When had the town house lost it?

Honeycutt handed him his hat and walking stick; the man was as immaculate as the hall but more alive. Perhaps museum wasn't the word he was looking for. Mausoleum might suit better. 'Where to, Your Grace?'

'To see Miss Treleven,' Vennor gave his waistcoat a final tug.

'Very good, Your Grace,' Honeycutt said with the air of one who'd known the answer long before he'd asked the question.

The Treleven hall didn't feel like a mausoleum, Vennor noted as he left his things with a footman. The space was smaller than Newlyn House, but it was brighter. Livelier. There were flowers in a vase of coloured glass on the console and sunlight streamed in through the large fan-shaped window above the door, adding to the warmth of the butter-yellow walls. Under his boots, a polished oak floor gleamed, decorated by a patterned Turkish throw rug.

'Vennor, my dear boy, it's so good to see you!' Lady Treleven, red-haired and as lovely as her six daughters, sailed into the hall, hands outstretched. If not for the hints of faded red at her temples, she might have been one of them. 'Marianne's upstairs in the reading room. Shall I take you up? I assume you've come to see her.' She had her arm through his and had him halfway up the stairs before he could answer, filling him in on the latest news. Perhaps Marianne got her nose for a good story from her.

The thought made him smile as he let her bright chatter wash over him. This was in part what he'd come for, to be some place that felt like home, a place where he wasn't judged, where he wasn't the Duke, where people weren't looking to him to make decisions. He'd spent much of his childhood at the Treleven home in Cornwall, surrounded by the girls and all the noise and love of their household. He'd never felt like an only child—not with six 'sisters'. Perhaps that had been his parents' intention to make up for what he lacked by way of siblings. If so, it had served him in good stead as an adult. Here was a place he could be himself.

Lady Treleven opened the reading room door. 'Marianne, look who's here,' she sang out cheerily. 'What a pleasant surprise.'

One look told him Marianne disagreed. Marianne didn't think his intrusion was quite so pleasant. Vennor saw her startle, then saw her cast a guilty look at the newspaper clippings spread out on the table. 'Vennor, what are you doing here?' He heard the nervous catch in her voice as she rose, moving towards them—or was it that she was moving *away* from the table? He'd wager she was hiding something. His curiosity regarding the table grew.

'I was in the neighbourhood and thought I'd drop by.' He resisted the tug on his arm attempting to lead him away from the table. What did she not want him to see?

'I'll send up some tea,' Lady Treleven offered. 'I am sure you won't have eaten yet, Vennor, or, if you have, you're hungry again. You'll have to excuse me, I've a charity meeting at Lady Bretton's.'

He waited until Lady Treleven's footsteps had faded on the stairs before he made his move, snatching up a news clipping from the table. 'What are we working on here?'

'Give me that!' Marianne grabbed for it but he held it out of reach with a laugh. Suddenly, they were young again, living only in the moment. Vennor darted away, putting the table between them.

'Vennor, if you don't give that to me right now, I'll tell Lady Lester you want to dance with all her daughters at the next ball!' Marianne threatened, her dark eyes blazing as she chased him down. She leapt for it again, a most unladylike jump, but to no avail, except to force him up against a wall. Her body pressed to his in the most noticeable way and her breasts—very nice, round, firm breasts, he might add—thrust taut against the bodice of her gown as her arm stretched towards the clipping.

'You wouldn't dare,' Vennor breathed, trying to defend himself against the dual threat of Marianne's suddenly noticeable breasts and Lady Lester's daughters. The Lester girls were no mean commination. There were five of them, each one more ill-mannered than the last, the bane of any ballroom.

'Don't try me on this, Vennor. Give it to me. *Now.*' Marianne was ferocious as she held out her hand for the paper. He was familiar with this ferocity of hers. One summer she'd thrown his clothes in the river when she'd discovered he'd gone swimming without her.

He relented—at least he *meant* to relent—but, as he handed the paper over to Marianne, his eyes lit on the headline.

Vigilante stops robbery on the East Docks!

Out of reflex, his hand closed about Marianne's wrist. 'What is this?' But in his gut, he knew what it was. She was pursuing the Vigilante despite her promise last night. Anger began to simmer low in his belly. No matter what his own private agenda was regarding the Vigilante, he'd extracted that promise from her last night for her own good, in order to keep her safe, Did she not see that? Less than a day later she'd broken her word. She'd never intended to keep it.

'Marianne,' he growled, 'have you broken your promise?' They weren't playing any more. In his desire to protect them both, the words came out more harshly than he'd anticipated. Marianne paled, either from his tone or from discovery.

Somehow breaking a promise was worse than telling a lie. Breaking a promise to Vennor was even lower than that. Marianne felt her face flush, embarrassed at having been caught out. 'I promised you I'd do nothing *rash*. Hunting the Vigilante from my reading room is hardly dangerous.' Marianne wound a long red curl around her finger.

'Then why the need for the subterfuge?' Vennor's blue stare was penetrating. Marianne fought the urge to fidget, reminding herself she wasn't a little girl any more. The ten-year difference in their ages was no longer an insurmountable chasm. They'd become equals in adulthood as well as friends. This morning, however, it was easy to forget that. Up close like this, the new awareness hummed between them. She was cognisant of his height, of the breadth of his shoulders, the physical power of him that accompanied the low-toned growl of disapproval. 'It's what you mean to do with the research that's the problem, Marianne. You don't intend to leave the project here in the reading room.' While she'd appreciated his ability to know her mind so well last night, it was an inconvenient talent this morning.

'How do you know that?' She tested his surety with a question. Perhaps he was merely fishing for a confession.

He wasn't bluffing. 'You curl your hair when you're nervous or hiding something.' Vennor flashed her an apologetic smile. 'Sorry, it's the curse of having a long acquaintance with someone.' The moment relieved the tension of the brewing quarrel as the tea tray was delivered. It occurred to her as they took their seats in the cosy bay of long windows amid the rays of morning sun and wisps of teapot steam that Viscount Hayes would never know her half as well; all her quirks and tells would mean little to him. Some piece of her would be lost with Hayes.

'I didn't *want* to lie to you.' She poured out the tea, with an eye to Vennor's perennial sweet tooth—one cube of sugar and a splash of milk. 'It was just that you were so adamant that I not do it.' She passed him the cup and saucer with its painted blue violets. 'I've always been able to count on your support, but you made it clear I did not have it in this endeavour.

What was I supposed to do? I can't just give up.' She took a sip of her own tea and fixed him with a stare over the delicate rim as she drew her battle lines. 'I have to do this whether you like it or not.' She didn't need his support, but she did need his understanding.

'Why?' came the simple question. Marianne wished the answer was as straightforward.

'I think this is my last chance, Ven. This is my third Season and I have a viscount at my feet. To refuse him and return for a fourth Season will raise questions, to say nothing of the financial expense for my parents.' She paused. They'd been more than generous with her, but her mother had made it clear that her patience was running out. A girl in her third Season must wed or be viewed suspiciously. Popularity would not protect her then. 'If I cannot make a breakthrough with my writing this Season, I think I must set those ambitions aside and choose the traditional path.' That was the gentle ultimatum she'd arrived at last night. She *had* considered Vennor's caution about the Vigilante and decided she could not give in to it.

Vennor's expression softened and she shook her head. 'I don't want your pity, Ven. This is what the world is like for women.' It wasn't fair. A woman had only two choices: marriage or outcast. In her opinion, both choices marginalised a woman's potential. 'We're not all dukes who can choose what they want to be and do.' Even second sons had more choice than she did as to how her life was arranged.

Vennor was quiet, thoughtful. 'It's not pity, Marianne. It's appreciation. I wish the world were different. Maybe it will be, later, although that does you little good now,' Vennor said at last. 'But why him, a man who immerses himself in the slums and violence? For all you know, he's a madman. Perhaps there's another story out there to chase?' The last was wishful thinking on Vennor's part, though. She'd racked her brains before coming up with even this idea.

'He's not mad, Ven. He's a very good man,' Marianne said quietly, eyeing Vennor with questions of her own. If he knew her down to the curling of her hair, she knew him just as well. The 'curse of long friendship' went both ways. Mad was a strong word. Vennor was usually not a judgemental man and she admired that about him. That he should use such a word without substantive evidence was out of character. But there was no reason for it that she could think of outside his concern for her well-being.

'You're romanticising him, like half of London.' Vennor cautioned.

'No, I'm not.' She set down her teacup and held out her hand. 'Would you let me show you?'

Chapter Four

Vennor surveyed the reading room table, a long, polished mahogany affair, covered in three years' worth of clippings with a certain amount of trepidation. Marianne had made good use of that length this morning, arranging the clippings in chronological order. He scanned the headlines as she talked.

Masked man averts attack in Hyde Park!
Masked man strikes again!

'These are the early accounts, the ones where he hadn't acquired a moniker yet or a routine.' She led him down the table, an underlying excitement in her voice. 'Then look what happens. He settles in. "The Vigilante Patrols Covent Garden with a Vengeance!" "The Vigilante Patrols the East Docks!" "The Vigilante Seen in Seven Dials." He left the safer environs of Mayfair's fringe and devoted himself almost exclusively to the London slums.'

Marianne was talking about the dates now, but his thoughts and his gaze were drifting from the clippings to her face. She was stunningly beautiful in her passion for the subject, her dark eyes alight with intelligent thought. It was like seeing her for the first time as the reporter she was meant to be.

'Some have already speculated about who the Vigilante is.' She picked up a clipping to illustrate her point. 'Some think he's a criminal himself, while others think he's from the stews. But I think he might be more than a crime fighter. I think he might be a revolutionary.' He had seen her impassioned for a cause before, from begging him to splint a duckling's wing when she was six to raising funds for Christmas baskets in Porth Karrek. But he'd never seen her like this—emotions and logic working together. It was impressive, really. *She* was impressive. No wonder she was frustrated. She had the ability to be an amazing reporter if given the chance…which she wouldn't be.

'What?' Marianne broke off her explanation. 'You're staring, Ven.' She rubbed her cheek. 'Do I have something on my face?'

'No, I was just caught up in the story,' Vennor stammered, caught off guard by the interruption. Caught up in *her* was more the case. 'Go on, you were saying he might be a revolutionary. How do you reason that?' He wanted to hear her interpretation, despite the element of awkwardness in hearing himself described when he knew better. He wasn't half the man she thought he was, just a man looking for justice, a man looking to make sense of a world which for him had been upended three years ago, a man who no longer knew who he was so he took refuge behind a mask.

'It's in his code. He is no respecter of class in the best sense. He protects the poor when no one else does. The constabulary hardly raise a finger in the places he frequents. Last night, he protected a flower girl, someone the finer world views as no better than a prostitute. He stood up for her because she deserves protecting, no matter the circumstances of her birth.'

Marianne paused and fixed him with her blazing gaze. 'Let me ask you this, Ven, as a man with a title. Would any of the lords in my court have done the same? I have no doubt Lord Hayes would stand up for me should I be unsuitably approached, but I am a lady of gentle birth. Would he have even looked twice at the flower girl in distress? Or, worse, would they have seen her distress and assumed she somehow deserved the poor treatment she was given? My point is this: without the Vigilante, the flower girl has no recourse to help or opportunity simply because of the luck of her birth.'

'You admire him,' Vennor said quietly when she had finished.

'I envy him,' Marianne corrected. 'He has purpose in his life, like you and the Cornish Dukes.'

Vennor smiled wryly. He thought so, too. It was the very reason he was loath to give up the mask. She was wrong about the latter, though. The Cornish Dukes, his circle of fathers and sons, had purpose, but not him. She gave him too much credit there. But she'd also given him an opening in which to make his argument. If she wouldn't leave the Vigilante alone for her own sake, perhaps she would for the Vigilante's sake. 'If you admire him, why do you want to unmask him?'

'A hero should be acknowledged,' Marianne replied, stacking up the clippings in careful order. 'It might even bring awareness to his cause, gain him a wealthy benefactor.' Little did she know that he needed neither.

'If he wanted to be acknowledged, he wouldn't wear a mask,' Vennor argued. 'Have you thought that unmasking him might be the end of him? Then where would your revolution be?' Where would his cause be? There'd be social scandal in the *ton*, to say nothing of the retribution he might face from the crime lords whose industry he'd disrupted.

Tell her, his conscience whispered more insistently. *Tell her and protect yourself. She wouldn't dare expose you.*

But she would be furious he'd hidden it from her and her plans would be ruined. Those were just the considerations of what it would do to their relationship. There was also the fact that he hadn't even told his best friends. Inigo, Eaton and Cassian had no idea of the masquerade. He felt no small twinge of guilt over that. Perhaps he ought to tell them first, *if* he told anyone? There were practical considerations, too, such as how did one simply insert that bit of information into a conversation? Yet it was hard to let the opportunity slip past him. He owed it to her. At some point, he *should* tell her on principle alone. She'd laid her soul bare for him today. It had taken courage to share her thoughts on a subject she knew they disagreed on. Yet she'd trusted their friendship enough to do it. She would not understand why he couldn't do the same. Still, he'd not come here to argue with her. He'd come to apologise and he hadn't done that yet.

He handed her the last of the clippings. 'You're very good at your craft, Marianne. You are far better than a columnist, I need you to know that. I also need you to know that I believe in you even if I can't support you going after the Vigilante. I see why you want to do it. He's all any of the ladies talk about. But it's not safe for you and, in the end, *if* you did find him, I want you to consider the danger unmasking poses for him as well.'

Marianne gave a slow, considering nod of her head. 'What if I didn't unmask his identity? What if I were to do a series of interviews with him? The public could learn more about him, I could prove to my editor I can be more and he can keep his identity hidden.'

'You would still have to find him and there is danger in that,' Vennor reminded her. Normally, he applauded Marianne's tenacity and creativity. Not so today. He wished there was a way to distract her from this course, another task he might set in her path that would give her the purpose she sought.

Vennor shifted his stance, stepping out of the sun's glare. The sun had moved, too, and now it flooded the room in full, turning the entire reading room into a place of cosy warmth. Like the hall downstairs, this room, too, was so unlike his house with its pristine, untouchable museum quality. One did not *live* in his house. And perhaps he hadn't been. Perhaps it was time for that to change. Maybe Marianne was the person to do it. He held out his hand. 'Come for a drive with me. I've brought the phaeton and the weather's brilliant. I've got a proposal for you.'

Marianne let the spring breeze bathe her face as they drove. It felt good to be out of doors. It felt good to be with Vennor without the constraints of the ballroom and its tension. Last night had been…different, throwing into sharp relief what sitting on the high seat of Vennor's phaeton represented. If she accepted Lord Hayes when he proposed, everything would change. *This* would change. There would be no more drives in the park with Vennor, no more tête-à-têtes beside fountains, no more confiding of secrets, no more arguing in the reading room. A certain chapter of her life would close.

Vennor nudged her toe with his boot as they tooled through the park gate, the place still deserted at this time of day. 'What are you thinking, Marianne? You are miles from here.'

'Can't a girl enjoy the weather?' Marianne slanted him a teasing look from under the brim of her straw hat.

'I might believe it if I thought that was the case, but *you* were thinking.' He smiled back, looking entirely boyish and entirely too handsome as the breeze played with his hair, golden blond in the sunlight.

The sight of him almost took her breath away, as did the realisation: what a handsome husband he would make someone. It was no wonder hostesses begged for his presence at their parties. The wonder was that she hadn't noticed, *really* noticed, the firm cut of his jaw, the slight squaring of his chin with its subtle dimple, the blueness of his eyes and the faintest of lines that had begun to web at the corners—further proof that they weren't children any more. She would be twenty-one in a few weeks, which meant he would be thirty-two in August. There was certainly nothing childish about Vennor Penlerick—he was full-grown and in his prime. Was this how other women saw him? As a *man*?

Marianne sighed. 'I was thinking how this is likely our last Season. I might marry Lord Hayes and you've got to marry someone. You'll be thirty-two, Ven.' She'd been so caught up in the drama of her own situation she hadn't thought about his. It was a marvel he hadn't married already, given his unique circumstances. 'I think we've put it off as long as we dare. The others have married.'

He looked over at her, his brow furrowed. 'I thought you weren't sure you wanted to marry at all.'

'I'm not sure I do,' Marianne affirmed, thinking out loud. 'It's just that I don't like being left behind and that's what's happened. The town house is quiet this year.' Her three older sisters had married and had residences of their own now. None of them had come up to town. It was just her and her parents.

'You have the twins,' Vennor reminded her.

She shook her head. 'It's not the same.' The twins, Isabella and Catherine, were still at home and wouldn't be out for another two years. There was a great chasm in age between her almost twenty-one years and their newly turned sixteen—a far larger chasm than the decade that spanned the difference between her and Vennor. 'I miss my sisters,' she confessed. They'd gone ahead into marriage and motherhood without her. 'It's not that I can't ride over and see them when I'm home. It's not the distance. It's hard to explain. I visit them, but I no longer share their lives. Their lives are shared by others now. To be honest, a part of me envies those husbands and babies; I'm angry at them for stealing my sisters away from me.'

She let out another breath of frustration. 'Sometimes I think I'm only considering Lord Hayes because he's the means by which I can catch up to them.' She could follow her sisters into matrimony and motherhood, no longer left behind. 'Don't you feel the same, Ven? Your friends have married.' Surely, he felt the loss of them.

'I do.' Vennor pulled the phaeton over to the verge and set the brake. 'I miss them and envy them their wives, their children, their purpose.' He jumped from the high seat and came around to help her down. Did she imagine it, or did his hands linger at her waist? They stood close, shielded by the carriage from passers-by, her skirts brushing his boots, his eyes steady on hers, two blue flames, and her pulse raced as it had last night. It was becoming a most disturbing new reaction to her old friend.

His hands flexed at her waist and she was aware of the silence around them, the distant trill of birds in the trees, the rippling susurration of the stream beyond the verge. 'Missing them, wanting what they have, those are not reasons to throw yourself into marriage any more than filling my nursery is a reason for me to do the same.' His voice was low, for her alone. 'Promise me, Marianne, promise me you won't marry to satisfy your parents or society, or because you feel you have to catch up to your sisters.'

The knuckles of his hand skimmed her cheek, sending a little frisson of warmth through her. For all the secrets they'd traded over the years and all the confidences they'd shared, he'd never talked to her like this, never looked at her like this, before. 'You are too precious, Marianne, to throw yourself away in a lukewarm match. Promise me.'

She was tempted to say something slightly flippant like 'you've been asking for a lot of promises of me lately', but the look in his eyes decided her against it. This was no laughing matter and he was in earnest. 'If there's no one who catches my fancy? Who makes my heart pound? Then what?' she asked softly.

'Then don't wed, Marianne. Don't settle,' Vennor whispered treason.

'My parents would not like hearing you give this advice.' Oh, how she wished she could follow it. Wasn't it the very counsel of her own heart? She shook her head. 'My mother has been clear this Season that they've tolerated my "experimental tendencies" long enough. I believe her words were, "Now it's time to grow up and put aside childish things".' It was time to conform after a lifetime of nonconformity. She'd grown up being the 'different Treleven'. She was a writer when her sisters were all musicians. She loved the glamour of the Season where all her sisters preferred the quietude of Cornwall. Difference was tolerated only to a certain degree and she knew she'd been afforded a good deal of grace in that regard. But that grace had run out.

'Ah...' Vennor's single word carried a wealth of intuition with it. 'You're not the only one crossing the Rubicon this Season, it seems.' Something stirred behind his blue eyes, a consideration that both thrilled and unnerved her. What did he mean by that comment? Perhaps she would pursue it later. She did not want to be distracted from the issue at hand, whatever that was.

'But Rubicons are not what you wanted to talk about.' Marianne stepped back and he released his hold on her waist. 'You said you had a proposal for me. What is it?'

'Something I should have discussed a long time ago.' He gave her a wry smile. Her heart gave an odd lurch and for a moment she had a wild notion of Vennor making a proposal to her in truth. To save her from settling, perhaps? 'Would you help me pack up my parents' things? I should have done it ages ago, but I can't do it on my own.'

He wanted her to help him pack? Marianne blinked, clearing away her fanciful vision. She took a moment to gather her words and hide her...her what?

Disappointment? Shock? *Had* she wanted Vennor to declare himself in some way? Was that the reason for her racing pulse? In all logic, though, there were no grounds for such a proposal. They were *friends*. Friends told each other secrets. Friends did not propose to one another. 'It would be my pleasure,' she said softly. 'I'll bring my mother. She'll be an invaluable help.'

She understood it was a privilege to be let into what had become the very private world of Vennor Penlerick. He'd not allowed people to mourn with him, to help him when his parents had passed. That he'd asked for her help was proof of their deep friendship and the trust that went with it. She should be pleased. 'This is a big step, Ven. Why now?' There was a tightness at his mouth despite his smile. Whatever had prompted his decision, it had not been an easy one to make, one that he was still struggling with.

'Spring fever, I suppose. It's the season for new beginnings.' He used one hand to gesture to the trees with their green leaves. 'There are new buds and new foliage. If we were in the countryside, there would be baby sheep and goats, calves and foals. There is newness everywhere except in my house. I looked around the place this morning, truly looked around, and realised my house wasn't a home any more. It needs life, Marianne.'

She sensed there was more to it than that, but she didn't push. Vennor would reveal his thoughts when he was ready. This was clearly a difficult step for him to take, but a necessary one. She would do her best to help him take that first step back to really living, back to being happy, back to being the Vennor she remembered, who laughed without provocation, who found joy in the simplest of pleasures, who didn't face the world with a bland mask of urbanity. She reached for his hand and gave it a supportive squeeze. 'We'll come in the morning.'

Chapter Five

He had come to visit Miss Treleven and she had the audacity to be out! Justin Moore, the fifth Viscount Hayes, slapped the bouquet of flowers against his trousers, scattering blooms on the pavement in his abject disappointment. If she'd been out shopping, he could have tolerated it. Women lived to shop, after all. But out driving with His Grace, the Duke of Newlyn, he could not.

Hayes called to his driver, giving an address on the East Docks, a place where he'd be welcome and where comfort could be had. He slammed the carriage door shut and settled back against the cushioned seats, anger fuelling the whir of his mind. He'd been making exceptional progress this month with Miss Treleven. It was all the talk at White's. He was enjoying this rare bout of popularity brought on by his association with the Incomparable. There were even wagers in the betting book—not *if* she would accept his proposal, but *when*—proof of how far his suit had come and how well it had been received. His courtship was a well-placed master stroke to capture the Season's reigning Incomparable. She needed to marry. Her star was at its zenith and everyone knew she'd get no better offer than a viscount.

No one thought there were any 'ifs' left to argue about. Or at least they hadn't until Newlyn had started making the rounds in May. It was too bad the reclusive duke hadn't stayed in seclusion. Hayes tugged at the cuffs of his shirt so they peeped out an equal distance from the blue superfine sleeves of his jacket. He had originally ignored the alarm bells rung by Newlyn's presence. After all, Hayes had been at Miss Treleven's side in April, having come up to town early for that express purpose. He had been established before Newlyn had even ventured from the town house. Besides, Newlyn had had ages to woo Miss Treleven based on their family association and he hadn't made a move. That he was squiring her about on the rare occasion he put in an appearance was nothing more than duty.

No, he hadn't been worried and wasn't worried now, he reminded himself. However, it was becoming deuced annoying to lose her regularly for supper, to have Newlyn come waltzing into a ball at the last minute, as he had last night, and claim the prized dance while other men had worked for her attentions all night. And it wasn't just supper dances *now*, was it? She was out driving with the man, being seen with him in the park. People would start to wonder if there wasn't something more than duty behind it and, if they wondered about that, they would start to doubt him.

He couldn't afford the doubt, not if it came from the men to whom he owed money, men who had taken his upcoming engagement as collateral against sums advanced. Miss Treleven's dowry was respectable, but that wasn't what he'd promised against. He'd promised against the other intangibles that came with wedding her and geographically settling himself firmly in the territory of the Cornish Dukes, ready to take advantage of opportunity when it came. And it would come. He had plans, a reckoning three generations in the making, and a deathbed promise to his grandfather to uphold. The Penlericks had taken enough from the Moores over the years. It was time for a little payback.

Hayes lifted the window curtain long enough to ascertain his location and let it drop. He was nearly there. His blood started to hum at the prospect of Delilah's, his whorehouse of choice on the East Docks. Elise would be surprised to see him. It had been two years. A slow smile spread across his face as his hand moved to his member, rousing himself. 'Steady, boy,' he murmured. He had two years' worth of tricks learned on the Continent to add to his repertoire of skills and appetites. Elise would earn her keep.

His carriage pulled to a halt and he was quick to jump out and dismiss his coachman with instructions to return in three hours. There was no sense in having his coach linger and risk discovery. The whole point of frequenting Delilah's was to *avoid* discovery.

If he wanted it known he visited brothels, he'd stay in Mayfair. He found it useful that the *ton* regarded him as a very traditional peer and an upstanding Tory. He preferred it that way. Jock Treleven would not approve of his dirty little secret.

He inhaled the smell of brine and humanity as he rapped on the door. The East Docks hadn't changed one bit. They still stank. The stench would be all over him by afternoon's end, but never mind. He'd be home in time to clean up and sup before attending the evening's entertainments, his anger at Marianne Treleven's duplicity spent most avidly here instead of ruining his reputation for even-temperedness in London's ballrooms.

He was quickly let in by the large bouncer who guarded the door. Delilah's was nothing more than an old converted warehouse, exposed brick walls and women in various states of dingy undress lounging on ratty sofas. What the place lacked in décor, though, it made up for in discretion. Delilah herself swanned forward to greet him in a low-cut red gown made of cheap silk. 'Milord, you are returned. Shall I have Elise wait for you in her room?'

'Yes—and send up a riding crop. I'm sure she's been very naughty while I was away.' He mounted the stairs, his blood running hard now, his arousal rampant against his trousers. Half the thrill would be in laying that crop against the creamy smoothness of Elise's buttocks until she cried out from the sting of it. The other half was in knowing the *ton* didn't suspect a thing about his proclivities. Having a secret life was often its own aphrodisiac; it was what made it possible to get through insipid evenings filled with debutantes who were more like wax figurines from a museum. Outside Elise's door, he paused to give his arm an experimental swing. He felt alive again.

The house *was* a mausoleum. Marianne *felt* it the moment she stepped into the hall of Newlyn House. She'd not been here since the funeral wake for the late duke and duchess. Vennor had not exaggerated. The heels of her shoes gave an echoing click on the black-and-white tiles, the only noise in the house. Not even Honeycutt who'd answered the door had made a sound.

'Lady Treleven, Miss Treleven, what a delight to host you today.' Honeycutt helped them with their shawls as Marianne gave the hall an assessing glance. It was a visual affirmation of the silence, devoid of any signs of life. The console along the wall was polished to a sheen, but it was missing warmth; there was no vase, no flowers that might offer a touch of domesticity, or a sense of welcome for a visitor.

Marianne exchanged a look with her mother and began making a mental list. She had three items on that list by the time Vennor joined them in the hall. 'Lady Treleven,' he greeted her mother, 'thank you for coming and you, too, Marianne. I hope I haven't displaced any plans?' His tone was light. By all accounts, he might have been as he always was, full of humour and confidence, but Marianne saw the tell-tale tightness at the corners of his mouth, as only a close friend might.

Her heart went out to him. He'd not arrived at this decision easily. This was hard on him. But so, too, must be seeing the house this way, living in it this way; Newlyn House had once been lively and inviting; it had exuded the personalities of the Duke and Duchess themselves. That personality had died with them. Yet Marianne had a sneaking suspicion that the house hadn't changed since the day the Duke and Duchess had walked out and never come back. Vennor was surrounded by the past, by the last moments of their lives. How did a man face such a dilemma? To pack up the memories of his parents in order to move forward, or to honour those memories by leaving things as they were? She did not envy Vennor the choice.

'I thought we might start upstairs in the wardrobes. You'll know what is best saved or given away.' He gestured to the stairs and ushered them ahead of him, but Marianne turned to Honeycutt before she ascended the steps. 'Please send to the flower markets. I want bouquets for all the public rooms.'

Honeycutt made a small bow in her direction, relief on his usually stoic face. 'With pleasure, Miss Treleven.'

Vennor gave a low chuckle behind her. 'You've been here five minutes and you're already giving orders.'

Marianne lifted her chin in teasing superiority and

shot him a glance over her shoulder. 'It's why you asked me to come, isn't it? I'd hate to disappoint you.'

Whatever levity they'd manage to conjure up died the moment they opened the door to the late Duchess's chambers. Stepping inside was overpowering. They were assailed by memories of the woman they'd known. The room smelled of her, the faint scent of rosewater lingered in the musty, closed rooms. It *felt* like her, too. Her things lay about the room as if waiting for her return—the hairbrushes and perfume vials at the vanity, the dressing gown that lay on the bed. Marianne swallowed hard. No wonder Vennor hadn't come in here. One could almost believe the Duchess would come out of the dressing room at any moment and sweep them into one of her famous hugs. 'Vennor and I will do the Duchess's chambers. Mother, if you could take some maids and do the Duke's?' She turned to Vennor. 'You need to establish yourself in the ducal chambers as soon as they're ready. They are yours now.' By rights, he should have been in them years ago, another sign of how deeply entrenched his grief was.

She started with the gowns. The Duchess had possessed exquisite fashion sense. Her gowns carried a timeless quality to their design that kept them in fashion even after three years. 'You should make gifts of some of these. We'll select a few to give to her lady's maid and to the other maids if you wish. They can remake them or sell them to a second-hand shop for extra money.' Marianne handed the gowns to Vennor one by one. 'Arrange piles on the bed; one for the maids, one for charity and one to pack away.'

Having a purpose helped Vennor relax and some of the tightness left his mouth. 'You're good at this. I know how to balance estate ledgers and write legislation, but I haven't the foggiest idea how to clean out a woman's closet.' He tried for a laugh.

'Well, I do.' Marianne smiled encouragingly, 'This first batch will be for the maids.' She laid the gowns across his arms, telling stories as the pile grew, recalling this dress and that—the lavender dress the Duchess wore to her coming-out ball, the green gown she wore to the art show at Somerset House—and commenting on the Duchess's oft-complimented style. 'Even in Cornwall, I envied her carriage ensembles whenever she called.'

She was rewarded with a smile from Vennor. 'You make remembering a blessing, not a curse.'

Marianne laid the last of the gowns in his arms. 'I'm glad. She wouldn't want you to be sad, Ven.'

Vennor deposited the gowns on the bed and returned for more. 'I'm not sad, I'm mad. I'm angry.' He leaned against the door frame, his blond hair falling forward in his face. She fought the urge to push it back, to mother him just a bit, but he wanted pity no more than she did. 'I keep asking myself why would anyone want to kill them? What did they ever do but help others?'

'Street thugs don't make such distinctions.' Marianne hated the pain on his face. It was such a handsome face, it deserved to be smiling. 'Thugs don't know their victims.' She paused at the emotion flickering across Vennor's face. 'They loved you, Vennor. You were the best of sons.'

Vennor shook his head as she handed him the Duchess's jewel case to take into the bedroom. 'I should have been better.' There was that bitterness again, the bitterness that had crept into him since their deaths. Most people didn't notice. He didn't let them. He was so...*careful*...with what he let everyone see—even his friends. Perhaps *especially* his friends. This was a rare moment when his guard was down as they settled on the bed with the jewel case. She saw the naked honesty of his words and was tempted to take advantage of his vulnerability and see what lay beneath the bitterness. But she knew Vennor too well. He would not welcome the intrusion. If she pushed, she would lose him. It would be better to wait and let him come to her with the things that weighed on his mind and his soul, even though her impatience argued she'd already given him three years. How much more time could he want? Her curiosity needed to take second place to his need.

They dealt with the jewel case in silence. Most of the Newlyn jewels were kept in the family vault. The items in the case were merely some of his mother's personal pieces and would be stored until a later time. Vennor shut the case and looked around the room. 'I suppose you should order new bedding and curtains to update the space,' he said, but he sounded reluctant.

Marianne shook her head. 'You should wait. These are in fine condition and your Duchess will want to style the room to her own taste. It seems a waste to redo the room just to have it made over again.'

Vennor arched a blond brow. 'My Duchess? Are you trying to marry me off again, Marianne? This is the second time in two days you've mentioned my marrying.' He was only half-mocking.

'Well, you've got to marry sometime, Ven.' But to whom? Not just any debutante would do. Perhaps that was why he resisted? There was no one who sparked his interest. A wife should have that, at least. 'Would you like Mama to pick some out for you?'

His response would have been comical if they hadn't been so serious. 'Would you have me marry for less than love? My parents didn't. Eaton's, Inigo's and Cassian's parents didn't.' Vennor pressed the argument for its own sake. She knew as well as he did that most dukes certainly did marry for less than love. They married for duty. In many ways, it was a duke's only duty, just as she had a duty to marry well for the sake of her family. 'They managed to combine duty and love. Perhaps I can, too.' His wistfulness tugged at her. Perhaps he could. Hadn't the others succeeded in doing so with their own recent marriages? Perhaps he had every reason to hope, yet she felt the urge to ask the honest question.

'Of course I wouldn't have you marry for less than love, it's just that love is so very hard to find, isn't it?' She did not love Lord Hayes, she knew that much. Marianne ran through the list of girls out this Season. There were several pretty ones with good credentials, but none that she could see Vennor falling madly in love with. He needed someone more…lively. She pleated the bedcovering between her fingers. 'Ven, what if not all of us get to fall in love? What if a good match is the best we can hope for?'

That was the fear, wasn't it? That he might spend his life searching for something that didn't exist. Like his parents' killer. What if he never found the man? What if he never found love? What if the two things he hungered for the most eluded him? When did one stop searching and yield to the inevitable? What did he say to Marianne's question? That it was indeed a possibility? 'I will marry, just as soon as I catch their killers.'

'But what if you don't?' Marianne was studying him with dark, intelligent eyes. 'It's been three years. Surely the thought has crossed your mind.'

'You sound like Inigo and Cassian. They think I ought to give it up, too,' Vennor snapped.

'I'm not saying you should give up. The two don't have to be mutually exclusive. Why does marrying have to come *after* finding the killers?'

A hundred answers rocketed through his mind.

Because I don't know who I am. I have no purpose beyond being the Vigilante.

Because I am consumed by the search. Who would I be if I abandoned the search?

Because I have nothing to give a wife right now, not even myself.

Because I don't want to fail her the way I failed my parents.

He'd been failing them long before their deaths, refusing to marry the girls selected by his mother's best matchmaking efforts, failing to take up the callings his father had laid before him. But he could share none of this with Marianne. The reasons were too private, too shameful to admit out loud, even to his friend. She wouldn't want to believe them. She insisted on seeing the best in him even when he couldn't see it in himself. She would want to argue they weren't true.

'It hardly matters; there's no one I am interested in, so it's a moot point.' His mother had spent years tempting him with this friend's daughter and that friend's niece. They were all nice girls but, in the end, they were all the same.

Marianne straightened, her posture tensing as an idea occurred to her. 'Ven, do you *like* girls?' Her tone was hushed and a brave flush coloured Marianne's cheeks at the mention of such a scandalous subject.

'Yes, I like girls,' Vennor answered, although it had been a long time since he'd been with one. *I like you.* The thought blazed across his consciousness. It wasn't a new thought. He'd always liked Marianne on a subconscious level. Liking her was a given. He'd never questioned it, never examined the reasons for it.

Today, watching her manage his house, his staff, his own emotions about moving forward, the realisation took on more obvious import. She would make a fine duchess for the dukedom of Newlyn and they rubbed along well together. 'Rubbing along' was a rather lukewarm endorsement, but perhaps a lukewarm assessment was best. This was hardly the time to examine what liking Marianne meant and how deep that liking ran. Neither of them knew their own minds. He was struggling to find a life of his own outside his role as the Vigilante and she was struggling with her own path. It would be easy to abuse the friendship, to use it as a distraction from the real issues facing both of them.

He should keep Marianne at arm's length until they'd resolved their own individual issues.

His mind issued a warning. *If you wait, it might be too late. What if she marries Hayes?*

His heart had done a strange little flip of its own accord this morning on seeing her in the hall, listening to her issue the orders for flowers. She seemed right at home at Newlyn House. She'd known exactly what he'd needed. She'd made him laugh while sorting the dresses. She'd transformed his grief into fond remembrances with her stories. That scared him. She was drawing closer, and he *wanted* her closer, at a time when he needed her further from him, a time when he needed to be alone to finish the journey.

He got off the bed, the large room suddenly too small for the both of them. His eyes seemed to have nowhere to look but at her face, at her sharp dark eyes, at the redness of her lips and at that full mouth of hers as she gave as good as she got in an argument. What was wrong with him? Since when had Marianne's mouth become a source of interest? Yesterday, he'd been noticing her breasts. Since when had she become a woman who drew him on merits other than friendship? Since when had the temptation arisen to do something about it? Yesterday? At the Fordhams'? Or had that temptation been there all along, lying dormant, just waiting for a time to raise its head?

He turned towards the window and drew back the curtain, determined to keep himself from drowning in the dark pools of her eyes, eyes that saw him, knew him, as others did not. Did she feel it, too? This new attraction? These new thoughts? Or had this all been brought on by his loneliness?

Marianne gave him no relief, the soft floral scent of lilies of the valley cut with vanilla announcing her presence as she came to stand beside him. She stood close—friendship had made them casual with one another.

'Are you all right, Ven?' She was looking up at him, a tiny furrow of concern on her brow. It would be a simple matter to capture her mouth with his, to test the attraction.

No, damn it, he wasn't fine. He wanted to drag her to him and kiss her hard on the mouth, wanted to see if the current between them was shared, to see if it was more than a distraction, an excuse for facing his realities. What would Marianne say if he acted on that impulse? What would she do? Would he ruin their friendship for ever? He found that friendship was too precious to him to risk it. Even if she shared the nascent attraction, what then? He had even less to offer her than anyone else. How could he live with himself if he failed her, too? And how could he not fail her? It seemed as if he was in a double bind. He'd fail her if the attraction was short-lived because the unsuccessful foray would be between them for evermore. He'd fail her if the attraction was real because he could offer her nothing but his brokenness.

'Ven, you look queer. I think we've done enough for today.' She looped her arm through his. 'Let's go downstairs and see how Honeycutt is coming with the flowers.'

Yes, he thought. Because if they stayed here, all hell was about to break loose in his mother's bedchamber.

Chapter Six

Spring had broken loose downstairs in their absence. Vases of bright yellow daffodils and colourful Dutch tulips populated sideboards and consoles, adding much-needed colour and a sense of lively warmth to the house. The simple transformation was not lost on Vennor as he helped Marianne and her mother with their shawls. 'The flowers are a lovely addition,' he complimented, his hands lingering a moment longer than needed at Marianne's shoulders. 'Thank you for this.'

'Flowers are just the beginning.' Marianne smiled over her shoulder and for a moment they might have been the only two people in the hall. Thank goodness they weren't. He might have been tempted beyond restraint, tempted to steal that kiss, to experiment with the thoughts that had seated themselves in his mind. 'We'll do the ballroom next.'

Vennor chuckled at that. 'Why? What do I need a

ballroom for?' He would have thought she'd do the drawing room next or the private sitting rooms.

Marianne merely gave him an impish grin that boded no good. 'You never know when you'll need one. Maybe it's time to bring back the Newlyn Charity Ball.'

She was smiling, but she wasn't joking, the little minx. It made him nervous. She had plans. 'Why would I do that?' He could think of nothing worse than hosting a ball. His mother had spent months arranging the charity ball and he didn't have either the time or the inclination. 'I don't know that I want the *ton* roaming through my parents' home like tourists.'

'Not your parents' home, Ven, your home. That's what today is about and tomorrow, and the next. Making this your home.' Marianne's hand cupped his jaw. 'I know it's hard, but this is your place now, the seat of your power when you're in town. You have to show everyone you're back.'

'I never left. I hold my seat in the House of Lords and I attend select events.' He'd not once let the Penlerick presence in the House of Lords lapse. He'd taken up his father's seat immediately, despite his grief. He looked over Marianne's shoulder, in the hopes of appealing to Lady Treleven for help, but there was none. She was vigorously nodding her head, a sharp gleam in her eye.

'Marianne's right, Vennor.' Lady Treleven jumped into the fray. 'Attending "select" events means you go out little and show up late.' She wagged a motherly finger in his direction. 'I know what you're up to, not showing up until the supper dance and then claiming Marianne. You're hiding. That's not being socially available.' He knew it, too. He just didn't want to be 'socially available', as Lady Treleven put it. It meant dancing with the debutantes and the wallflowers, with hostesses' daughters and nieces—all the things his mother had asked him to do. It meant less time to play the Vigilante. He couldn't be patrolling the East Docks if he was dancing attendance on the likes of Lady Lester's daughters.

Lady Treleven was firm. 'It's time to signal to society that you're ready to keep up the Penlerick reputation for entertaining. At the very least, you need to resurrect your parents' charity ball for the London orphanages.'

Vennor scoffed at the idea, feeling beset. Even Honeycutt, who was exceedingly busy straightening tulips in a vase as an excuse for eavesdropping, was no help. 'Forgive my disagreement. The only thing a ball will signal is that I am ready to wed. Every matchmaking mama in London will line up for an invitation.' The only thing worse than the *ton* roaming through his house was a ballroom full of girls wanting to marry his title. He hadn't the time for that this Season. 'Maybe next year,' Vennor opted to politely table the idea. 'I think it might be a bit much for me this year, with the Season already underway.'

'We'd plan it, wouldn't we, Mama?' Marianne joined her mother at the door and slipped her arm through her mother's. Forces joined. 'You wouldn't have to do anything except show up.'

'I have all of Her Grace's notes about the ball; the caterer she used, the florists and the decorators,' Honeycutt offered. 'Shall I get them for you?'

'That would be lovely, thank you, Honeycutt. See how easy it will be? Why, it's practically planned already.' Marianne beamed.

'I don't think that will be necessary, Honeycutt.' Vennor glowered at the unhelpful butler. 'The ladies need to be off, I'm sure.' With luck, the collective ardour for such an undertaking would diminish to more manageable proportions tomorrow. He moved towards the door, opening it himself with a bow. 'I will see you tonight, Marianne, at the Gaspards'. Shall I call with the carriage at half past seven?' Perhaps on the ride over, he could talk her out of her latest madcap idea.

'Or perhaps I can talk you into it,' she murmured, reading his thoughts as she passed him.

Well, she could try. Vennor shut the door behind them and girded himself to face that traitor Honeycutt. He would stand firm on this. There would be no ball.

There *would* be a ball, Marianne thought resolutely, settling in the landau. The folding hoods had been retracted so they could take advantage of the fine weather on the drive between Portland Square and Curzon Street. Marianne was in high spirits. If only Vennor's spirits were as elevated. Today had been full of progress on that account, though. She had pushed him in some ways, like the mention of the ball, and given him his privacy in others. But she had not coddled him. The time for that had passed, if it had ever existed. Vennor had not coddled himself, had not wallowed in self-pity when his parents died. He'd taken up the dukedom immediately and relentlessly, working harder than his friends had felt he ought. But he'd made himself a recluse in the process. A duke had a social duty as well as a political one and Vennor had done little of the former.

'You did well today, my dear,' her mother complimented as the landau merged into afternoon traffic. 'Vennor can't possibly have failed to notice what an excellent manager you are. Any home of yours will run smoothly.'

Marianne tilted her head to study her mother. It was an odd comment to make. 'I don't think Vennor particularly cares whether or not I can write out a dinner menu.' She *could* run a large house. Her mother had included home management as part of the education of all her daughters once they turned thirteen, but just because she was an apt hand at it didn't mean she *wanted* to do it. She wasn't like her sister Ayleth, who'd married an MP and absolutely prided herself on running his home.

Her mother arched a brow. 'I wouldn't be so sure. Today allowed Vennor the opportunity to see you with new eyes. I rather think he took that opportunity.'

Coming on the heels of her own new awareness of the edge, the spark—whatever one wanted to call it—between her and Vennor, the comment made her uneasy. What did it mean if her mother saw it, too? There were indeed 'new eyes', as her mother put it, and not just his, but hers as well. This afternoon, at the window in his mother's room, there'd been a moment when she could have sworn Vennor had wanted to kiss her.

And her curiosity had wanted him to.

The moment had gone as quickly as it had come, but not the wanting—*that* had lingered along with his hands on her shoulders in the hall and she had *welcomed* it. She did not, however, welcome her mother's intrusion. The gleam in her mother's eye was positively alarming. Anyone who looked at Sarah Treleven and saw a pretty, biddable woman in her midforties didn't look hard enough. She was a veritable tigress when it came to her daughters. It was no wonder, Marianne thought, that Rosenwyn had hidden her courtship with Cador Kitto until the very end. Now, all her mother's tenacity and energy was focused on her.

'Vennor must marry. His delay does not eradicate the need. His reluctance is obvious.' Her mother adjusted her parasol against the sun.

'There's no one out this Season who catches his eye.' Marianne suddenly felt defensive of her friend. Maybe Vennor *was* right to refuse her mother's help in matchmaking. Her mother would have him wedded in no time.

Her mother waved a dismissive hand. 'There are plenty of girls this Season. There's Leah St John. She's lovely and plays the piano exquisitely. There's

Amelia Helmsley. Her father's an earl and her manners are divine, as is her dowry. If I had a son, I'd send him in her direction without hesitation.'

'They hardly know him.' A queer, unpleasant flutter had taken up residence in her stomach at the thought of Vennor marrying either of them. They were both nice girls, yet she didn't want them with Vennor. Vennor was…hers. He'd always been hers. It was Vennor who'd given her piggyback rides through the summer woods, Vennor who'd always talked the others into letting her tag along on fishing trips. It was Vennor who'd captained the boys' team in charades against her girls' team. She found now that she didn't want to share him. Did Vennor feel this way when she waltzed off with Lord Hayes? She supposed she'd have to get used to the feeling. It was one thing to theorise about Vennor marrying, it was another to accept it as inevitable. The latter was far harder to get used to. Her mother was right. Vennor had to marry someone and the sooner the better.

Her mother gave her a pointed look. 'There's you.'

Marianne stared. 'Me? Vennor should marry me? I can't marry him,' she stammered. 'He's my *friend*.'

'He wants to be more than your friend, that much was plain today.' Her mother pressed, 'Surely you are not that naive, Marianne? He invited you to fix up his home. It's on the same level as being invited to the family pile in the country. Everyone knows what *that* invitation means.'

'Because he trusts me,' Marianne argued against the notion. 'You heard him today. He feels like an object of gossip. He doesn't want people in his home who are looking to resurrect the old scandal.'

'Trust is a desirable quality in a mate. Being a duke is no easy task. It would be a comfort to him to have a wife who knows him so well that a look can speak volumes, to have a wife who will have his back and stand at his side, who won't have an affair or speak ill of him. Why not marry a friend? Who better to be all that to him than a girl he's known all his life, who's become a woman more than capable of running his home, raising his children and loving him as only a long-standing friend can?'

'I cannot believe you're suggesting that. We are friends,' she repeated, fully aware that the phrase did not defeat any of her mother's reasons, only fuelled them. 'What about Lord Hayes?'

Her mother gave an elegant, one-shoulder shrug. 'I didn't say *you* wanted to marry Vennor. Goodness knows he's got baggage to boot, with his reluctance to rejoin society, and who knows where he spends his time when he's not working for Parliament? He's buried himself in work so he doesn't have to face his emotions and one of these days his dam will burst. He won't be an easy husband for any woman.'

'Then why tell me all these things?' Marianne blurted out, feeling angry. What did her mother mean to suggest? One moment she was singing Vennor's praises and the next she was maligning him, which in truth did surprise her. Vennor had always been her mother's favourite of the four.

'I'm merely telling you what Vennor is thinking.'

Her mother was unfazed by her outburst. 'I've not brought three daughters to the altar without knowing what goes on in the heads of young men.' She twirled the handle of her parasol thoughtfully, a little smile touching her lips, and Marianne could see a hint of the debutante she used to be. 'Forewarned is forearmed, my dear. If you can anticipate the situation, nothing will surprise you. Vennor is thinking of courting you. If he decides to do so, you need to be ready.'

Vennor wanted to court her?

The thought chased her into the reading room at home. Marianne shut the door firmly behind her, but the idea followed her anyway. Perhaps if it were distasteful to her it would be easier to shut it out. But it wasn't. It was a curious idea.

What would it be like to be courted by Vennor? What would change between them? *Was* it even possible for things to stay the same? If not, what would they lose? Would it be worth it? A kiss would change everything, she was fairly certain of that, and yet she wanted that kiss, wanted to know what his mouth would feel like against hers. Did all men kiss the same way? Would it feel the same as Hayes's?

Hayes had kissed her once a few weeks ago after the art show at Somerset House. Perhaps she shouldn't have allowed it, but she'd never had a real kiss, only a few rowdy pecks as the result of parlour games back home. It had been a chaste brush against her lips, hardly anything to cause a girl to be led into sin. If that was all there was to it, Marianne wondered what all the fuss was about. There had to be more.

Her sisters blushed happily whenever they discussed their husbands, but they wouldn't tell her a thing, apparently preferring to keep it a secret between themselves. Thank goodness there were books, a highly invaluable resource for completing a young girl's education if she knew where to look—and Marianne did. A back section at Hatchard's had been quite enlightening.

Marianne opened the drawer in the reading table and took out her notebook along with a folded map of London. The idea that she might soon need to choose between Vennor and Hayes was a false dichotomy based on an equally false premise. Her mother saw only the two choices, both based on the assumption that she would marry at the end of the Season. Marianne spread the map out on the table and studied the red X's. She knew differently. She didn't have to choose marriage. She didn't have to choose Vennor or Hayes. She could choose herself. *If* she found the Vigilante.

Some honest work was exactly what she needed. *This* was her calling—being a reporter, not a lady of the *ton* whose most useful writing skill was setting seating charts and menus.

Vennor might let you keep your writing. With him, it could be different.

The thought whispered around her head, gaining veracity with logic. Vennor already knew of her secret writing career and he encouraged it.

Realism's arrow pierced the idea at its heart. Vennor encouraged her writing currently because it posed no risk to himself. Whether he approved or not, his Duchess couldn't write a news column for a gentleman's magazine. If someone found out, the scandal would be enormous. He would be shamed. No, being a duchess was the greatest cage of all. Society's eyes would ever be on her just as they were on Vennor now. No wonder he chose seclusion.

The column! She'd nearly forgotten. It was due tomorrow. She needed to send it this afternoon so that it would be waiting for her editor in the morning. Marianne opened the drawer again and pulled it out. Thank goodness it was ready to go. The day had flown by working with Vennor. Her hand stilled as she folded the paper. Was it possible that was what was behind his request for her help? Had he thought to keep her too busy to pursue the Vigilante? He'd made no secret of his disapproval in that regard. She recalled feeling that there was more to his request than the answer he'd given her yesterday in the park. The possibility put her at war with herself.

How dare he sabotage her!

But no. It wasn't sabotage. He cared for her, he was worried for her safety. He knew how much this meant to her, how much she was counting on this.

He thought the Vigilante should stay masked.

Even if it was sabotage, look at the lengths he was willing to go. He was willing to come out of his grief, to finally pack up the town house and make it his own. She knew what that meant to him and what it had cost him emotionally to do it. He'd been facing dragons today. She'd seen it in his face. Was he really willing to go that far just to keep her safe?

No matter his motives, she couldn't allow it to stop her. She had to do this. Whether he meant to court her, or whether he meant to protect her, her best course of action was still trying to prove herself as a journalist, to give herself another choice besides marriage when the time came. She needed to find the Vigilante and she couldn't do that sitting at home.

She stared at the map, tracing the X's. He hadn't been to the East Docks for a while. He was due for a visit. Maybe she would start there. She grimaced. It was the beginning of a plan, but it was not the whole plan. She couldn't just wander the East Docks. She'd be no better or luckier than Angeline Mercer. She might be deader, though. Vennor's concern wasn't erroneous. It would be dangerous, but the Vigilante only came out at night. There were no daytime sightings of him reported, *ever*. She had no choice. She splayed her hands on the table. She would go tonight. There was no sense in delaying. Any night would be just as dangerous and she might not find him the first time out. If she needed more than one outing, she'd need all the time she could muster. While she was there, she would ask around about him. Perhaps he had a lair? He must go somewhere during the day? He didn't stop existing at sunrise. If she were lucky, perhaps word of her search would reach him and he might come looking for her, which would make things all that much easier.

The thrill of the hunt started to thrum through her as she made a list of supplies and details. What to wear? She'd need a dark cloak, money for a hack and a weapon. She hadn't acquired a pistol yet. She'd been counting on Vennor for that, but there was no way now that he'd help her get a pistol knowing what she intended it for. She did have a small knife, though. It would have to do.

A little frisson of fear snaked down her back, mingling with the thrill, as the reality of what she proposed to do sank in. She was going to journey into the slums of London. At night. Alone. That was what a good reporter did, she told herself. If she meant to be a serious journalist, it meant taking serious chances. It was easy to write titbits for the society column. She only had to walk into ballrooms, which were safe, brightly lit and mostly populated by people she knew. She shook off her misgivings. This was *exactly* the test she needed. Was she cut out to be a serious journalist? Could she do the things that were required? If not, perhaps that was a sign that she *should* choose a more traditional path.

Satisfied with her list, she turned to her next task: subterfuge. She needed to elude Vennor, who was expecting her at the Gaspards', and her parents who had their own plans this evening. Marianne glanced at the clock, it was nearly six. Vennor was planning to call for her in an hour and a half. She took out writing paper and scribbled hastily. It wouldn't serve her purpose to have Vennor miss getting her note. The last thing she needed was for him to show up here and for her to be gone.

Chapter Seven

The note arrived just as he was finishing his preparations for the evening. Vennor lifted his chin, letting his valet tie his cravat. He was more than a little disappointed by the news. He'd been looking forward to the Gaspards' *with* Marianne and listening to her arguments as to why he should host a ball. He wasn't going to do it. She was not changing his mind on this, but it would be entertaining to watch her try. That wasn't the only disappointment, though. The larger disappointment was that she'd chosen to attend the Mayfield rout with Lord Hayes instead.

His valet finished the work and stuck a sapphire stickpin into the snowy folds and stepped back. Vennor approved the work with a quick, absent-minded nod, his thoughts on Lord Hayes. It was the Hayes part that bothered him about Marianne's note. She'd chosen the Viscount over him *after* their little duel in the hall over the ball. He could still see that challenging smile she'd tossed him and how her eyes had said *this is not over.* But suddenly, four hours later, it was. It wasn't like her to change her mind, not when they had unfinished business and she was not besotted with Hayes. He'd seen them together. She was cordial with Hayes, but nothing more. Had she been pressured into it by her parents? Had something happened?

Vennor fingered the note. Had she picked up on the spark between them and decided it was best to establish some distance? Perhaps she'd even divined his thoughts this afternoon. But even that rang false. Marianne never ran from a fight or from awkwardness. If she *had* divined his thoughts, she would confront him. He could see her now on the Gaspards' dance floor, asking in the middle of the waltz, 'Ven, did you mean to kiss me today?' with the same bluntness she'd enquired whether he liked girls. The scene made him chuckle even as it set off warning bells. Something was definitely afoot. That decided it. He took his silk hat and swordstick from his valet. 'Appleby, send word to the coachman, there's been a change of plans.'

He would attend the Mayfields' instead, if for no other reason than to assure himself Marianne was fine.

She wasn't at the Mayfield rout. It seemed she'd changed her plans yet again. For a girl who *never* changed her mind, changing it twice in one night seemed highly irregular. Vennor took two tours of the ballroom just to be sure before he felt forced to approach Hayes, a man who seemed determined to view him as a rival. Hayes informed him in clipped tones that indicated his own disappointment at her absence and his disapproval of Vennor's presence—or perhaps it was Vennor's search for Marianne that upset him—that Miss Treleven had decided to stay in for the evening due to a headache.

A headache made no sense at all to Vennor. If she was unwell, why tell him she'd decided to attend the Mayfield ball? Why not just tell him she was staying in? Because Hayes would believe the headache scenario and he wouldn't. Marianne hadn't had a headache a day in her life. She was the healthiest person Vennor knew. Of course, he didn't bother to mention it to Hayes, who was already prickly enough.

Vennor excused himself and made another circuit of the ballroom, stopping to make small talk here and there, all the while his mind running through Marianne's messages. They were clearly hiding something. Why had she wanted he and Hayes to think she was somewhere different? Why was such subterfuge necessary? Was she working on something for her column? But that made little sense, too. Coming to balls *was* her work; it was where she got her information and the Gaspard and Mayfield balls were well attended. She'd easily have material for a week from any one of them.

A worried nugget began to form. Had she gone after the Vigilante? Was she even now out in the streets of London, hunting him? The thought sent a new kind of terror through him. Marianne was adventurous and brave, but that didn't mean she was street savvy. He began to move through the crowd, his pace quicker now, fuelled by concern. He didn't want to think of the trouble she could get into: drunks, pimps, brothel-snatchers, cutpurses.

His thoughts were sprinting ahead of him. Did she know enough to leave her jewellery at home? Had she dressed appropriately or had she gone out in a white ballgown, thinking to convince her parents she was actually at the Gaspards' with him? Oh, good Lord! Her parents thought she was with him! Jock Treleven would kill him if anything happened to her.

At the kerb he gestured for his carriage. 'The Treleven town house, on Curzon. All haste,' he instructed. He *hoped* he would find her at home with a good explanation for her lies. But the Treleven town house was dark when he arrived. It didn't stop him from hopping out and knocking on the door. Servants would know where the family had gone. Sir Jock and his wife were at a musicale, they informed him, and Miss Treleven was spending the night with a friend.

That confirmed it. He sank back against the squabs of the seats. Marianne was abroad in London. Alone. Where would she go? She could be anywhere and he could not be everywhere. Vigilante or not, he was only one man. He didn't know what was worse, Marianne wandering the whore grounds of Covent Garden or the crime-riddled lanes of the East Docks where throats were slit nightly. The danger ratio decided it. There were at least constabulary in Covent Garden at this time of night. She had the chance of having help there if she ran into trouble. There'd be no help at the docks.

The East Docks it was. He called instructions to the coachman and began to transform. He reached under the seat and pulled out a box for his valuables. He undid his cufflinks, slipped off his gold signet ring and removed his carefully placed sapphire stickpin from his cravat. He took inventory. Had he missed anything? No. Good. Now, what assets did he have? He did not have his usual hidden knife. The Vigilante never went out unarmed. Tonight, the unplanned foray left him feeling naked. What he did have was his short sword sheathed inside his walking stick and his fists. They would have to be enough. There was no time to go back to the town house or to his cache on the docks. He'd lost enough time already at the Mayfields'. Every moment he delayed put Marianne at risk.

He fingered the black silk in his pocket. He didn't *want* to wear the mask. He was dressed in evening clothes and a person of discernment would be bound to think the Vigilante a gentleman with his sword-stick and his apparel. It could imperil his identity, but wearing the mask might be the only way to protect her. It would certainly be easier to locate her. People would talk to the Vigilante one way or another. The Vigilante could put out word that she was not to be harmed. As long as he wasn't too late. Please, dear Lord, he thought fervently, don't let me be too late.

She'd never been out this late alone before. Marianne pulled her hood a little closer around her face and her hand gripped the handle of the little knife in her pocket. The feel of the smooth hilt offered reassurance as she skirted a muddy pool and tried to ignore the tell-tale smell of faeces and rotten food coming from an alley. She focused on the next step; she needed to make enquiries. She couldn't go randomly through the streets simply hoping to find him. She would stop in at the taverns and ask.

The first tavern was a dimly lit place that smelled of unwashed humanity. Marianne stepped inside and nearly gagged. She was not the only woman present, but she *was* the only one not draped over a man or two. No matter. She knew what to do. Shoulders back, head up. Walk with purpose and no one would bother her. No one interfered with a woman on a mission. But that only made her more conspicuous as she strode up to the bar. The barkeep was a heavy-jowled man with a scar on his cheek. He gave her a long, slow perusal as he dried a mug, but said nothing.

Marianne slid two coins across the scarred counter. 'I am looking for information about where to find the Vigilante,' she said in her best authoritative tone.

'You and everyone else.' He spat on to the floor, his small eyes fixed on her as she fought the urge to flinch. But she didn't dare show any weakness, not in a place like this. 'Nobody knows where he comes from, or where he goes. Nobody knows where he's going to be or when.' He spat again. 'Keeps the bosses on their toes, he does.'

'Does he have informants? People who can contact him? How does he know where to be?' Marianne pressed, the instinctive interviewer in her rising to the fore. 'Surely there's a way to reach him. Can I leave a message for him?'

The barkeep reached for another mug to dry. 'You can leave a message at the Vigilante's Post down on the docks. Not here, though. He doesn't exactly hobnob with anyone. He's put some of these fellas out of work. Can't say he's entirely popular with everyone in these parts.' He guffawed. 'I can see by the look on your face you hadn't thought of that.' He nodded towards the table by the window. 'Every one of those boyos over there would like to slit his throat. He's cost them jobs working for the bosses collecting dues.'

'They're extortionists, you mean.' Marianne let her gaze slide to the table at the window. The four men were big burly types, the sort with meanness rolling off them. No wonder they were given a wide berth.

'I don't know if I mean that or not. That's a pretty fancy word, for these parts, miss. We call them insurance men.' The barkeep reached for the coins and pocketed them. 'If I were you, I'd be moving along. I don't know where you came from with silk flashing beneath that cloak, but I can guess. This ain't no place for you. You're making my working girls jealous and my customers horny for something they don't have to buy.'

Marianne was happy to take the man's advice. The men at the window were making her nervous. She had other places to look for the Vigilante and if they turned up nothing, she could always try to locate the Vigilante's Post. She stepped out into the cooler, slightly fresher night air.

She'd taken no more than ten steps when the tavern door opened and shut behind her, spilling men into the darkness. She counselled herself to keep walking, not to look back. It was perfectly ordinary for men to leave a tavern. The act did not require her attention. It had nothing to do with her. But a rough voice in the darkness put paid to that notion.

'You, there, you're looking for the Vigilante. Why don't we join forshes?'

The last part was slurred. At least one of the men was intoxicated. Marianne walked a little faster. The men followed.

'Weesh is looking for him, too. The bloody bashtard stole our jobsh.'

Now she *was* worried. These were the men from the table. The extortionists. She looked about for a place to duck into, but the street she'd turned up was dark, not a light in sight, and she had no idea where she was. The docks weren't laid out with street signs and grids like Mayfair.

She started to run. She'd worry about finding her way out later. Right now, she was worried about her safety. Footsteps pounded behind her, laughter and shouts of drunken merriment following. 'Come on, lassie, we just want to have a little fun!' Drat, at least one of them was sober.

Marianne turned a corner here, another corner there. She slipped on crooked cobblestones, regained her balance and kept going. A stitch took up residence in her side. She took another turn and nearly ran into a brick wall. Dammit! A dead end! She was trapped in a dark alley. She looked about furtively for a doorway, a staircase, anything that might lead anywhere away from here. There was nothing. Fear gripped her as she pressed herself against the wall. She could hear them coming, breathing hard from their efforts. Her own breath was ragged. She tried to control it, tried to stay quiet. Perhaps they would overlook her in the dark. She slid a hand into her pocket and drew her knife in case they didn't.

Luck was not with her. Her dress betrayed her, peeping beneath her cloak. She didn't cover it fast enough. 'She's down there!' one of them cried and they came crashing into the alley.

'Stay back. I am armed.' Marianne brandished her blade, but it seemed too tiny to be of consequence against men of their size and girth. And she was far too inexperienced to make the most of her weapon. They rushed her, one man grabbing her wrist and gripping it hard until the knife clattered to the cobblestones. A second man grabbed her other arm.

'You and me can be first, then Eli.' The third man laughed, working open his trousers. Marianne kicked at him and struggled against her captors, but they were too strong, weighing her arms down.

'The Vigilante will hear about this.' Perhaps a threat would get them to reconsider.

'Maybe he will. It'll be too late for you, though,' he leered, pressing himself against her.

Marianne spit in his face and earned the back of

his hand in a stinging blow across her cheek. Her head bounced hard enough to see stars and for a moment she struggled for consciousness. Dear heavens, she *had* to stay alert. If she didn't, she wondered if she'd ever wake up. Perhaps they'd slit her throat once they'd finished with her.

'I have money.' Marianne tried one last time, but it was hard to make the words. Her cheek stung and there was blood in her mouth.

'I'm not interested in money at the moment.' He had a hand beneath her skirts. 'Not unless you have a sack full in your—'

The man didn't finish his sentence. There was a cry of pain from behind him and a swift, dark form dispatched the fourth man. He dropped to the ground, unconscious before he fell. The two men holding her arms dropped them in a panic, but there was nowhere for them to run.

'Leave the lady alone.' Low, gravelly tones cut through the darkness.

'Or you'll what?' The third man wasn't as impressed as his comrades. 'There's three of us and one of you, Vigilante. Those are tough odds. Perhaps we'll finish you off and get back to business.'

'You're welcome to try.'

Marianne gasped as a swordstick flashed in the Vigilante's hand: a gentleman's weapon! The three men advanced on him in a semicircle, their own more rugged blades drawn. Her initial relief at the Vigilante's sudden appearance was quickly replaced with a new fear. She was going to get the Vigilante killed.

How did one man take on three armed men? She edged to the side, keeping her back against the brick wall, and inched towards safety. If she could get behind the Vigilante, she could run. But where? Into more trouble? Perhaps she should stay here and do what she could to help.

The man on the left moved first, but he was a lumbering ox of a man who was slowed by his bulk. The Vigilante met his stabbing thrust easily with his swordstick and sent the man's blade skittering out of reach. He struck hard with his fist and the man sagged against the brick wall. The Vigilante whirled to face the remaining two attackers. They came at him in a coordinated effort to overpower him. The Vigilante let them come, luring them close enough to land a powerful boot in the soft belly of one and slice the other down the length of his arm. Winded and bleeding, they stumbled down the alley, yelping in pain.

It had all been over in less than two minutes. The Vigilante had handled them as if they were child's play. He sheathed his swordstick and kicked at the two unconscious men left behind by their comrades before turning to her. 'Are you hurt?'

'No, thank you.' Her voice trembled. 'Just bruised.' She gingerly touched her cheek. 'You came along just in time.' She took the handkerchief he offered and pressed it to her lips, breathing in its sophisticated scent. The expensive cloth came away bloody. At the sight of it, her hands began to shake. The reality of what had nearly happened settled in. Her boldness had almost got her raped in an alley, perhaps killed.

She didn't want to think of what would have happened if the Vigilante hadn't been there. She'd been lucky tonight and Vennor had been right. This was a dangerous mission and she'd acted foolishly in coming alone…or in coming at all. She began to tremble all over again.

Chapter Eight

Marianne's body flooded with the twin reverberations of the ordeal and the elation of rescue, of having survived. Her body wanted to celebrate, but all it seemed capable of doing was shaking. Her knees went weak, unable to hold her. She stumbled against the Vigilante and his arms were there, drawing her close, his body all warmth and safety.

'You'll be all right in a bit; it's just shock,' he offered as assurance. She could hear his heartbeat where her head pressed against his chest, its own rhythm strong and hard, still coursing from the fight. Beneath the sweat of his exertions, he smelled like his handkerchief, all fresh starch and something else familiar—sandalwood and nutmeg?

'Breathe with me,' he coached, drawing a long, slow breath she could feel against her cheek as his chest rose and fell. 'That's it. Good girl. Breathe again. Now take another.' They stood that way, in the dark alley, her wrapped in his arms, for a long while. She could feel his heartbeat slowing into its normal rhythm. Even when the shaking had subsided, she was reluctant to leave the shelter of his arms. This man had saved her at considerable risk to himself. Facing down four men was no small feat despite him having made it look easy.

She raised her head and looked up at him, her curiosity starting to reassert itself now that danger had passed. The black silk mask hid the top half of his face, covering his hair and the upper portion of his features, leaving only his mouth to view, as well as a strong, square chin—quite the stuff of heroes, to be sure. The conjecture in London drawing rooms about his good looks was not falsely rooted if those features were anything to go on. He might be a gentleman in disguise, after all, given his clothes, his swordstick and the expensive scent of his linen. Her gaze rested on his chin. Was that a dimple hiding there? In the darkness it was hard to tell if she'd seen anything or not.

He was alert to her perusal and did not allow her to stare. 'Let me get you home.' His voice was a low growl and she had the impression that he was trying to disguise it, that this was not his natural tone. He took her by the hand, leading her out of the alley towards a main street, where it was slightly lighter. Gas lamps had not been prolifically deployed in this part of London. Still, she hoped for a better look at the Vigilante's face. He seemed to be aware of that risk, too, though, and carefully kept his face averted, his pace two steps ahead of her.

They walked several streets in silence as he searched for a hack. This was not hack territory at this time of night. He was quiet, speaking not at all now that she was recovered. There were no questions, no enquiries into what she was doing there, no scoldings. If there was going to be any conversation it would be up to her, she decided. This was her chance, the chance she'd come looking for. There *had* to be conversation.

'I want to thank you, sir. For what you did,' Marianne said, hoping to begin a dialogue, but her opening salvo was met with more silence. She tried again. 'Why do you do it, sir? Patrolling the streets? Exposing yourself to danger every night?' He didn't even attempt to acknowledge the question. They were approaching a larger inn with bright lights and music. A hack waited out front. Her time was running out and her temper was running hot. How dare he ignore her as if she were inconsequential now that she was rescued? She'd not expected the Vigilante to be so uncouth. 'You can at least look at me when I am talking to you!' She grabbed his arm. 'I risked my life coming to look for you tonight.'

That did it. His stoicism cracked. He whirled on her then, brilliant blue eyes flashing through the holes of his mask as he hauled her into a side street, the rough brick of a wall scratching at her back. 'And I risked mine coming to save you, you little fool!' He was mad, and fierce, and...aroused.

Marianne realised too late his silence was a sign of his restraint, of how tightly leashed he had kept himself in order to get her back to safety. And now, with her persistent questions, she'd inadvertently demanded an explanation for his silence, insisted that he slip that leash to vent his myriad emotions. It was like adding oil to an already raging fire. But he was not the only one with emotions riding high. Hers were, too. She wanted to make him pay for his lack of acknowledgement, for his rudeness after he'd exhibited so much caring, as much as he wanted to make her pay for her intrusion. She saw the consequence of such heat too late to prepare herself. They were both spoiling for a fight, or perhaps something else.

'Do you have any idea what could have happened?' His body was close to hers, close enough to feel the heat of him, anger radiating from him. There was something else in that pulse of energy directed at her. It was almost as if he was restraining himself, holding back from the urge to claim her as his own, to assure himself in that claiming, in that marking, that she was safe and unharmed. Her breath came short and her lips parted of their own volition. Perhaps it was all the invitation he needed to know he'd be welcomed after the boors of the street. He did not need to be asked twice. His mouth came crashing down on hers.

She met him in a collision of tempers and emotions. This was a different kind of argument and she was not unwilling to engage. What sprang between them was instant, hot, consuming—a naked arousal that refused to be masked in politeness and flirtation or by the initial surge of anger between them. The aftermath of the danger had burned away any need for pretence. She wanted and he wanted, each of them kindling the other's spark.

The kiss did not stay angry for long. Their tongues duelled and her teeth pulled at the tender flesh of his lip, sucking hard. His mouth moved to other parts of her, mimicking those actions at her earlobe, tracking hard kisses down the length of her jaw, the column of her neck. Her eyes were closed tight against the harsh pleasure racking her body, or perhaps in thrall to it, she couldn't decide which.

She was aware of him intimately behind her eyelids; she felt his ragged inhalations as his body pressed against her; the scent of him, the touch of him, engulfed her. He became more familiar with each kiss, each caress. Nutmeg and sandalwood floated through her memory and her mind's eye saw what her gaze did not, the peek-a-boo dimple at his chin, the sharp blueness of his eyes, the unnameable something in his touch that rang with its own familiarity. Items that had escaped her in the heat of battle, in the initial heat of passion began to coalesce into their own sensory vision. She *knew* him, this man. The Vigilante was not a stranger, not to her. It was why he didn't want to speak, why he'd tried so hard to disguise his voice.

But who did she know who would think to look for her here tonight? Who would be both angry and aroused by her actions? Who dared the things that had been dared tonight? He sucked hard at her throat and she gasped with the shocking pleasure of it, inhaling once more the sensual smell of him, and she knew with her eyes shut, what her eyes wide open had missed, had denied.

'Vennor!' Her eyes flew open, her hand swiping for the mask and dragging the black silk from his head before he could stop her, his golden locks catching the street light. 'Vennor, it is you!' Her heart both pumped with elation and then sank with disappointment. It wasn't the Vigilante at all. Her temper returned 'How dare you! How dare you make me believe you were him! How dare you let me think I'd found him. You knew how much this meant to me!' In her anger, she raised her hand and struck him hard across the face.

Somewhere in the depths of London a clock struck midnight. Everything had been stripped away. There were no gallant heroes and there would be no great unmasking to bolster her reporting career. There was no grandeur. Everything had become pumpkins and mice. How dare he take her dream and make a mockery of it.

She didn't believe him. Vennor nursed his jaw and strove for comprehension. In all of his imaginings of how it would go when he told her, he had not once entertained a scenario where Marianne doubted him. Nay, not just doubt him, but actually thought he was deliberately masquerading as the Vigilante to either appease her desire to find the Vigilante or to throw her off the scent entirely with an enormously fabricated lie.

'Marianne, I can explain—' Vennor said, but she

interrupted, bristling with fury. Her outrage had not defused with the slap.

'You'd better be able to explain.' Her eyes flashed and he saw in their dark depths hurt mixed with the anger. She'd not slapped him solely because she was mad. She'd slapped him because she felt betrayed in the most extraordinary and cruel of ways. It was that which decided his choice. He could take the out presented by her disbelief and protect his identity by letting her understanding of the situation become the truth, or he could argue for the real truth of the matter until she believed it. The lie only saved him tonight. He had no illusions that she wouldn't try again to find the 'true' Vigilante and, if she did, he'd have to answer for not one but two lies. In the interim, there'd be the tension over his attempt to pretend to be the Vigilante and undermine her efforts at unmasking him.

Their friendship would pay the price in the short- and long-term if he went that route. But if he made her see the truth, they might get through this. It wouldn't be without a price. She'd be angry he hadn't told her before. Her dream would be finished and it would be his fault. But perhaps there was room within that for understanding.

'I can explain, but not here.' Vennor's brain was starting to function again. He retrieved his mask and tied it over his face. If they were noticed, it would be far better to be seen as the Vigilante. There were things to discuss, but not here in a dark alley after midnight, a scenario made clear by the sounds of brawling issuing from the tavern as two men spilled drunkenly out into the street, grappling and wrestling, intent on doing bodily harm to each other. He'd already defended Marianne once tonight, but that didn't mean he wouldn't be called upon to do it again. The white silk of her ball gown glimmered beneath her cloak and he grimaced.

'What was I supposed to wear?' Marianne snapped, following his gaze. 'I had to convince my parents I was going out with my friend. I couldn't very well wear rags.'

'You could very well have stayed where you were supposed to be, with me at the Gaspards'.' But they could debate that later. He grabbed her wrist, his voice gruff. 'Come with me.' He would take her to the warehouse; there was no other choice, even though it required retracing their steps back into the heart of the docks. He needed safety, privacy and anonymity for them both and the warehouse was his only guarantee of getting it.

They walked rapidly through the dark streets. Well, *he* walked rapidly. Marianne trotted behind him, almost running, trying to keep up with his long strides. There were drunks and cheap whores out, but no one bothered them. At the sight of the Vigilante, most fell away and slunk back into their alleys. They reached the warehouse without trouble and Vennor led her to an obscure side gate chained with a lock. 'There's a lantern behind that post,' he instructed. 'There are matches, too. Bring them.'

'Where are we?' Marianne looked about as she

brought him the lantern and matches. 'Are you breaking in?' He struck a match and, voila, there was light.

'The warehouse is abandoned. I don't think it constitutes breaking in if no one's there.' Vennor passed her the lantern, his tone terse, his own emotions still running hot over the events of the evening. 'Hold it up so I can see the lock.' He bent to the lock, working its combination until the shackle came free. He pushed the gate open. 'After you, please.' The less he had to explain to Marianne the better; there was already so much and he hadn't even allowed himself to think about that kiss yet.

Marianne was undaunted. She swung the lantern around the deserted work yard. 'I know this place! This is the old Penlerick warehouse.' She smiled, but not at him or for him. She was still too mad for that, still too disbelieving. She smiled with pride over solving the puzzle. 'I came here once with my sisters. Your father had just received a shipment of Kashmir shawls and he gave us first pick.' He remembered that day, the four oldest Treleven girls all crowded around the trunks, oohing and aahing and wrapping themselves in shawls. The drab warehouse had been bright and lively with their laughter.

'Upstairs. Now,' Vennor growled. 'And for goodness' sake, don't be flashing that light around for everyone to see.'

'Who's to see besides drunkards and whores?' Marianne challenged. 'No one's working this late and we're behind a gate.'

He took the lantern from her and all but dragged

her upstairs in his earnestness to get them to safety. He would not rest easy until they were in his little self-appointed apartment, the door barred against intruders and the night. Fear washed over him afresh as they climbed the stairs. He should be more patient. *But by God, he'd nearly lost her tonight!* He could not be patient with foolhardiness and they weren't out of the woods yet.

He unlocked the door at the top of the stairs and she slid him a sideways glance. 'What is this?'

'The Vigilante's lair.' He bolted the door behind them and set the lantern on the wood table. They were safe now.

Marianne's eyes were wide with wonder and speculation as she took in the space and began to recalculate her disbelief. She turned in a slow full circle. When her eyes met his again, they were rife with questions. 'So, it's really you? You're the Vigilante?' Vennor nodded as she took a seat on the low, wide bed which was shoved against a wall. 'Well, it's a good thing we've got all night. That might just be long enough for you to tell me everything and then explain why you haven't told me before.'

The whore at the street corner gathered her thin shawl about her in satisfaction as the lantern went out, hidden from view. She'd found the Vigilante and now she could find him again if she needed to. There was peace in that and hope, too. She gingerly touched her split lip where it was still puffy and swollen. She'd endured a lot over the years for the sake of money, but no more. The man who came to visit her grew more brutal, his demands outpacing his payments. The Vigilante had stood up for a flower girl. Perhaps he would stand up for her if she asked him to.

Her customer had used her sorely once before. People had died because she couldn't stop him the first time. Now, he was back after a long absence. This time it would be different. If she needed to, she could step forward. She could get help. But that was for later. This was not a step to consider lightly. To betray her nameless lover would be to put herself in great danger. If he found out, he would come for her, she was sure of it. It was too soon yet for such risk. She could endure a bit more and she needed something more substantial to report that would move the Vigilante to action. Rumours would not do. She walked slowly back to the brothel, taking comfort that, when or if the time came, she would have help.

Chapter Nine

This time, Marianne believed him. She sat cross-legged on the bed, her skirts tucked about her, as Vennor finished his tale. She had to remember to close her mouth every so often, so incredible did she find his story. Of course it was true, she saw that now. It explained his social absences, the reasons he showed up late and left early when he did attend an event. It explained how and why he hadn't given up the investigation of his parents' deaths. But knowing Vennor's secret didn't solve anything. It merely complicated things. The more it explained, the more she questioned if she really knew Vennor at all.

Marianne blew out a shaky breath. 'Why didn't you tell me from the start? More to the point, were you ever going to tell me?' The hurt and anger she'd felt over the discovery was still there. Explanation and understanding had not mitigated it. If anything, it had intensified her sense of betrayal.

Vennor stopped pacing and faced her. 'I didn't

want anyone to know. I thought it would be safer for them, and for me, if I kept that piece of my life separate. If I were discovered, I didn't want my friends to become leverage to use against me. Nor did I want to embroil them in scandal.' He shrugged. 'And maybe I was just too embarrassed. I knew what Inigo would say. Every time I thought about saying something, I could hear Inigo's voice in my head, lecturing about the danger, about how there was no heir if I fell, about the futility of searching a cold trail.'

That sounded like Inigo. 'But not about the scandal,' Marianne defended their friend softly. 'He would have been worried for you, that's all.'

Vennor managed a wry smile. 'Can I tell you something? I saved him once, as the Vigilante. Brenley's thugs came upon him one night. It was three to one and Inigo was struggling.' Vennor gave a chuckle as he remembered. 'When I was sure he was all right, I ran home as fast as I could, for fear the first place Inigo would go would be my house. I was the only other one in town. Cassian was on honeymoon and Eaton was in Cornwall. I was right. I had ten minutes on him. He came banging on my door shortly after midnight.'

Marianne laughed, too. The story broke through some of the tension that crowded the space, but she wouldn't let the story derail them. Vennor had explained, but there was more to accomplish in this little room with its low bed and wooden table. How many nights had he slept here, unwilling to go home to the town house and its memories? 'I understand why you didn't tell Inigo or the others. But why not *me*?' She returned to her original question. 'I thought we were friends, Ven. Friends who told each other *everything*.' She'd told him so many secrets over the years and she'd thought he had told her all his secrets, too.

Vennor came and sat on the bed beside her. He reached for her hand and threaded his fingers through hers in a familiar gesture. 'At first, I didn't think it would last. I thought it would be short-term, that either I'd find the clues I was looking for or I wouldn't, and that would be the end of it.' He gave her a sheepish grin, 'I wasn't sure I'd be any good at it, either. Perhaps some pride was at stake.' He laughed.

'But it did last. The Vigilante is a celebrity now,' Marianne argued.

Vennor shook his head. 'And now I am in so deep I can't leave it. I kept thinking I couldn't tell you because you'd be angry I didn't tell you sooner. Looks as though I was right,' he teased and she smiled. Pieces of themselves, of who they were together, were coming back, slowly conquering the anger and betrayal, but she feared those pieces might not fit back together in the same way as before. She'd seen a new side of Vennor tonight—a man who could pick locks, who could fight four men in an alley with deadly intent. The man she'd seen wasn't an urbane duke, but a far more primal creature, and a far more passionate creature.

'I should have told you,' Vennor confessed. 'Not knowing didn't keep you safe. In fact, it did just the opposite.' His voice dropped. 'God, Marianne, when

I realised what you'd done, where you'd gone, I bolted out of the Mayfields' ballroom only to realise you could be anywhere.' He stopped, his head bowed, and she felt him shudder. 'What if I'd chosen differently? What if I'd gone to Seven Dials instead? I wouldn't have been there. Those men, Marianne, they were all over you. If I'd failed you, I would never have forgiven myself.'

'Hush, everything is fine.' Marianne stroked his back, comforting. She could handle her own fear, but not his. 'You guessed right and all's well that ends well.'

He peered up at her through blond locks. 'Has it ended well, Marianne?'

'I'm unhurt beyond a bruise or two and a need for carefully applied rice powder tomorrow,' she tried to joke, but his question could not be brushed away with humour. 'I don't know,' she answered honestly as she took up his hand again, her fingers flexing as they slid through his. Physically, the evening *had* ended well. She was indeed unhurt, which was no small thing given what might have happened. But other things had been, if not exactly hurt, then definitely changed; their understanding of one another and most certainly of their friendship had been tested by fire tonight in more ways than one. The steel of their friendship was bent. Might it be forged anew? What would it look like? She respected that he was leaving that decision up to her. It was a testament to his strength of character that he had the confidence not to force his own preferences on her.

'Can you forgive me, Marianne? For keeping it from you?' Light from the lantern cast shadows over the planes of his face. The imprint of her palm on his cheek had begun to fade. He was not the only one who needed forgiveness.

Marianne nodded. Forgiveness seemed a good place to start for them both. 'Can you forgive me for breaking my word to you and for slapping you?' But forgiving wasn't the same as forgetting and she thought it would be a while before they fully overcame what the other had done, as evidenced by the silence that hung between them. Despite their joined hands, there *was* distance. She could forgive him the deception, but she couldn't forget what her discovery would cost her. 'I suppose this means I can't publish my story,' Marianne said at last. 'Perhaps I couldn't have published it anyway. Perhaps it was an ill-fated idea from the start.' Not just the story, but the whole thought of being a journalist, of escaping marriage. The realisation swamped her, threatening to overwhelm her. Her choices were gone now. She'd not lived up to the ultimatum she'd given herself. She needed to succumb to marriage. Perhaps it was true, that one could not escape one's fate.

'When do you know it's time to give up?' She leaned her head against his shoulder with a sigh. Tonight had turned her world upside down. 'I was so hopeful when I left the house tonight. I never dreamed it would all fall apart.' Never dreamed she'd be attacked, never dreamed the Vigilante would rescue her, that he would turn out to be her best friend, that her best friend would turn out to be someone she'd only thought she knew, or that her best friend would kiss like sin itself and that she would kiss him back.

'If there's a time to quit, I haven't reached it yet.' Ven's arm was around her, drawing her close to the warmth of him against the coldness of the room. 'I hope you haven't either,' he whispered into her hair.

She looked up at him. 'Have you found leads, then? Is the investigation truly alive and well?' She hoped for his sake it was. Three years of nothing was a long time to live on hope alone.

'No, there's been nothing new since Bow Street closed the case. It took me six months or so to figure that out.' Vennor leaned back against the wall, taking her with him.

'So, why do you persist in playing the Vigilante?' Marianne curled up in the arc of his arm. She was getting drowsy and he was deliciously warm.

'Because they need me. These people need the Vigilante. I can be their hope when there is no other.'

Marianne smiled in the dimness of the room. 'So I wasn't far off the mark the other day when I called the Vigilante a revolutionary.' *This* she could reconcile. The Vennor she knew had been raised under the aegis of the Cornish Dukes whose legacy was civic service and care for all of humankind regardless of station. The Vennor she knew would want to see every last person fed and clothed, sheltered and protected, educated and employed in gainful use of their services. It was the primal ferocity she couldn't account for. 'Dukes can do that, too, you know. You can save people without wearing a mask and lurking in dark alleys.'

'Not these people you can't,' Vennor murmured. 'They need more than food baskets and charity, Marianne. They need a protector, someone who will stand up for them against unimaginable evil.' His hand ran up and down her arm in a slow, idle massage. 'Just last month, I rescued a girl from a brothel. She'd been sold to the madam by her father for gin money and she was going to be sold again that night to anyone who paid enough gold for first rights to her.'

'How awful.' Marianne suppressed a shiver. She'd had a taste of that brutality tonight. 'What happened to her?' She imagined the Vigilante as he'd been tonight, all in black and masked, racing to the girl's aid, carrying her away in his arms.

'She's a maid in Nikolay Baklanov's employ now on Leicester Square.' Nikolay was a Russian prince who ran a riding academy in town. She'd met him once—a tall, dark-haired fellow, very striking, as was his wife. 'But I can't put them all into the households of my friends. It would be too suspicious, for one thing, and there's just not enough work for another. My friends only need so many maids and footmen.' Vennor sighed, the burden of the Vigilante weighing him down. 'Right before Christmas, I found a baby left in a tavern alley in Seven Dials, wrapped in rags.'

'Did you take it to an orphanage?' The thought of Vennor with a baby in his arms made her smile. He would be an extraordinary father. But the story didn't end the way she'd thought it would.

'No, the baby died before I could get help for it. I couldn't save it. I was two streets from the orphanage and I just felt the life go out of it, felt that last little breath against my chest.' The pain in his words silenced her. There was no comfort she could offer. Reassurances would sound pitiful. 'That baby needed more than a charity basket. That baby's mother, whoever she was, needed more, too. I can't even imagine what level of despair drives someone to think their child has a better chance in an alley than with them.'

She could not imagine it either as she hugged him. 'I'm sorry, Ven.' She was quiet for a while, thinking. When she spoke again, her words came slowly, her mind still forming around an idea. 'People need to know how bad it is. People need to understand that a charity basket isn't enough, that it doesn't bring real change, that the only thing that brings real change is education and the opportunity for honest work in return for honest wages.' She sat up, and brushed her hair out of her face, her excitement growing as renewed purpose flooded her. 'I can't tell the Vigilante's story now and perhaps you were right—I never could. But there are hundreds, maybe even thousands, of stories that need to be told right here and I can tell them. I can interview them, with the Vigilante's help. Together, Ven, we can tell their stories and we can make change happen.'

'All four of us—the Vigilante and M.R. Mannering included, eh?' Vennor was grinning for the first time that night. His thumb ran thoughtfully over her knuckles.

'I like that...you smiling. It means we might survive this.'

Vennor laughed. 'I would hope our friendship could survive one mishap.'

She looked down at their hands. The new awareness between them was rising again now that other issues had been settled. Would they survive *that*? To explore it might be the real threat to their friendship. 'But it wasn't just one mishap, was it?' It was time to beard the other ghost in the room. 'You kissed me tonight.'

Vennor's hand tipped her chin up, forcing her eyes to meet his, his mouth close to hers as he whispered, 'I don't consider that a mishap, and I'd like very much to do it again.' With a gentle movement, his mouth closed the short distance between them, taking her in a slow kiss that was as thrilling for its languor as the kiss in the alley had been for its ferocity. Her mouth opened to him, his tongue tracing her lips, tasting her mouth, coaxing her to taste his.

This was a deliberate kiss, a kiss for savouring. There was no danger, no anger to get in the way of passion's exploration. She wanted to drink and drink from him until her thirst was satiated; she wanted to press her body against him as she'd done in the alley; she wanted to feel his strength against her. The terror of the street seemed far away. She lay back on the wide bed, her arms wrapped around Vennor's neck, his body warm against hers, desire driving her. She was safe here because this was Vennor, both the man she knew and the man she did not. She was eager to explore them both with her mouth, her hands and even her heart.

Chapter Ten

His body answered her eagerness with an enviable earnestness of its own that could, for a while, transcend the reasoning of his mind as it called out cautions at every kiss and caress. Her touch was a hot flame branding him as surely as it soothed him. What they were doing right now on the mattress of his makeshift bed posed a greater risk to their friendship than any secret he'd kept from her. . .

Passion once engaged could not be withdrawn or forgotten. These moments would exist with him for ever—the sight of her bright hair tumbling about her shoulders in a lantern-lit cascade, framing her oval face with its slim, elegant nose and the enticing fullness of her mouth. Neither was he likely to forget how her body pressed against him, untutored but unerringly instinctive in the lift of her hips and the arch of her back, to all of which his hungry body cried out, *yes*!

They might have been able to explain away the

alley kisses as a one-time event born of extreme circumstances and perhaps even some identity confusion. He wasn't himself when he was the Vigilante, but an entirely different being who answered to no law except his own. Perhaps it was the same for her when she was M.R. Mannering and not the Incomparable. She hadn't known who she was kissing in the alley nor who was kissing her. But here, in the small boxy warehouse office-cum-apartment, they could not escape who they were. On this bed, they were Marianne and Vennor.

Marianne's hands reached for his shirt, pulling it free of the waistband of his evening trousers. Her hands slid beneath the fabric, warm and sure as they skimmed his torso and moved upwards over the flats of his nipples, his skin tingling with awareness at her touch, his nipples pricking to alertness. 'Vennor, you're hard everywhere.' Her hips wiggled against another source of hardness lower down.

'Did you think I wasn't?' He laughed in her ear, his body still outpacing his mind in terms of the wisdom of this course of action. His body found no reason to disguise the hardness that pressed against her thigh, unrepentant and obvious in its desire, although his mind was sprinting to catch up, to warn him that this must stop before Marianne in her recklessness, and he in his wanting, took things too far. 'Did you think I was a prettily dressed, soft fop of a man like the other ballroom dandies who flock about you?' Want made his voice harsh, harsh with restrained yearning for her, with a competitive male urge to stand out from her usual swains, to be seen as more than her friend.

She looked up at him with desire-drenched eyes. 'No, I never thought that. Still, having proof is entirely different to just assuming it.' Her hands worked the buttons of his shirt, apparently seeking eyewitness testimony. It was time to put a halt to this. The removal of clothing was a dangerous step closer to disaster and they were already in bed, already part of the way down that slippery slope, as it were. He'd never intended this room for pleasure.

Vennor stilled her hands. 'No, things have gone far enough for one night.' He rolled to his side and lifted himself up on one arm. 'We have a lot to figure out, Marianne. Until we do, we need be careful not to burn the ships, eh?' The metaphor sounded better than saying they needed to keep their options open, although the intention was the same.

He kissed her on the tip of her nose, not trusting himself to keep a kiss on her mouth chaste. He'd already stolen one dream from her tonight, although she'd recovered from it admirably. But he'd be damned if he'd steal another from which recovery would not be possible. No matter how his body burned with the temptation to take her, he knew that to do so would force them into the one thing neither of them felt ready for: marriage. After the passion there would be despising and all that might have had the potential for love would become hate.

'I don't want to go home.' Marianne faced him, mirroring his posture, her length stretched out alongside his, her red curls falling over the prop of her hand. 'Tell me about the Vigilante and not the things you've already told me. Tell me his stories, his adventures. Tell me what he does all night.'

He was reluctant. 'I'm not a hero, Marianne,' he warned. 'I don't save them all. Sometimes it doesn't work out; sometimes I can't get there in time.'

She nodded solemnly. 'I know. No one expects you to.'

'I wouldn't know where to start.' If he did start, he wasn't sure he would stop.

'Start with this room. Is this why you haven't reopened the warehouse? Because you needed a lair?' He'd closed this warehouse two weeks after his father's death.

'I have a new warehouse on the India Docks. It's bigger and better able to handle the larger cargoes as our shipping interests expand.' All true. It was also not a constant reminder of the past the way this warehouse was. There was more to this place than just a reminder of time he'd spent here with his father. He couldn't expect Marianne to understand that without also understanding other dynamics he was loath to discuss. It was questions like these that had caused him to choose self-imposed isolation early on. There were no simple answers. Every answer posed another question and demanded a deeper exploration of himself, a step further into the darkness.

'Is that the only reason, Ven?' Marianne's soft voice probed. 'It always just seemed so sudden to me, that is all, coming out of the blue after your father died.'

Vennor flopped on to his back, his arm outstretched, inviting her to join him. 'I thought you wanted to hear stories of the Vigilante,' he teased, settling her against him. His blood had cooled to a comfortable simmer, enough to enjoy the simple pleasure of holding her. 'Let me tell you about the time I rescued a puppy from the Thames.'

Marianne laughed, 'The Vigilante has quite the repertoire, not just damsels in distress.' Her hand was light on his chest, resting, not playing, not seducing, just lying there with a comfortable ease. There'd always been that easiness between them. He was glad it was still there, that the night hadn't destroyed it in favour of other things. It was hard to come by. He could not say that he'd found it with any of the women with whom he'd engaged in affairs. The comfort, sometimes, but not the ease. There was always a wariness, a holding back, that he had to be something for them, that they expected him to be the heir, to be the *thing*. He wasn't allowed to be human. He knew instinctively that no matter what happened, no matter what paths they took after tonight, he would never duplicate what he had with her. Who else would want to hear about rescued puppies?

'Our erstwhile dog, you see, had been chasing a cat, only the cat was much nimbler on the bridge. The puppy lost its footing and fell in.' He tried to make light of the story. It had happened early in his career and it had been one of the more foolish things he'd done. He'd heard the puppy crying in the dark swirling waters as it struggled to paddle to shore, then begin to panic when it realised it wouldn't beat the current. He'd jumped in, boots and all, for the dog, risking a ducal dynasty for the sake of an errant puppy. Honeycutt had been furious when he'd come home dripping, a muddy dog under his arm.

'Where's the puppy now?' Marianne was curious.

'He's in the mews behind the town house. He took a shine to one of my grooms.'

'We'll have to visit the puppy.' Marianne snuggled closer. 'Who else? Tell me more.'

'Children, women, boys, all sorts.' Vennor sifted through the stories in his mind, looking for a suitable one. He would shield her from some of the bloodier tales. Now that the first story was out of the way, the dam on the reservoir was starting to crumble and it was becoming easier to talk about his escapades; the tales began to flow, one after another, as the night slid by. Marianne was a good listener, interspersing an exclamation or a curious question, encouraging him to elaborate, and with each telling he felt lighter, that the burdens he carried alone were eased. He'd not talked to someone like this, cathartically, and meaningfully, since his parents had died. There was so much more to say, so much he was not ready to talk about it yet, but this was a start.

The lantern had burned down, leaving them in complete darkness, and still they talked until dawn edged the night and Marianne grew uncharacteristically still beside him.

'Marianne, are you awake?' he murmured, smothering a yawn of his own when he got no response. He placed a soft kiss in the tangles of Marianne's curls and whispered the simple words, 'Thank you.' What a gift she'd given him tonight. To share the Vigilante with her, to talk about how he'd been spending his life, was nothing short of an immense relief. Vennor shut his eyes, holding her close, the night catching up to him at last.

'Catch.' Hayes tossed a red wig to the whore and shut the door behind him, locking it. 'I don't want us to be disturbed. I have something particular planned for tonight, Elise.'

She caught the wig and disappeared behind the dressing screen. 'Is there someone you'd like me to be, my lord?'

'A fine lady who needs to be punished.' Hayes sat down on the bed and pulled off his boots, beginning to undress. 'Don't bother with anything more than a dressing gown, Elise, and a little rice powder. I don't want to look at the cut on your face. You know I don't like blemishes,' he scolded. For the price he paid her, one would think she could remember the little things that made him happy. Then again, she wasn't a high-priced courtesan who had an education in nuance. But high-priced courtesans weren't generally in the market for the type of play he preferred. So he settled for Elise, a self-taught street whore. Her skills consisted primarily of lying on her back and making the appropriate noises.

Not with him, though. Hayes untied his cravat and laid it aside for later. A crop to the backside ensured rather more genuine sounds. He pulled out his shirttails and lay back on the pillows, his member rousing as he thought about what was to come. They would start with a confession, he would make her disrobe for him, stand before him naked, then he'd tie her to the bedpost and take a crop to her until she begged for repentance, and then, only when she was penitent and he was bursting with arousal, would he give her a penance. She would kneel before him and take him in her mouth. Elise was very good with her mouth and the whole time he could pretend it was Marianne Treleven who knelt before him in supplication, whose full, sensual mouth was on him, who begged him for mercy. Would she beg for Penlerick's life if he asked it of her? What would she do to save her friend? Or perhaps he was something more than a friend? The events at the Mayfields' had been telling in that regard, an affirmation that his instincts were right—recently, the potential for something more between Marianne and Penlerick had indeed blossomed.

Penlerick's appearance at the Mayfields' had made that abundantly clear. The man had been desperate to find her, desperate…beyond the concern of a friend. Hayes had rather enjoyed thwarting Penlerick's efforts. He'd been absolutely no help at all. He wondered whether Penlerick had gone to her house and whether she'd actually been there. There was always the possibility Marianne had chosen to avoid the company of both men. It hardly mattered what the outcome was; it only mattered that Penlerick had been willing to chase after her. Hayes hadn't been willing. In his book, a man never chased after a woman. It gave a woman too much power. The pursuit of courtship was as far as Hayes was willing to go to work himself into a woman's good graces. Of course, the ends justified the means. There would be time enough after marriage to re-establish the appropriate hierarchy between husband and wife.

He calmed his rampant thoughts and shifted on the bed. There was no use in spending himself before the play could commence. Once they were married, Marianne would be his to use as he desired. He would demand abject obedience and humility from her. He would make her pay for shunning him as she had at the Mayfields' ball, as she had for every supper dance that ought to have been his. She knew very well what his intentions were, she could not pretend innocence there, yet it was Newlyn she favoured, further proof that things could not be as platonic as was rumoured between them.

He could imagine throwing her across his knee and drawing up her skirts, taking his crop to her white buttocks so that she'd remember him every time she sat down. He squirmed, wishing Elise would hurry. By Jove, he'd never been this hard in his life. The only fly in the ointment was Newlyn himself. As long as Newlyn was around, there was a chance he would not make it to the altar with Marianne. The trick would be earning her consent to wed. If Newlyn were to declare himself, Hayes wasn't sure of the outcome. The only guarantee his plans could proceed as originally intended would be to ensure Newlyn was dead.

He fingered his member idly, giving it a slow stroke up and down, revelling in the unyielding rigidity of himself. By the heavens, he was like Thor's hammer.

He didn't just want to take Marianne from Penlerick, he wanted to take the dukedom, everything the Penlericks had worked for, everything they'd stolen over the years from the Moores. With Penlerick out of the way, Marianne *and* Cornwall would be at his mercy and it would feel good to have revenge at last.

'How do I look?' Elise came out from behind the dressing screen, the red curls of the wig falling over the full swells of her breasts which were barely hidden behind the cheap, satiny fabric of her dressing gown.

A slow, cruel smile took his face. 'Perfect.'

He would leave her a little extra, he thought as he finished dressing. The little room was darkening now as dusk fell. They'd played away the afternoon, but he had one last piece of business to discuss. 'My dear, do you know any men who might be interested in some work?'

She moaned, not quite awake. He strode towards the bed and gave her a shove into alertness. 'I'm not through with you yet. Answer my question.' He brought the crop down on the mattress with a resounding whack. That got her attention. Elise scrambled up, red wig tangled and askew, curls rioting everywhere as she pulled the bedsheet up protectively. He'd used her hard this afternoon, he thought with satisfaction.

'What kind of work, milord?' she asked with a wary tone.

'Work like last time, Elise. I'm happy to pay them handsomely—and you, too, for arranging it. Didn't I leave a tidy sum when I left for the Continent?' He paced the room, flicking at this frippery and that with his crop. 'You've been able to afford little luxuries. Perhaps this time, there will be enough to get a cottage of your own some place where you can leave this life behind, if you so choose.' He glanced back towards the bed. That got her attention. Freedom. It was what they all wanted, viscounts and whores alike. Freedom. The power to decide one's own fate. Freedom took money. With enough of it, freedom could be bought. People weren't so very different in the end. The only difference was in what they'd do to get it.

'Yes, milord, I might know of some men.'

He made a show of setting down a small stack of pound notes on the dressing table. 'Good, we can discuss it further when I come next time. Keep the wig, I'll want you to wear it again.'

Chapter Eleven

'Keep your hood up. I don't want anyone to get a good look at your hair or your face if we can help it,' Vennor cautioned for at least the tenth time since they'd set out from Mayfair, slinking out of the Tetlow ball shortly after eleven. 'Both are far too memorable.'

Marianne tugged the hood of her cloak up a little higher, not for her sake, but for his. Vennor was nervous. She didn't want him regretting having brought her. She understood the risks inherent in her presence. If someone connected her to the Vigilante, they might connect the Vigilante to Vennor. It was a minute chance. After all, no one in the slums knew her directly, but it was still a risk—word travelled fast in London.

She and Vennor had been careful in other ways, too, since that night in the East Docks, careful not to give away what had transpired between them in the warehouse apartment. Outwardly, nothing had changed. He still showed up late to balls, just in time to claim her for the supper waltz to Lord Hayes's ever-growing chagrin. If anyone had changed in outward appearances, it was Hayes, who was becoming more possessive by the day and more alert to Vennor's presence.

The coach jolted over the cobblestones, the ride becoming jarring as they neared the docks. Perhaps she only imagined Hayes's growing obsession because *she* was more aware of Vennor's presence than ever. Vennor's hand felt different at her back as they danced, his gaze held secrets just for her and her body trembled with the knowledge of it, of what they could do to one another. Yet they had not discussed it. That night in his arms lay between them, but neither had addressed it. She had hoped he would bring it up, not because she was a coward but because she wasn't sure how to begin.

She studied Vennor's face in the dimness of the carriage. He had not yet put his mask on and his features were stark with alertness, his body tense in anticipation of what the evening held. Did one simply come out and say, *I liked your kisses. I want you to kiss me again. And, oh, by the way, what does it mean, these kisses between us?*

It had occurred to her that Vennor had said nothing about it because it hadn't been life-changing for him and he saw no reason why the one interlude should alter anything between them. Why should he? They both knew he was in no hurry to marry and she'd been clear about her own hesitations in that regard. Maybe the question she ought to be asking herself was what did that night mean to *her* before she concerned herself with what it meant to him?

Marianne played with the strings of her hood, twisting them into a single strand before letting them spin upwards and unravel. The night had been precious as much as it had been passionate. She'd revelled equally in the stories he'd told her as much as she had the kisses. For a few hours she'd had her friend back, the one who told her everything, the one who'd slipped away from her in the intervening years. She'd held him in all ways that night, but the morning had come and with the dawn she'd lost her grip.

Across from her, Vennor tied on his mask, the dark silk transforming him once more into the powerful, physical stranger who'd rescued her. Her skin began to tingle with vivid remembrances of the Vigilante's hard, wicked kisses as the carriage came to a stop.

'We'll go on foot from here.' Vennor's tone was gruff as he surveyed her one last time for any obvious giveaways. He reached out and pushed a curl back into the depths of her hood, his touch gentle, at odds with his voice, as his fingers skimmed her cheek. 'There, that should do.'

'Who are we meeting tonight?' Marianne gathered up a satchel which held her writing materials, excitement beginning to take hold. This would be her first interview. It was really happening; she was going to get her chance. She was determined it would go well.

'*You* are meeting Mrs Broadham. She's the proprietress of a boarding house. *I* will be out patrolling the streets. There are new Indiamen in port and the sailors will be on shore leave with money in their pockets and high spirits.'

'She sounds respectable.' Marianne's high spirits deflated a bit. She'd been hoping for a prostitute or a runaway. She'd rather be out watching the Vigilante at work, making sure Vennor didn't do anything rash, but she knew better than to push her luck. She'd come this far. For now, that would be enough.

Vennor chuckled. 'She can tell you about all the people who live in her house. She can give you variety and quantity to choose from, Marianne. As for respectable, don't let the name fool you. I don't think there's ever been a Mr Broadham. She says he's at sea, but he hasn't been home since I've known her. Mighty long voyage, if you ask me.' He paused, his worry returning. 'You know I can't go with you. I can't sit there with you. It would give too much a way.'

It would be too dangerous as well. Not everyone liked the Vigilante—the barkeep she'd met the first night had not lied. Those who liked crime, who made their living from lawlessness, were not friends of the Vigilante's cause. He stayed alive because he kept moving, because no one could ever predict when he'd turn up.

Marianne nodded her understanding. 'I'll be close by, though.' He reached across the darkness and squeezed her hand. 'You should be safe at the boarding house.' She thought he said that as much for her as for him as he handed her out of the carriage.

The boarding house, she noted, was in Blackwall, not far from the East India docks. From the sounds in the streets, the Vigilante would have his choice of fist fights, drunken brawls and robberies to select from tonight. Vennor saw her into Mrs Broadham's care before disappearing back out into the streets.

'What would you like to see first?' Mrs Broadham's voice was brisk with the roughness of the docks. 'The Vigilante says you're a reporter wanting to tell stories about people who live in the East End.'

'That's right.' Marianne stood a little taller at the realisation. Tonight she *was* a reporter, not a debutante. It was the first time she'd thought of herself that way. She'd have to remember to thank Vennor for that. What a gift he'd given her. 'A tour of your establishment would be welcome.' Marianne pulled out her notepad and pencil. 'I'll just take some notes as we walk.'

'Humph.' Mrs Broadham made a sound through her nose and Marianne gave a surreptitious twitch of her cloak to cover up any tell-tale signs of her skirts. Mrs Broadham narrowed her gaze 'I've never met a woman reporter before.' Marianne did not reply. In all likelihood, Mrs Broadham hadn't met *any* reporters before, male or female.

'A story could be good advertising for your boarding house,' Marianne offered, gingerly stepping past a hole in the wall that might very well be home to a family of mice.

'This is the dining room.' Mrs Broadham gestured to the spacious room off to the left of the hall. It was plainly furnished with a set of two long, scarred wooden tables, their planks grey with wear, but their tops scrubbed clean. Various shapes and sizes of chairs were pulled up to the tables. 'We can feed twenty-four people and we do when the house is full of boarders,' she boasted proudly. 'Two meals a day.'

They toured the sitting room where guests gathered in the evenings. The steps creaked beneath Marianne's feet and she noticed the treads were worn. 'So close to the water, it's hard to keep the damp from settling in,' Mrs Broadham explained. Marianne nodded, writing as fast as she could. The roof was in no better shape. Several of the rooms held buckets that collected drip water. In spite of Mrs Broadham's pride in her establishment, the place was run-down and in need of repair it was unlikely to get. The boarders' rooms were small, holding a cot and perhaps a small set of drawers that stood next to the bed, lit with a single tallow candle, if they were lit at all.

'Boarders supply their own candles,' Mrs Broadham pointed out. 'And their own extra furniture if they want it.' Clothes hung from pegs nailed into the walls and rooms smelled stale, and not all the rooms had windows. Some of them housed four people, or whole families.

Mrs Broadham knocked on one door and it was

opened by a birdlike woman with wispy, faded blonde hair. 'Mrs Simon, I hope it's not too late for a visitor.'

Mrs Simon juggled a toddler on her hip, a little boy of maybe four clung to her skirts, and an older girl sat on the single bed in the room, peering shyly at Marianne. Marianne smiled back as she stepped inside. 'This here is a reporter. She's doing a story about the boarding house,' Mrs Broadham explained to Mrs Simon, who looked all too glad of any visitor who was over the age of eight and embarrassed at the same time. The small room was even tinier with six people in it.

'Lila, off the bed, let the lady sit down.' Mrs Simon made a shooing gesture with her free hand.

'No, that's not necessary. I'm happy to stand,' Marianne offered, partly out of a desire not to discommode poor Mrs Simon any further and partly out of a sense of self-preservation. Regardless of Mrs Simon's best housekeeping efforts, Marianne wasn't entirely sure she trusted those blankets. 'Mrs Simon, may I ask you some questions?'

It turned out Mrs Simon was quite talkative once she got over the surprise of having a guest. 'And Mr Simon?' Marianne asked as the interview progressed. 'Does he work here on the docks?'

Mrs Simon juggled the toddler, asleep now in her arms. She'd not put him down yet. There was no crib, no trundle. 'No, ma'am. Mr Simon is dead. He was killed in Greece two years ago with the English troops. We're fortunate he left us provided for, though...' her eyes were misty when she looked up

'…thanks to my widow's pension and we have a roof over our heads thanks to Mrs Broadham.' She offered a smile of gratitude to the landlady.

'Now, Sally, don't be making me out to be a saint, 'cause I ain't.' Mrs Broadham's tone was brisk and thick. 'You're a paying customer like everyone else, that's all.' But Marianne's instinct hinted otherwise as a smile passed between the two women. Whatever the widow's pension didn't cover, Mrs Broadham clearly overlooked.

But what about clothes for the children? Marianne thought. What about medicine when a child took ill? What about toys and the occasional luxury? The pension wouldn't cover incidentals as well. Yet Mrs Simon was grateful for her little room and the leaky roof over her head. Marianne offered her thanks and let Mrs Broadham usher her out of the room to complete the tour.

She hoped her emotions didn't show on her face. She'd seen poverty before. There was plenty of it in Cornwall and she saw it when she delivered baskets and Christmas presents with her sisters. But city poverty felt different, she was realising. There was a hopelessness to it, an endlessness, and it made her angry. London was one of the largest cities in the world, with resources galore. How dare a portion of its citizens go hungry, go sick, go cold.

Vennor had warned her that she knew nothing of this world. She'd been so sure she was prepared for what she might find, but she had not been prepared for this—and this wasn't even the worst of it. How did

Vennor do it? How did he stand it night after night? How did he convince himself he could make a difference when the scope of the problem was so vast?

Mrs Broadham concluded the tour of the house and invited her for tea in the kitchen while they waited for the Vigilante to return. The tea was warm if not aromatic. The leaves had been used several times prior, but the warmth was all Marianne needed as she wrapped her hands around the chipped cup. 'How did you come to be acquainted with the Vigilante?' It had occurred to Marianne that there might be more than one story here, even if she couldn't tell it to the papers.

Mrs Broadham smiled, her harsh features softening at the mention. 'Two years ago, he cleaned out a gang of "insurance men" on this street. The men were charging money to make sure no one broke our windows or set fire to our homes, or brought harm to our persons when we went out. Of course, the people they were really taking money to protect us from were themselves.' She wiped her hands on her apron. 'The price kept going up, too. A couple of my neighbours couldn't afford to pay.' The woman's voice caught and Marianne nodded in empathy. She'd seen the burnt-out remains walking up to the boarding house. 'I just knew I was going to be next. I barely had enough boarders to make my own rent, let alone enough to pay the insurance men.' Mrs Broadham shook her head. 'No one wanted to stay on this street once word got around about what was happening. The insurance men were driving themselves out of business, only they were too stupid to realise it.'

'What did you do?' Marianne probed gently.

'I left a note for the Vigilante. Anonymous, of course. I couldn't let the insurance men know it was me. Can't get caught, though. Not everyone likes him. The post is covered in broadsheets, so it's easy for other notes to blend in. I wasn't sure he'd see mine, but he did and within a week the gang was gone. They haven't been back since.' She was beaming now. 'In a very real way, he saved my life.' She gestured to the house. 'This is all I have. Where would I go? What would I do? I owe him more than I can say.' And she'd passed that kindness on to Mrs Simon and who knew how many others. The Vigilante's justice was like ripples on a pond.

A knock at the back door interrupted their discussion and Marianne stood up hurriedly. It would be Vennor and he'd want to be off quickly, stealthily. The two hours had flown by. At the door, the Vigilante pressed a small bag of coins on Mrs Broadham and they were gone, disappearing into the night, silently hurrying towards the coach on the perimeter of Blackwell.

Inside, the coach was warm and safe. Marianne leaned back against the squabs and shut her eyes, letting the tension that had kept her alert all night seep out of her. Vennor's clothes rustled with movement. He must be taking off his mask. 'How was it? Was Mrs Broadham helpful?'

'She was extraordinary. You were right, it was a good place to start.' Marianne paused. 'You were right, too, that I know nothing of that world.' She clenched her fists, the anger returning. ‘How can we let people live like that? I met Mrs Simon. She and her three children living in that tiny room. And yet that room was a gift.’ She punched the fine leather of the seat. ‘I want to send a basket to her tomorrow, a braided rug for the floor, new blankets, clothes for the children.’ She shook her head. It would be easy to do. There was a surplus of things at Treleven House to send. ‘But it wouldn’t be enough. It would bring them comfort, but not change.’

She felt Vennor’s hand close over hers. ‘Send the basket anyway. You can tell her it was in gratitude for her story.’ Marianne opened her eyes at his touch, seeing his face for the first time since they’d left the docks. ‘Oh, my heavens, you’ve been hurt!’ He had a bruise starting to blossom on one cheek. It was going to be a bad one if she could see it from here in the dimness of the carriage. She reached a hand out instinctively to touch it.

‘Ouch!’ Vennor drew back with a gasping laugh. ‘Why do people do that? Touch something that’s clearly injured.’ He put his own hand to it, cradling his jaw. ‘I’ll have Honeycutt put a steak on it. The other men looked worse.’

‘The other *men*? How many were there?’ That was cause for alarm. She didn’t like thinking of Vennor set upon and outnumbered, no matter that she’d seen him in action and knew he could handle himself.

‘Three, maybe four.’ He shook his head. ‘But I couldn’t let them steal the young man’s pay. He was little more than a kid, home at last from sea. The boy was about sixteen and skinny as a stick.'

Marianne peered out the window at the mention of Honeycutt. They were going the wrong way, back to Mayfair. She wasn't ready to return. 'No warehouse tonight?'

'No, we need to get you home.' Vennor reached beneath the seat and pulled out the box where he stored his valuables. He retrieved his watch and put it back in his pocket, but not before he checked it. 'Half past two. Your parents won't suspect a thing. We'll have you back before the Tetlow ball winds down.' Vennor's tone dropped, becoming more confidential. 'Are you glad you went?'

'Glad, mad, and I can hardly wait to go back. I understand now why you do it. There is so much to do, Ven. People need to know about this.'

Vennor gave a sharp snort. 'They do know, Marianne. I know what you're thinking. You're thinking you'll publish a story and people will suddenly *see* what's been there all along.'

'This time it will be different, though. M.R. Mannering has a *male* audience, Ven. This isn't just an article talking about charity projects to women,' Marianne insisted, her excitement rising. 'Men have the power of legislation, the power of real action.'

'Marianne, they already know. They simply don't care. I don't want you to be disappointed. I sit in the House of Lords and argue with these men for every inch of reform I can get.' There was quiet realism in Vennor's tone. She chose to ignore it. Quiet realism had never done anyone much good in her opinion except to create lives of silent desperation.

'This time it will be different,' Marianne repeated defiantly, thinking of poor Mrs Simon and her three children. 'I will make them care.' First, she had to make her editor care. He had to want to print her story. Well, she would find a way, that was all there was to it.

She could feel Vennor grinning in the darkness across from her. 'If anyone can, it's you, Marianne. It's what I admire most about you.' Tonight, she wanted a little more than admiration from him. She wanted him to leave his proper seat and sit beside her. She wanted him to take her in his arms, pull her against the muscled strength of his body, to kiss her again. She would have liked to have gone to the warehouse tonight instead of back to the Tetlows'. It somehow seemed wrong, hypocritical even, to return to chandeliers and champagne after the squalor of the boarding house.

'It's what the ruse demands,' Vennor said softly in the darkness, reading her thoughts. 'We have to go back.'

Marianne reached beneath her seat and retrieved her own box of valuables. She pulled on her gloves and threaded her dance card about her wrist with a sense of surrealism. 'Will you dance the Roger de Coverly with me?' It would be the last dance of the evening. Suddenly, she couldn't bear the thought of being in anyone else's arms. Perhaps he couldn't either. His answer came out in a husky single word.

'Yes.'

Chapter Twelve

He must be out of his mind to involve Marianne like this in the secrets of his life, but once begun, there was no going back. She'd been out with the Vigilante three more times since that first visit, interviewing like mad. There was no going back in other ways, too. That much was patently clear as Vennor sat down to breakfast amid the delicious assault on his senses: sausages and eggs tempered with the aroma of brewed coffee and the fresh-baked yeastiness of Cook's cinnamon buns. All his favourites. Someone must have made the suggestion to Cook. That someone was likely also the one who'd suggested the curtains be drawn back. As a result, the spring morning drenched the parlour with all its sunlight and warmth while a tall vase of long-stemmed tulips in a profusion of colours stood sentinel on the crowded sideboard.

It didn't take long to guess who was responsible. Marianne's stamp was everywhere these days. Vennor sorted through the newspapers left beside his plate, pressed and ready, until he found what he wanted: the newest edition of *Gentlemen's Weekly.* He turned immediately to M.R. Mannering's column and smiled.

> *Dear Readers,*
> *Along with my usual report on the doings of the* ton, *this will also be the first instalment of a new series regarding other citizens of London with whom we share the city and with whom we should also share the burden of living...*

Vennor drew a breath. She'd done it, then. She'd got the story published. Well done, Marianne.

Of course, Marianne would complain. She'd had to share column space in order to get it printed, but if he knew her, she'd find a way around that, too, given time, just as she'd found a way into his home with her cleaning and sorting and flower vases.

You invited her in, his conscience prompted.

Yes, indeed he had, but he'd never bargained on how much impact that invitation would have. The house sparkled these days. It had always been clean—his staff would tolerate no less—but the house had its life back now. More than that, it was slowly becoming *his.* Marianne had adroitly seen to it and was still seeing to it. He'd been informed there was wallpaper to select.

Vennor set aside the column and tackled a second serving of eggs. He'd need his strength. Marianne was due here at noon and he could well imagine what the afternoon would entail. His own eagerness to see her gave him pause. He'd just seen her a few hours ago. They'd gone into Seven Dials last night, sneaking out of Lady Hardcastle's masquerade, and sneaking back in before the masquerade concluded. Marianne had interviewed a prostitute with remarkable sensitivity, drawing the nervous girl out with her questions. He'd watched from the shadows, impressed.

He had to be careful of his eagerness, had to be aware of its source. Was it from the excitement of sharing his secret life with someone at last? Was it in being released from his self-imposed loneliness? Or, did his eagerness stem from those kisses in the East Docks? The intimacy in the warehouse apartment? They'd not repeated that intimacy in the two weeks since then and his body was hungry for more. Nor had he addressed it with her. Neither of them had brought it up.

He debated whether or not he should at this late date. Perhaps the window for discussing it had passed. But the aftermath lingered, suggesting otherwise. He felt it when they danced, when they touched, when their gazes met. His body thrummed with it. But he could not pursue it. He could not be the man she needed until he understood himself, until he settled his own debt with the past. Nothing could come of it but disappointment for them both.

No good could come of this. Something was brewing and at *his* expense. Things had been off these past weeks with Marianne and he was determined to know why. Hayes drummed his fingers on the surface of his desk in an angry tattoo. 'Is there anything else to report?' He glared at the two men he'd hired to watch Marianne Treleven. Information was everything. No one would take him by surprise, certainly not the Duke of Newlyn who had insinuated himself into Marianne's court and was now insinuating himself into much more.

'No, sir, it's just that she's always there,' one of the men offered with trepidation. There, in this case, meant Newlyn House. 'She and her mother are there almost every afternoon.'

The man beside him jostled him with an elbow. 'How bad could it be if her mother's there? It's likely they ain't tupping one another.'

Tupping. A disgustingly vulgar word. But what could one expect from the East Docks? These East Docks men wouldn't ask questions, they would just take their money and do what they were told. For now, that involved watching Marianne.

Hayes thrust two bags of coins forward on the desk and dismissed them with an abrupt wave of his hand. He didn't want to hear the rest of it. He almost wished they *were* trysting. Her mother's presence made it far worse than an illicit rendezvous. He could blackmail them both with that. But this decent, chaperoned visiting could be serious. There were only so many reasons young women and their mothers visited dukes at home and most of those reasons involved marriage. Hayes brought his fist down on the desk. Damn it, he was not going to lose Marianne to Newlyn. She was the key to all his plans.

He needed to act. He needed to do something more than dancing attendance on her since that wasn't working, not with Newlyn increasingly on hand to steal her away. He glanced at the calendar sitting to the side of his desk. It was the first half of June. He'd not meant to stake a more formal claim until next month, but his original plans had not counted on any strong competition. Well, perhaps ardour would hold some sway with Sir Jock Treleven when he pressed his suit on short acquaintance. Hayes called for his secretary. 'Send a note over to Treleven House and request a meeting for this afternoon.' All the better to do it when it could be man to man without interruption. If his informants were to be believed, Marianne and her mother would be otherwise engaged.

One look at Vennor's gaze told her he didn't find selecting wallpaper for the drawing room nearly as engaging as she did. But to his credit, he was persevering. 'I think the grey will be suitable, Mr Howser. We will leave you to your measurements.' Marianne wanted the issue settled as quickly as possible for Vennor's sake. She wanted him in a compliant mood when they addressed the ballroom.

They left Mr Howser and his staff and headed towards the ballroom. Vennor was still smiling; that had to be a good sign and he seemed in overall high spirits despite their late night. Marianne threw open the walnut double doors to the ballroom and sailed inside, throwing her arms wide in a twirl before reaching for Vennor. 'Come and dance with me.' She drew him out into the centre of the floor. Sunlight streamed in through the dusty bank of French doors that lined the far wall. Beyond the vast wall of glass lay the town gardens of Newlyn House. 'Do you know, I've never danced in here.' She spoke without thinking, caught up in the whirl of their impromptu waltz.

Vennor's smile faded. 'You would have danced at the charity ball if they hadn't been killed.'

'Yes.' She had to brave it out now and own up to her misstep. She'd not meant to remind him of anything sad. 'I remember looking forward to that growing up. My sisters would tell me such fabulous stories of that night.' Her eldest sister had attended twice and Ayleth and Violet had each attended once. 'How the chandeliers would glisten...'

She looked up to the ceiling where a pair of shrouded crystal masterpieces hung. What she would give to see those chandeliers unwrapped and shining! Vennor turned her at the top of the ballroom, the two of them in perfect step in their silent dance, but his hand burned at her back as it always seemed to these days. The excitement of the Vigilante's trips to the slums, the interviews, the secrecy of slipping out of balls, the joy of seeing her article printed in the magazine, even if it was short and had to share space with her column, all of it was nothing compared to the reckless thrill conjured by Vennor's touch; it could ignite her, body, memories and all.

Oh, how she wanted a repeat of that night in the

warehouse, to have his hands on her, his mouth, his voice low and husky as he shared a piece of his heart with her. She did not fool herself that he'd told her everything, but it had been a much-needed start. She didn't want it to end there, not for him or for her, yet it seemed it had. Unless she did something about it. She'd waited long enough for him to bring it up. She fixed Vennor with her gaze, a light smile on her lips. 'Will it always feel this way from now on when you touch me? Like I'm burning up from the inside?'

She had surprised him, she saw it in his gaze, the quick rapid blink of his eyes, twice, and then nothing as he recovered. 'Maybe. Perhaps in time it might wear off.' Vennor swept her through another turn fast and light, trying to distract her.

'Maybe I don't want it to wear off.' She'd come this far, she might as well go the distance.

'What we want and what must be aren't always the same thing.' That urbane mask she hated so much was starting to slip into place again, hiding him from her.

'Do you not want to kiss me again? Did the kiss mean nothing?' she asked boldly. Now that she'd started, there was no turning back. 'You *can* tell me the truth, Ven. Was that night in the East Docks a mistake? Something you regret?' Although her pride might take a hit, she had to know.

He gave a harsh laugh. 'You ask the most awkward questions. I don't regret it, but I do think it was a mistake.' Their waltzing slowed. 'It doesn't matter if I liked it or if we want to do it again. We simply can't. What can come of it but harm?' His voice dropped, low and sincere, edged with pain, proof that he *had* thought of their kisses in the intervening weeks. She'd not been alone there. 'You and I don't want to marry at the moment. Yet how else does this end but in marriage? How long do you think we could restrain ourselves from folly if we indulged in kisses again? Surely you are not ignorant of my wanting you.'

No. She was not. She'd felt the proud hardness of him pressed against her leg, felt the heat of him, seen the desire in his dark blue eyes, and he had seen hers and heard it in her moans. That was dangerous tinder. 'Maybe you don't have to play the gentleman, Ven.' The suggestion was out before she could call it back or check her boldness. But it was not a lie.

'Marianne, you don't know what you're saying. I could not ruin you. A friend does not...'

'I'm not asking you to be my friend in this matter.' Marianne was quick to reply. 'I may never marry, Ven. Why should I not take pleasure where I can find it? There are women who do and who live respectable lives if they're discreet.'

'You are too young to make such a decision.' Vennor was all caution. They'd stopped dancing and stood still in the centre of the room, their bodies touching, their hands still linked. Vennor's breath came hard as if he were still exercising. 'What about Lord Hayes?'

She hadn't even thought about Hayes seriously in the past two weeks. She'd been too swept up in her reporting, in her small success of a story and in being overwhelmed by Vennor, his revelations, house clearing, kisses and all. The rest of her life—ballrooms and gowns and a court of suitors—had paled by comparison. 'Perhaps I'll refuse him, if he even asks.' She wasn't sure he would any more. Their courtship had stalled. He stood in her court, danced with her, sent the daily bouquet to the house and watched her from afar. But there was nothing more, other than bristling in Vennor's general direction.

'You are being too glib, Marianne.'

'No, I just know what I want,' she challenged. She wanted him. It had taken the night in the East Docks to show her *how* she wanted him—as more than a friend.

He opened his mouth to argue, but her mother's interruption forestalled further debate. 'There you are!' Lady Treleven was slightly trembly, her hands clutched firmly together at her waist, her voice shaky with excitement. 'Your father has sent a note. We need to hurry home.'

Marianne felt a wave of panic grip her stomach. 'Is it the girls? Rose's baby?' Oh, dear, not her sweet little nephew!

'No, it's nothing like that.' Lady Treleven's face broke into a smile. 'Lord Hayes has been to speak to your father. I think he may have asked for your hand. Isn't it exciting? We must go home at once.'

The panic did not recede from her stomach. Only the reason for it was replaced as they hurriedly gathered their things and made their way to the hall. She'd not expected this, not when she'd decided she wanted something else, *someone* else, altogether. What could possibly have motivated the unemotional Hayes to do something as impetuous as ask for her hand after only a month's acquaintance? She glanced at Vennor. His face was pale, his urbane mask firmly in place.

Say something, do something! she cried silently. But he said nothing. He merely nodded and saw them out, the look in his eyes saying it all: *This is why we can't.*

It occurred to her on the way home that Vennor could have stopped this if he'd wanted to. He simply hadn't wanted to. What was he afraid of? Surely it couldn't be her father. Her father would welcome a suit from Vennor. Her father looked upon him as a foster son. Vennor had a title, wealth and he was a family friend. He was all one could wish for in a *ton*nish marriage. There would be no resistance save what he voiced himself, surely Vennor knew that. But it was still a marriage, still a trap that neither of them was keen to spring.

That brought Marianne up short. Did she truly not want to marry or was it just that she didn't want to marry Hayes? If Vennor offered for her, would his rescue solve anything? Did she want to be married? Vennor didn't, not until he had settled the issue of his parents' deaths. She didn't want him sacrificing himself for her. She folded her hands in her lap, calm settling over her. Perhaps, in this case, she would have to rescue herself.

Chapter Thirteen

The house was buzzing when they arrived home. Marianne could feel it in the expectant air that greeted them. Lord Hayes had been here to visit her father—did she know? Her maid had whispered the news, eyes saucer-wide. A whirlwind courtship, how romantic! So that was how he was framing his early proposal. Marianne pressed a hand to her stomach, trying to quiet the riot of butterflies that fluttered nervously within as she marshalled her arguments should they be needed. Perhaps she was worrying for no reason. Maybe her father had dismissed Hayes's proposal because of that haste. Or maybe not. Her parents had been pleased with Hayes's attentions earlier in the Season. There was no reason for that impression to have altered. Her father would listen intently. He would see the male's side of the argument and all the practical reasons he ought to give his permission. Her father wanted what was best for her and he would think Hayes fitted that criteria.

'Marianne, is that you? Are you home? Come in here and bring your mother. I want to speak with you,' her father's jovial tones called out from his office. He sounded happy. She feared the worst. She also feared disappointing him. He was anticipating a celebration of sorts, but she couldn't give him that.

They all took seats, Marianne sitting on the edge of hers.

'What is it, Father?' Marianne smiled and tried to look quizzical, as if she had no idea about the reason for the summons.

'We have things to talk over. You got my note?' Her father beamed at her and her heart sank further. Oh, dear. Hayes must have been devastatingly persuasive. Her father's eyes were bright and why shouldn't they be? When a man had six daughters, marriage was an enormous accomplishment and he'd managed it three times already. He was halfway there. 'Lord Hayes called. He's asked for your hand. He understands it's a bit premature. He had not meant to ask until later in the Season, but he wants to make his intentions known in a more formal way.'

'Why does it need to be formal?' Marianne was quick to respond, perhaps too quick. She needed to present a calm front. Her parents would wonder why she protested so vociferously when in May she'd been open to the suit. 'We hardly know each other,' she amended. 'Did he give a reason? Because I'm not certain I'm amenable to an early engagement.'

'What does it matter if it's now or in six weeks?' her father replied, surprised to meet with any resistance. He wasn't used to it or prepared for it. None of her sisters had resisted when men had asked for their hands, although Cador Kitto had asked Rosenwyn first before going to their father, something their father had taken a bit to get over.

'I'd like to finish my Season before deciding, that's all. A girl is only young once and I do love London in the spring.' It was all true.

'*Before* deciding?' Her father was sharp. He'd not missed her strategic wording. His earlier bonhomie was gone, replaced now by the father who could be stern with his recalcitrant daughter. 'It sounds as if you aren't sure at all about Lord Hayes whether it be now or six weeks hence. You've spent considerable time with him. I admit to believing this was a *fait accompli*, that the two of you had an understanding.' He cast a worried look at her mother, looking for enlightenment, wondering what he'd missed before looking back at his daughter. 'Marianne, have you been leading the Viscount on?'

'No!' Truly, she hadn't been. She'd thought she could consider going through with it if she must, but that was before unmasking the Vigilante, before she'd seen the work that could be done in the East Docks, before Vennor had kissed her. But she could say none of that. If her father knew what had happened with Vennor, he'd never let her within a foot of him again. It would break the family's friendship.

Her mother broke in gently. 'Is there someone else, dear? Is that why you aren't sure of Hayes any more? I agree with your father. I thought you were set on him.' She couldn't blame her parents for thinking that. She'd certainly behaved that way, hadn't she? The dutiful daughter had always been a convenient cover for getting away with more illicit activities. Now, she was caught in a trap of her own making.

'I thought I could do it, but I'm not sure I can,' Marianne confessed, her gaze going from her father to her mother.

'Why in sweet heavens not?' Her father's patience was much shorter than her mother's. She'd inherited her high spirits and temper from him. 'Well? You must have an answer, dear girl,' he insisted. 'An upstanding man has come offering marriage. He cannot be turned away out of hand.'

But if there were a reason? Marianne sifted rapidly through her knowledge of Hayes. What vices did he have? Had he ever once done anything inappropriate that might cause alarm? Unfortunately not, to her knowledge, but perhaps that was a reason in itself? She tried it out. 'He's not terribly exciting.' It was excruciatingly embarrassing to have this conversation with her parents. What would she say if they asked her what she knew about exciting?

'Thank goodness for that.' Her father's greying brows shot up in disbelief. 'He's titled. He's well behaved. He's not riddled with vices like half the *ton*. He's exactly what a man hopes for his daughter.' He wagged a finger at her. 'Exciting is dangerous and inevitably disappointing.' He tossed her mother a look of exasperation that clearly said this was a woman's domain. He was out of his depth. 'An exciting man will lose your dowry at the gaming hells, or flaunt his bas—'

'Or worse,' her mother concluded for him with a sharp look. She rose and held out her hand. 'Come, Marianne. Let us talk in my sitting room.' Marianne did not miss the look her parents exchanged. They were, as usual, united when it came to the well-being of their children.

Her mother shut the sitting room door behind them and favoured her with a soft smile, misleading though it was. It did not match the blunt words that came out of her sweet mother's mouth. 'I trust that we can speak more openly between the two of us, mother to daughter.' Marianne nodded, but she'd misjudged her mother's acuity. 'I assume what we mean by Lord Hayes being "not exciting" is that the Viscount is a terrible kisser and Vennor is not.'

Marianne looked at her mother, stunned. 'How did you know?' The question was an admission, but there seemed little reason to keep it secret now. Perhaps it had never been a secret. She recalled her mother had been the first one to suggest Vennor was contemplating courting her.

Her mother gave her a stern look that rivalled her father's. 'I've done my best to let each of my girls find their own way.' She paused as they sat down. 'Still, I feel it's my duty to you to intervene if I think you are in danger of making a poor decision. I did not intervene soon enough with Rosenwyn and her earlier disaster in London. I will not make the same mistake with you. So, I fear I must be blunt, Marianne. How far have things gone between you and Vennor?'

There was worry and genuine concern behind her asking, and guilt, too, as if she herself were to blame for allowing them certain leniencies based on the family connection. Still, the reasons behind her mother's question were akin to a slap in the face. Marianne had not considered her actions in that light—a betrayal of her mother's trust. 'I was counting on both you and Vennor having the good sense not to let things get out of hand.' Nor had she thought about how her behaviour would reflect on her sweet mother who'd raised her to know better.

Marianne looked down at her hands, swamped with self-reproach. 'Just kisses, Mama. That's all.' But she hadn't wanted that to be all, had she? If it had been up to her, she would have quite the transgression to report. She'd wanted so much more from Vennor. He'd been the one with enough sense to put a stop to things that night when her hands had crept beneath his shirt. Guilt was one thing, regret was another, and she did not regret what they'd done. She would do it again given the chance—and, oh, how she hoped she might be given the chance.

'Good.' Her mother nodded, relieved it had only been kisses. 'I suppose the next question is do you think Vennor will offer for you?'

'I don't know.' Marianne answered somewhat truthfully. Vennor had been very clear that he could not think of marriage until the crime of his parents' death was resolved, but would he actually want to marry her then?

'Nor do we. Vennor has not mentioned any intention to court you, although I had hopes he would, as you well know. I don't want to be brutal, but I think in this case we must assume that not knowing his intentions means there are no intentions. My dear girl, if you are waiting to see if Vennor comes up to scratch, you will risk losing Hayes. Have you considered that Vennor's presence *is* the reason Hayes is eager to press his suit more formally? If you deny him, he will take it as a sign that you prefer Vennor's suit.' Her mother drew a breath before delivering her proclamation. 'I think we have to let Vennor go. You've had a bit of a fling, but you need to make it clear to him that it ends now—or better yet, that there was nothing there to begin with.'

Marianne had been studying her hands, but at her mother's words she looked up in shock. She'd not expected her mother's edict to be an eradication of Vennor, not after her veiled, hopeful implication a few weeks ago that something more might be brewing. 'But his house? We have to finish the projects. We can't simply walk away from him.' It would break him. He might not understand the ways he needed her, but he did need her. And she needed him. She'd just got her series of articles accepted for publication in the magazine, she had interviews to conduct, the Vigilante to assist. They could not leave each other now.

'I'm not talking about severing ties completely. I'm talking about putting things to rights. His friends will be in town. There will be plenty of people to assist him, like Cassian's wife, Inigo's wife. There will be no reason for you to be alone with him. Whatever *tendre* exists between the two of you will fade naturally. Hayes will see that there is no threat from that quarter.' Her mother took her hand. 'You will see, in time, that it's for the best. Exciting men are often broken men who are missing something inside. They seek to fill the gap with worldly things and they put on masks to hide the hurt. In the long run, a girl is better off with the steady man.'

A man like Hayes. She understood the moral of her mother's lesson. What girl, who'd been out three Seasons, put off the chance to marry a title? 'Is that what you chose, Mama? The steady man?' Her parents had always seemed very much in love. She'd assumed theirs had been a fortunate love match.

Her mother met her gaze evenly with her own dark eyes. 'Yes, I chose the steady man and I've not been sorry. I've had a wonderful life, a secure life, and six daughters to love. I want such blessings for you, too.'

'What if there are other kinds of blessings besides marriage and children? Maybe I don't want to marry at all. Maybe it's not a question of Vennor or Hayes.' Marianne tested the waters very delicately. 'What if I want a career? I've wanted to try my hand at journalistic writing, at promoting an awareness of the social problems we face.'

Managing men and matrimony had not fazed her mother, not even the announcement that she'd kissed Vennor. But this did. To her credit, her mother did not flinch, but she did blanch. 'I don't know what to say to that, Marianne. It's certainly unorthodox. Lord Hayes would not allow it, nor would there be time for it. A viscountess has responsibilities.'

'Then maybe Hayes isn't the one for me. Don't you see, I need time to decide not just on a husband, but on the whole course of my life.' Vennor understood that because he needed time, too. 'I want Father to tell Hayes I need time, that it's too soon.'

Her mother nodded thoughtfully now that it had come down to negotiating positions. 'In exchange, you need to give Lord Hayes some hope that all is not lost. Distance yourself from Vennor, Marianne. Let him be surrounded by his friends, let Lord Hayes see that Vennor no longer singles you out.'

It was the best bargain she was going to get out of today. 'Yes.' Marianne offered the word, but she already knew it was a lie. She could not give him up any more than she could give up her writing and now the two were intertwined. Her heart lurched. All she wanted was Vennor. She wanted to tell him everything—the good and the bad. She wanted his arms about her, his encouragement whispered at her ear, she wanted his mouth on hers, stopping her troubles with his kiss. She wanted his touch to burn away her thoughts. She wanted to live in the moment with him in the East Docks helping people, tomorrow and society be damned.

He'd been damned generous with her tonight and all she could do was snivel. Hayes felt his ambivalent mood ebb at the sight of Elise curled up on the bed, knees drawn up tight under her chin, arms wrapped about herself, the red wig in tangles about her shoulders. 'Those two men you recommended have worked out well.' He set down a pouch of money on the little table hard enough to make the bag jingle temptingly. 'I hope they're as discreet as you say they are. I can't have them blabbing what they know to anyone.' That they were following Miss Treleven about Mayfair and reporting back to him. He didn't want his creditors getting wind of anything that smelled like desperation or worry that his engagement wasn't going to take place. Nor did he want Sir Jock Treleven to learn of it.

'They're trustworthy,' Elise murmured.

'They'd better be, for your sake,' he reminded her. 'I'll take it out of your hide if they so much as whisper a word about their task and who they're doing it for.' So far, so good, though. Their information had paid off. It had allowed him to hedge his chances by getting to Jock Treleven with his offer first. If he had delayed, the prize might have slipped from his grasp. Now, he had to do his part and decide how best to eliminate Newlyn from the game. 'Do you think your friends might be up for something a little bloodier?' he asked.

Elise was wary. She lifted her head from the bed. 'They might be. Do you mean like last time?'

'Possibly. I haven't decided yet. The men we used before, are they still available?' He knew very well they weren't. He'd seen to it that they'd met their own bloody ends once he was done with their services.

'No, I haven't seen them. I think they took ship to the Americas.' Elise sat up, tucking a sheet about her. There was a sudden boldness to her that surprised him. 'I don't want to have anything to do with any more murder.'

Hayes laughed. 'You hardly had anything to do with it last time. You don't even know who they killed.'

'And I don't want to know,' Elise said quickly, her eyes flashing with a bit of fight. Panic often brought that out in people. She'd have to be handled carefully. He couldn't have her getting nervous and telling someone.

'No matter. I'm sure you know some men who can be hired. It hardly makes you guilty to simply put the opportunity before them and let them decide. Start looking. Perhaps some of your clients might be inclined. As always, I'll pay you a handsome commission.' He hadn't decided if it would come to that. There was always a risk when a third party was involved, but the trade-off was that it was so much easier to distance oneself from the crime when one wasn't actually holding the smoking gun, or knife as the case might be. 'Elise, be a good girl and help me with my cravat. I have a ball to attend.' And with luck, Marianne Treleven would not only be in attendance, but compliant as well.

Chapter Fourteen

She could not be compliant about this, even though politeness and good *ton* demanded she offer Lord Hayes a gentle set down when he asked for her decision, which he would most surely do tonight. He was in confident spirits this evening as they danced, no doubt anticipating an affirmative response from her. She would disappoint him. She hoped he would understand that she neither liked nor disliked him. She simply didn't want to marry him.

Lord Hayes took them through the turn at the top of the ballroom with his usual steady precision, nothing at all like Vennor's reckless, whirling speed that left a girl breathless. For the first time since she'd come out, Marianne didn't want to be at a ball, didn't want to be dancing.

It didn't matter that this was one of the most sought-after invitations of the early Season, that the crush tonight was peopled with the brightest stars of the *ton*, or that the food and decorations were nonpareil. She made mental notes of the glittering ballroom to record for M.R. Mannering's column later, but her heart wasn't in it tonight. Instead, her heart was yearning to be in Blackwell, interviewing women at Mrs Broadham's, checking on Mrs Simon and the children. Part of her wondered if that was where Vennor was tonight. He certainly wasn't here. Had he gone out alone? Was he even now righting wrongs and being useful while she waltzed hypocritically with Lord Hayes amid the opulence of a silk-strewn ballroom?

If there was any good to have come from today's surprises it was that she knew her own heart. She could not marry Hayes, no matter what happened with her writing. She fixed her gaze on his face, listening abstractedly to him talk about an incident at his club, all the while wondering why Vennor should rouse such passion in her while Hayes could rouse none. The two men shared certain attractive features: both were blond, both were tall, but Hayes's shoulders weren't as broad, his arm not as muscled where her hand lay on his sleeve. His embrace did not inspire a feeling of welcoming security.

It was the eyes, she thought; Vennor's eyes were alive, but Hayes's eyes were blank, empty. Vennor had purpose. Hayes had the ennui of unexercised privilege. What did he get up for in the mornings? The irony was that he should have something that motivated him. He was a peer, a man with a title, money, land and the ability to shape the world the way he desired through his seat in the House of Lords. Yet from those resources he'd fashioned nothing.

Unlike Vennor, who'd seen his father's reform legislation move through Parliament and spent his nights masquerading as the Vigilante.

Unlike the other Cornish Dukes, who each, in their own ways, made Cornwall a better place to live for all.

Unlike herself, who wanted to inspire others with her writings to see justice done. Lord Hayes would want to keep her in line. She didn't want to be kept in line. She wanted to soar. It had taken Vennor and the Vigilante to help her see that. She knew her heart. She just needed to act upon it.

'Miss Treleven, would you like to walk in the garden?' The dance had ended and Lord Hayes was eager for his answer. In a few moments he might wish otherwise. 'The fountain is pretty at night. I should like to show it to you.'

'Of course, that would be lovely,' Marianne managed in response. They were speaking in code. They both knew what he really wanted to discuss. Marianne's stomach clenched. Despite her commitment to her own decision, there would be consequences. Everyone knew he was courting her. She was an Incomparable; everyone watched her and who she was with. Everyone knew Viscount Hayes meant to offer for her. People would wonder what had happened. He would look foolish if he was refused. She would look like a jilt. People would say she'd led him on. People would also say she'd never do better. People would speculate on the reason for it; they might even attempt to drag Vennor into the scandal. The best she could do to save face for them all was delay the inevitable, as she'd promised her mother.

'You've been distracted. Might I assume it has something to do with my visit with your father today?' Hayes enquired as they strolled slowly through the garden, stopping to admire the statuary as they made their way towards the fountain.

'Yes, it does, in fact.' They might as well get right to it. 'I was surprised that you would wish such a thing on so short an acquaintance. You hardly know me, milord, nor I you.'

'Justin. It's my name. You might start with that.' There was more warmth in his tone than she'd ever heard, but she wasn't entirely sure the warmth was from affection or from anger.

'That's just it. A start. Hardly enough to base a lifetime commitment on. I need more time to consider and in all honesty I think you do, too. Haste is unseemly and unnecessary. We can decide if we suit at the end of the Season.'

Hayes's eyes were keen, piercing. 'Is that the real reason you resist or is there someone else I am being measured against?' There was a boldness to Hayes tonight she'd not encountered before.

Hayes covered her hand with his where it lay on his sleeve, a gesture that was more possessive than polite. Her hand was trapped. 'His Grace the Duke of Newlyn, perhaps? A man with hopes of your hand cannot find that arrangement encouraging.' It was calmly said with a hint of self-deprecation, but Marianne was not fooled. This was a command, an *order*, on par with her mother's edict earlier today to stay away from Vennor.

Marianne bristled. This was a taste of what married life with Hayes would have been like—implicitly wrapped orders she was expected to obey without question. 'You worry for naught. Newlyn is an old family friend. He can't be expected to remodel his home without a female touch and he has no one to hand.'

Hayes smiled, but coldly. 'Then let your mother act as hostess. She is an expert. I wouldn't want Newlyn to get the wrong impression. A woman's touch, a woman's presence, can put all nature of notions into a man's head. I would protect you from the wickedness of men, my dear.'

Marianne pulled her hand away. 'I am quite capable of protecting myself, milord. I appreciate your understanding in regards to my need for time. I cannot possibly decide the matter between us right now. If you would excuse me, I need to return inside.' He had not offered her understanding or granted her permission to delay, but she'd seized both. A gentleman would not contradict her, but just in case the idea crossed his mind, Marianne fled up the path before he could protest and she didn't stop there. Her slippered feet took her out of the ballroom, past the kerb lined with waiting carriages and down the street to Portland Square, unconsciously guiding her trajectory to the one place, the one person, she'd wanted to be with since the moment she'd left him that afternoon. Marianne dashed up the steps of Newlyn House, one thought on her mind: to get to Vennor, to be with Vennor. It was the only thing that made sense any more.

Her hand was at the knocker before the darkness of the house registered and with it a thousand misgivings. What if Vennor was out? What if Vennor was *in*? And not alone? No, he wasn't that sort. He would not bring a mistress here, not to the rooms she'd so carefully done for him, for his fresh start. Honeycutt answered her knock, surprised to see her. 'His Grace is out, miss.' He was flustered, a rare condition for him. Perhaps he wasn't used to young ladies calling alone at night. That was a good sign.

Marianne took advantage, her brain starting to function. 'I'm happy to wait. I'll just wait upstairs for him. There are some additional measurements Mr Howser needs for the wall hangings,' she improvised with a smile as she sailed up the steps. There was nothing like action for affirmation. She wasn't asking Honeycutt for permission, just as she had not asked Hayes for his.

Upstairs, she stepped inside the Duke's newly redecorated chambers and shut the door with a smile. That had been easier than she'd expected. One victory down. She turned up the lamp and took a tour of the room before she sat. From the look of things, Vennor was settling in nicely. Her hand ran over the silver backs of his brushes, the length of his razor. She pulled the stopper out of his cologne bottle and took a healthy sniff—sandalwood and nutmeg, a spicy, masculine scent that was saved from sharpness by the undertones of vanilla. It was quintessential Vennor, a scent she'd associated with him ever since she could remember. She dabbed a bit of it on her neck and moved on. In the dressing room, his blue banyan hung from a peg, ready to be slipped on. She fingered the silk. Did she dare?

It was an admittedly wicked idea, but one that had merit. If he came home and found her sitting primly in his chair, he would argue with her. She hadn't come here to argue. She'd come here to claim. Now that her head was clear, she knew exactly what she wanted and there would be no turning back. It was a bit of a struggle to get out of her gown without help. She'd had to be creative about getting the hooks in the back and even a little destructive. She wasn't certain all the hooks had survived. But sacrificing a dress to the cause seemed a small price to pay against the bigger picture now that she was decided.

She wrapped herself in Vennor's banyan, letting the folds envelop her, the silk brush against her skin as the scent of him brushed against her nostrils. She settled on the bed to take down her hair with a smile playing on her lips. Tonight, she claimed her future. Tonight she would put herself beyond Hayes's reach, beyond the reach of any man who thought to limit her.

He had not protected Marianne from Hayes this afternoon and now there was another woman in need of protection. Vennor's hand closed around the note in his pocket, taken from the Vigilante's Post this evening. He'd gone out alone on a rampage as soon as it was dark, lashing out in his frustration at any criminal that dared to move. The East Docks had never been safer, but it did not mitigate the rage and the impotence in Vennor's heart that had brewed since Lady Treleven had dragged Marianne home in anticipation of a proposal from Lord Hayes.

Should he have intervened? Should he have raced to Treleven House and made an offer of his own even knowing that was something neither of them wanted? What did an offer solve? Yet he could not put the last sight of her out of his mind. She'd glanced his way and for a moment there'd been a flash of desperation, an appeal for help, for *him*. But it had been gone so quickly he might have imagined it. Marianne was used to fending for herself. He could only make matters worse.

Seven hours and four apprehended criminals later, Vennor wasn't sure he'd made the right choice. He felt miserable right now. She'd be dancing at the Medhursts' ball. Perhaps he should have gone if for no other reason than to puncture Lord Hayes's overinflated ego. What if there had been an announcement? What if Marianne had decided to go through with it? His stomach lurched at the thought. Surely she wouldn't, but what if there'd been pressure from her parents? What if she *couldn't* refuse?

He stopped walking, a sixth sense pricking at him. He focused on his surroundings, surprised to find that his feet had led him to the Royal Opera House with its distinctive columns. It was deserted, the evening venue having let out hours ago. It was not a place he came as Vennor the Duke or as the Vigilante. He'd not set foot inside the opera house since the night of his parents' deaths. The Newlyn box sat empty Season after Season—a fact that did not go unremarked.

In little over a week it would be the third anniversary of the murders.

Vennor reached up and tightened the ties of his mask, suddenly seized with a perverse desire to see the spot again—the alley where they'd lain. He'd seen it before, on the evening of their deaths, and the scene was indelibly etched in his mind.

His feet brought him to the alley and his mind brought the rest.

They'd still lain as they had fallen, the Bow Street Runners wanting to study the scene before the bodies were moved. His mother's throat had been cut and his father had been run through the stomach with a blade of some sort.

His mother had died first. His father had died trying to reach her, his hand outstretched towards her as he'd fallen. The depth of the blade's cut testified to a man driven to madness at the last. He must have plunged forward, desperate to reach her, heedless of whatever obstacle stood in his way. The blade had nearly speared him clean through.

Vennor had promptly walked away to vomit in privacy.

From the looks of it, his parents had been provoked and taunted before being violently slain. He could imagine his mother, her elegant head pulled back, held against her captor, a knife against her white throat, and his father outraged and…helpless? It had been hard to picture him thus. The Duke of Newlyn hadn't been helpless a day in his life. But he would have been that night.

He'd clearly drawn his swordstick because it had lain on the cobblestones beside him—but to do what? It would have been useless against a knife to his wife's throat. This had not been a hasty murder, no matter how Bow Street had insisted it was the work of thugs.

Thugs with swords? Swords were not the weapons of the street. Thugs wanted money, not blood. But nothing of value had been taken from them—not his mother's diamond necklace, nor his father's watch. There'd been plenty to take and his father would have handed those items over without hesitation to protect his mother.

Nothing Bow Street had concluded had rung true, yet nothing had emerged in the days, months and now years following to disprove the original hypothesis.

Vennor traced their last moments with his own movements. His father would have stood here, swordstick in hand. His gaze lifted to the brick wall. His mother would have been there. He took a step and then another, faster now. His father would have been quick. He would have stumbled here, the blade of his attacker taking him.

Vennor went to his knees in the alley, crawling, crawling and then stretching out, the cobblestones cold beneath his cheek, his hand reaching for the slipper on his mother's foot and falling short. Horrifying last moments. His mother's eyes had been wide, a scream frozen on her lips. Had she lived long enough to see his father reach for her? Long enough to see him fall? That would have destroyed her in those last moments. They'd been everything to each other.

The morbid guilt rose in his mind, refusing to be pushed back. He'd failed them. He was still failing them—just as he'd failed Marianne today. Three years and still no answers. Maybe it *was* time to give it up, to set aside his quest. If he did, he'd be free to offer for Marianne, to give her a choice beyond exile as a journalist or marriage to a man she didn't love for the sake of respectability. Marriage to him would be better than that, at least for a while, until she realised he wasn't half the man she'd made him out to be, that, in truth, he was a man without direction, a man who'd failed in the one task he'd set for himself.

Vennor stayed in the shadows, leaving the Vigilante's mask on as long as he dared, wanting to walk home, but dreading the arrival. The town house would be dark and he feared the ghosts were hovering close tonight. Finally, reaching his house, he stuffed the mask into his pocket and Honeycutt opened the door for him.

'You have a visitor, Your Grace.'

Ah, so it wasn't ghosts that were hovering close, but Marianne in the flesh. His blood began to pound as he took the steps two at a time. She was exactly what he wanted and exactly what he must resist.

Chapter Fifteen

Prepared as he was, Vennor stopped short at the sight greeting him. Marianne was sitting cross legged on his bed, draped in his banyan, her riot of red curls falling about her shoulders, a veritable siren if ever there was one—and a naked one, too. This realisation came to him as the lamplight played over her alabaster skin highlighting where his robe draped over her breasts. 'What in heaven's name are you doing here, Marianne?' His voice was rough with surprise and hoarse from desire.

'Waiting for you. You went out without me.' There was a scold in her voice at being left behind. She rose from the bed and moved towards him, a sylph in silk, the robe threatening to slip open, teasing him. He'd never seen anything so seductive, so tempting, that he so desperately needed to decline.

He ought to tell her about the note in his pocket, about the woman in need of help, but discussing the Vigilante's business was asking for the impossible when every part of his body cried out for her, when all he wanted to do was take her in his arms and kiss her senseless, and make her forget Hayes; he wanted to take her to bed and make love to her until he was senseless, too, his own nightmares and failures driven away. Today had been trying for them both and they'd reached for each other in their desperation.

He ought to have called for his carriage and taken her home. He should have demanded she get dressed at once but the words that came out were far different. 'Hayes has proposed?' He'd never hated another man so intensely as he did Hayes right now.

'I have asked for a delay in my decision, but I will refuse him.' She pressed a finger to his lips and stepped back, giving him a full view of her, her grip letting go of the banyan. The sides fell open to offer a glimpse of creamy breasts, full and ripe and ready for his hands. 'I could never marry him, no matter what the situation.'

All that mattered in this moment was simply that she was his. She was here tonight because she was his. *His.* Vennor dragged her to him, kissing her hard on the mouth, whispering one word fiercely, 'Mine.'

And Marianne answered back, 'Mine. For tonight, for however long it can last, I want you, Vennor. Only you.' There was a fury between them now the decision had been made. They were in a hurry to go forward. Their hands fumbled with his clothes. She worked the buttons of his waistcoat free and pushed it from his shoulders, tugging at his shirttails, impatient, eager, and he pulled the shirt roughly over his head, refusing to be slowed down by buttons.

'Trousers next,' Marianne breathed, her dark eyes sparkling like polished onyx in the lamplight.

Trousers, absolutely. He wanted only to be naked with her, skin-to-skin, as if in their mutual nakedness he could exorcise the demons that had driven them here tonight. Vennor worked the fastenings at lightning speed, pushing them down past hips and thighs, watching Marianne's face come alive with awe and desire. They were man and woman now, Adam and Eve in the garden for the first time. He lifted her, her legs wrapping around his hips, her arms about his neck, as he carried her to the bed.

He came up over her, arms braced, muscles taut, as he looked down on the glory of her, all fire and cream beneath him as he settled between her thighs as if he belonged there, as if their bodies had been made for each other. 'I want to worship you,' he murmured at her ear, trailing kisses like offerings to the gods along the curve of her jaw, the length of her neck, in the valley between her breasts. He lingered there as long as his body allowed, his hands caressing, his tongue licking, his mouth sucking while his body revelled in the response of hers. Every moan, every little mewl of delight thrummed as she came awake to passion's pleasures.

She arched against him, hips driving into his, and lingering no longer became prudent. He kissed her navel, his hands bracketing her hips in a firm, controlling grip as he reached the damp nest of her curls.

He blew against them, exhilarated by the long gasping sigh that followed and the hoarse whisper of his name on her lips. 'Vennor.' It was a plea, asking for something she could not name, did not know how to name, but something her body knew existed all the same.

'Yes, Marianne,' he breathed against her, his tongue finding the secret nub of her pleasure, licking it with a lingering stroke that both teased and consoled, working her to a frenzy as she arched and bucked beneath him, seeking the elusive capstone to her pleasure and drawing ever nearer. They were both primed to pleasure's brink when she shattered, her back arched, her hips thrust high against him. The scent of her completion was in his nostrils, an aphrodisiac nonpareil. He closed his eyes, letting his other senses feel the pleasure that rippled through her, wave upon wave.

He moved only after her body had settled, levering himself over her once more, taking in the smile on her face. 'I had no idea,' Marianne murmured, barely coherent in the wake of her fascination with the discovery. 'There's more, though, isn't there?' She said it as if she couldn't imagine there being anything more wondrous than what had just occurred.

'Oh, yes, there's more and it's even more wondrous.' Vennor pushed a curl back from her face, although he shared her sentiment. In the moment, it was hard to imagine anything more wondrous than having watched her achieve her pleasure and knowing he'd been the one to give it to her.

She wrapped her arms about his neck. 'I want it,

all of it, Ven. I want to leave nothing out.' Her thighs bracketed him, her knees bent, and again it felt as if their bodies were meant not just for this, but for each other, two interlocking pieces that had been separated for too long. He wanted it, too. Giving her pleasure had been just the beginning, a readying. While it had achieved that, it had left him in a rather heightened state of arousal. He would need to keep himself in check and go slowly with her this first time, something that was becoming a challenge to his willpower with each passing moment.

He kissed her, a long, unhurried meeting of lips and mouths as he raised her arms above her head, shackling them in his grip. His body began to move as he pressed himself against the opening to her core, teasing, preparing her. 'I will try not to hurt you,' he murmured in her ear. He would not take her blindly. If she showed any ounce of resistance, he would stop, he promised himself.

'I know. You could never hurt me, Vennor.' As if to prove it, she raised her hips, urging him on.

She was ready and slick as Vennor eased into her, slow but persistent until at last he felt the tightness in her relent. A smile took her face as he sheathed himself to the full, then he began to move, a rhythmic rocking that she soon joined, answering the motion of his body with the movement of her own. Her legs gripped his hips, holding him tight, her arms drawing him close as the rhythm intensified, overwhelming them until they were one another's anchors in the storm of pleasure sweeping over them. Marianne cried out, joy and laughter mixing with her moans, sounds of ultimate pleasure, ultimate happiness as he pushed them to climax, his own release rushing upon him in an irresistible wave. He'd have to resist, though, what little piece of sanity was left reminded him. He would see to her pleasure and then at last, he would not deny his, but he would mitigate it.

He felt her body tighten along with his and he gave a final thrust, pushing her into the bliss, and then sought his own release in the sheets, both of them heaving with the exhaustion of completion, both of them wrapped in one another's arms. This was love-making at its finest, two people claiming joy from the joining. But it was more than that, Vennor thought as he held her. This had contained something intangible that transcended his usual encounters. Some might argue that it was nothing more than ending three years of celibacy that had given this lovemaking its edge. But this had not been a purely physical joining. This had been almost otherworldly, a connection of souls. He'd lost himself in the act and found himself, too. No. Not in the act. He'd lost himself in *her*, and he'd found himself there, too, in her onyx eyes, in her cries of pleasure, in her intoxicating words, *'I want only you, Vennor.'* If only the night would last for ever. If only he didn't have to face the morning.

'Is it always like this?' Marianne murmured. She lay in the crook of his arm, her head resting against the hollow of his shoulder, her body soft and exhausted against the hardness of his. In these moments, she was satisfied. Mentally. Physically. Emotionally. The draining emotions of the day had no claim on her here.

'No, to be honest.' Vennor's voice was quiet in the darkness; perhaps he, too, wanted to preserve the reverence that followed in the aftermath. 'Sometimes, it's…' Vennor groped for the right word '…emptier.'

She smiled against his chest, privately pleased that he felt it, too, that it hadn't been just another liaison for him. 'Good.' She sighed. There could be no second-guessing her decision on Lord Hayes now. In his eyes she would be ruined. She had put herself beyond his reach even if he pressed the issue. She had a trump card to play now.

Vennor stirred, apparently the same thought occurring to him. 'Marianne, why did you come here tonight? Did you come to be ruined on purpose?'

'No, it's not like that, Ven. You mustn't think I used you for that. I came to take charge of my life. I came because I wanted to be with you and no other and I wanted no strings attached. I wanted it to be my choice entirely.' How did she explain her decision? Would her words be enough?

'You're thinking, Marianne.' His fingers played in her hair, gently combing through the tangles. 'Not having regrets already?'

'Never.' She let her own hand drift over the muscled expanse of his torso, tracing, exploring. Now that she'd claimed this, she wanted more of it.

'You're a ruined woman, now.' Vennor offered. Regardless of what her motives were, that consequence was certain.

'Not ruined. Complete.' Marianne looked up at him, taking in the strong jaw and the squared chin with its secret dimple. 'I could never feel ruined by what we did.' She levered up on one arm. 'I wish I could have gone with you tonight.'

'No, you don't. I went to the opera house. To the alley. I walked their footsteps.'

Marianne was silent. The ghosts were riding him hard tonight, then. He seldom went there. 'Did you find what you were looking for?' She could only imagine the horror he associated with that place.

'No, in fact, I did not. Am I just torturing myself now, Marianne? Should I let them go? Should I accept that I won't get the answers I'm looking for, that those answers might not exist? That maybe I want more than answers. Perhaps I want absolution, absolution for not being there that night, for not stopping it.' He'd not once spoken to her of his guilt. She wondered if he'd spoken of it to anyone? To Cassian or Eaton? Or Inigo? She waited, careful not to speak lest it deter him from continuing. She felt his chest rise with a deep inhalation and then the words came. 'I should have been there. I was *supposed* to be there.'

The pain in his voice was edged with a gnawing agony. The sound of it tore at her. Dear heavens, it shredded her heart to think this confident, strong man had carried this with him all along. It made her response that much more important. This guilt could not be dismissed with platitudes. She draped her arm across his naked torso, all strength and muscle beneath her hand, and held him close. 'Tell me, Ven. Tell me all of it,' she offered in soft tones. 'Let me share your burden. Please.'

There was a long silence, and she thought for a moment he would not take the invitation, but the intimacy of the night, the intimacy of their arms wrapped around one another was an irresistible cocoon, a safe space in the world where anything might be said. Vennor began to talk, each word setting free another part of the past.

Chapter Sixteen

'We'd had dinner together at a restaurant my mother wanted to try. She'd worn a new dress that had been delivered that day, a purple one with jet beading. Father ordered champagne and told her she looked spectacular.' Vennor remembered the evening as if it had happened last week, so vivid were those last hours. 'They were always so in love. They were always complimenting one another.'

'That must be why you're so very good with the compliments yourself.' Marianne laughed softly, encouraging him, and he let the darkness envelop them in rare, intimate privacy, grateful for the warmth of her against him.

'We had a good time at dinner. The meal was excellent, the champagne cold, and we laughed and talked about nothing significant.' Which had been a relief because it had been a tense week full of disagreement. His mother had diplomatically tried to bring up the subject of marriage and his father had not so diplomatically suggested he find a cause to take an interest in. He'd quarrelled with both of them.

'At the end of dinner, though, a message arrived from the town house,' he continued. 'A cargo we'd been waiting for had arrived. Someone was needed to oversee the handling of it and to sign receiving documents. The foreman had gone home sick earlier. The first chance I had, I offered to go and take care of the cargo. I was relieved. My mother had arranged for us to take the niece of a friend to the opera that night and I was not looking forward to meeting the girl. I left them at the restaurant, eager to be away, happy to have escaped another of my mother's matchmaking attempts. My mother was disappointed. She had great hopes that I might find the girl interesting.' He exhaled. 'She wasn't just disappointed in the outing fizzing out, she was disappointed in me. *I* had disappointed her.'

'How could *you* disappoint her? She loved you, Ven,' Marianne murmured.

'I wasn't taking my position as an heir seriously and pursuing marriage. I was in my late twenties, the only male of the line, really, and I was resolutely refusing to do my duty, my *most* important duty.' It hurt him to admit it. 'I quarrelled with her over it constantly. She was right to want it. I was selfish. None of my friends had married. Why should I? Of course, no one expected Eaton to marry because of his sterility, but I conveniently overlooked that when making my arguments.'

'Happy families quarrel, too, Ven, I assure you. I

have five sisters and there's always something fractious brewing. It doesn't mean we love each other less,' Marianne consoled.

'Well, I felt as if I'd failed her. More than just escaping the matchmaking, I'd volunteered to go to the docks because I wanted to get back at them both for pressuring me. I wanted to say, "See, I am making something of myself, Father, by taking an interest in the dukedom and in doing so it is forcing me to disappoint Mother." I had some idea of playing them off against one another. In retrospect, it was petty of me. I hugged my mother and I shook my father's hand, told him to have a good evening and that I'd see him the next day at White's for drinks. I never saw them alive again.' He had seen them, of course, lying in the alley.

Vennor's voice caught on the last, emotion threatening. 'They were stupid words. Stupid, stupid words,' Vennor growled, his breath ragged. 'I should have told my mother I loved her. I should have told my father how proud I was to be his son, what an inspiration he'd been to me. I should have told them how much I loved our little family, the walks we took at Karrek Sands, the picnics in the Trevaylor Woods, and that I was so grateful for them. I should not have begrudged their efforts to help me be my best. There was so much I should have said, Marianne, and so much I should have done.'

And now, nothing could bring them back.

So potent was the thought it might as well have been spoken out loud.

* * *

'They knew all those things, Ven.' Her heart was breaking for him, for this strong, devoted man who'd borne so many secrets alone these past years. It tore at her that he thought he had to carry them alone. She understood better now the reasons for that urbane mask he wore and perhaps even the reasons why he wore the Vigilante's mask as well.

'It seems the least I can do is solve the mystery of their murder and bring to justice whoever did that to them.'

'And to you,' Marianne added. Whoever had done this had hurt him as well. *She* wanted revenge for that, for having had the carefree friend she'd once known stolen and turned into a secret-keeping duke who felt he had no choice but to live in darkness. There *was* brokenness in Vennor. She saw that now. How perceptive her mother had been. He needed to grieve his parents and he needed to forgive himself. Only then could he move forward. 'If you'd been there, you could have been killed, too. There's no guarantee your presence would have changed anything.'

He grunted at that. 'The odds would have been even, two on two. There *were* two of them. The one who held my mother and the one who stabbed my father. Bow Street likes to pretend it's not clear there were two, but I saw it plain tonight. It could not have been just one.'

'Ven, do you think solving the mystery will bring you peace?'

'It *will* bring justice,' Vennor countered swiftly with a touch of fierceness.

'That's not the same thing,' she argued softly. Justice would bring closure to the tragedy, but it would not necessarily bring absolution.

'It might be all I can have, though.' His voice was hoarse with emotion.

'And the Vigilante? What can he have? What happens to him once this is done?' It was all of a piece, the Vigilante and the search for his parents' killers, but the Vigilante had become more than just the search. Did he see that? 'I think the Vigilante will be missed should he disappear. People count on him.' She thought of the Vigilante's Post in Blackwell where people pinned their grievances and needs. 'What will happen to the Mrs Simons of the world without the Vigilante?' The Vigilante might have started out as a clue seeker, but had rapidly become more. It was clear from her interviews that the people of the neighbourhoods he frequented relied on him for justice, for succour. He was their gateway to a better life.

'I don't know. I haven't figured that out yet.' He reached for her, kissing her softly on the mouth. 'There's a lot I haven't figured out.'

'I know what you mean.' Marianne gave a soft laugh, awareness rippling through her body as he moved over her. Her arms went around his neck. He meant to make love to her again. She stretched luxuriously beneath him in anticipation.

The lovemaking was different this time. Gone was

the tension of earlier, replaced by a slower pace, a languid exploration where neither was in a hurry to reach completion, although when completion did come it was just as overwhelming as it had been the first time, though with a bittersweet edge to it. The night was passing. She would have to leave the warmth of his body, the safety of this room where nothing else mattered, and make her way home.

Vennor helped her dress, his fingers lingering on the broken fastenings of her gown. He called for his coach and insisted on accompanying her home. He would not hear of her making the short journey to Curzon Street alone. She dozed against his shoulder on the drive, her body lapping up the warmth of his a little while longer. She would have liked to have driven like that for ever, the sky hinting towards grey, the city quiet except for the occasional rumble of carriages bringing late-night revellers home and Vennor beside her. She said as much. 'Shall we just keep driving?'

'Where to?' Vennor laughed.

'Anywhere, far from here.' Some place where there were no proposals from eager viscounts, or dead parents to mourn, or past regrets to forgive, or complicated futures to contemplate.

'That would only be fun for a while. You would miss everyone.' Vennor yawned and peered out the window. 'We're here. Shall I see you in?'

She shook her head. 'No, it would only complicate things. If anyone asks, I'll think of something to say.'

She'd have to be careful with her dress. There were a few hooks missing and her maid would notice.

'Marianne...' Vennor said.

'No, say nothing, Ven. I thought we agreed we don't have it all worked out. We don't have to have all the answers tonight. Let tonight be enough on its own.' She kissed him swiftly on the mouth, one last time. 'I'll see you tomorrow.'

She made her way into the house, feeling Vennor's gaze on her back. She smiled, a sense of completion and peace filling her to know Vennor wouldn't leave until she was safe inside. Of course he wouldn't. He'd fought for a flower girl. What more would he do for a woman he cared for?

Across the street, stiff from a long night's vigil, two figures hurried off into the fading darkness, free at last from their task.

Whack! His arm brought the crop down across her buttocks, anger riding him hard, hard enough to have him seeking Elise out before noon. The informants had brought awful news. Miss Treleven had come home at dawn in Newlyn's carriage. Whack! The air in the room whistled gratifyingly. Elise shrieked, but he would not stop. Marianne Treleven had played him, begging for more time, suggesting maidenly modesty at making a hasty match, leading him on, making him believe she would accept a proposal at the Season's end, only to run straight into Newlyn's arms.

It seemed to be a recurring theme, the Moore men

losing their women to the Penlerick males. His grandfather had lost his true love to Alfred Penlerick, Vennor's grandsire. That had been the beginning of the Moore troubles. It seemed Alfred Penlerick had not been content with stealing Evangeline Warnick from Henry Moore, but had gone on to defeat his grandfather at every turn—denying funding for roads that would have made transportation of goods from his grandfather's remote mills less costly, voting down legislation that would have lowered workers' wages, thus enabling his grandfather to turn a larger profit. The list of grievances was long, leading to the current financial situation of his viscountcy.

Exhausted finally, Hayes laid aside the crop, breathing hard. Elise was sobbing. 'Dry your tears,' he scoffed. 'I paid you plenty.'

She lifted her head, the red curls of her wig falling forward over her shoulders, a new fire in her eyes. 'You pay me for keeping your secrets. You pay me for finding you men to do who knows what. You pay me to dress up as some debutante who has eluded you. But you do not pay me enough to whip me within an inch of my life. I will not receive you again.'

'Oh, very good, my elusive debutante is something of a spitfire, too.' Hayes laughed dismissively at her chagrin. 'I do like a challenge.' Not that this was much of a challenge. He had used her hard this morning, an outlet for his anger over Marianne's betrayal. But whores were simple creatures to understand. It all came down to money and the occasional promise a man never intended to keep. Elise wanted more money. He would supply it. Even in his straitened circumstances, he was rich compared to a whore.

He tipped her chin up to meet his gaze with a hard thumb and forefinger. 'You're lucky I like you and I don't take the crop to you again, this time for your own insubordination. You think to blackmail me with my secrets. But you've forgotten one thing. You have no enforcement. Who would you tell? Who would believe you? Besides, what would you tell them? That I, a nobleman, asked you to find me a couple of men who could gather information? You don't know what for. You know nothing of interest to anyone. You don't even know my name.'

'I could tell them about last time,' she argued in a surprising show of spirit. 'You had someone killed. It's why you went away.'

Did she think that was leverage? He withdrew a knife from a sheath in his coat, a long slender, wicked blade for slicing. 'If you tell anyone, I would kill *you* before questions could be asked, just for betraying me.' He smiled and re-sheathed the blade. 'It's good to be clear about these things, Elise, don't you agree? We must always know where we stand with one another.' He might need to kill her anyway. She'd been defiant yet again. It meant she was thinking and thinking in a woman was always dangerous. Thoughts of freedom wouldn't be too far off. Women must always be managed.

As for Marianne, he would still marry her, although he'd rather not have been forced to take Newlyn's leavings. Did she think the loss of her virginity—if that was what indeed had happened in the interim between leaving the ball and arriving home—would dissuade him? Hardly. He was after much more from her than a body in bed. He would marry her even if she were a dowd simply for her property and her place in Cornish society.

Chapter Seventeen

He should offer to marry her. It was what a man did when he had compromised a virgin, even if she'd been the one to proposition him. Vennor stared at the blank sheet of paper before him on a blotter at his desk, the pen idle in his hand. It was nearly noon and he'd been staring at the sheet for an hour. He'd not slept when he returned home. He hadn't even tried. He sat up instead, watching the sun rise and replaying the night in his mind. He'd replayed it all through breakfast and was still replaying it, still wishing he'd handled things differently.

There were things he should have said to her, things they should have talked about, the business of post-coital expectations and such. He was not so out of practice that he didn't know his duty. But Marianne didn't want his duty and he was in no position to offer it even if she did. He would, however, if he thought for a moment she wanted a proposal. Of course, should circumstances require a proposal, regardless of what either of them preferred, he'd make it. If there were to be consequences, a child, from last night despite his precautions, he would do the right thing.

A child. That would certainly change everything. What they wanted as individuals would cease to matter. Vennor fiddled with his pen, picturing Marianne large with that child, picturing the child born, wrapped in a white blanket in Marianne's arms, then in his arms. A child who would not die, who would want for nothing, who would carry on the legacy of the Newlyn dukedom. *A son with Marianne.* Joy was followed by regret. A baby. Another person to fail, yet being with Marianne last night had been the most peaceful he'd felt in ages and he wanted it again.

'Your Grace,' Honeycutt interrupted his thoughts. 'You have visitors. The Earl of Tintagel has arrived, along with Viscount Trevethow, the Marquess of Lynford, and their wives. Miss Treleven is with them, too. I have taken the liberty of setting extra places for luncheon.' Honeycutt could barely repress his glee over the thought of serving luncheon for eight. It was a dead giveaway. Vennor knew immediately what had happened. Marianne had ambushed him. He set aside his pen and smiled.

The drawing room was a cacophony of laughter and exclamations. The noise of it could be heard down the hall, growing louder as he approached. Vennor had just a moment to survey the joyous melee inside before they noticed him, a moment to commit it all to memory, this joyous reunion of best friends: Cassian, tall and broad, looking confined in town clothes, but happy as he embraced Eaton, equally as tall and broad, his dark curls already escaping their careful combing; Eaton turned to embrace Inigo who was, as usual, immaculate and well groomed.

Their wives stood aside in their own cluster, looking like a spring bouquet in their pretty muslins, Marianne at their centre, her hair bright, her smile wide as she showed off the newly wallpapered drawing room. She looked as though she belonged here, not just in his house, but in his life, among his friends, among their wives, as if she were meant to take her place among the Cornish Dukes. It was a dangerous thought coming on the heels of his other thoughts this morning, thoughts of a future, of children.

This was not how he had imagined seeing her for the first time after last night, surrounded by friends, with no chance for privacy and the discussion that must take place. There was also the issue of the woman's note from the East Docks. He was going to need Marianne's help with that. Yet he could have watched her ceaselessly, noting every nuance, the way she tossed her head when she laughed, how she touched people, an easy tap here, a heartfelt squeeze there. She emanated abundant joy. She'd brought her joy into his house and now she'd brought his friends. Despite other pressing matters, Vennor could not begrudge her the little ambush-cum-reunion, although he did wonder what had brought it on.

Cassian caught sight of him at the door. 'Vennor, there you are, old chap!' Within a handful of strides, Cassian reached him, enveloping him in a tight embrace—the first of many, as he was swallowed up by his friends. Eaton followed Cassian, then Inigo, and then the wives came with kisses all in turn—Eliza, Penrose, and Audevere. Their welcome was overwhelming. Marianne slipped a hand through his arm in support when the greetings were over, perhaps understanding how he'd feel. The four heirs had not been all together since the funeral. He'd seen Inigo in town and he'd seen Cassian when the Hawaiian royals had been in London. But having everyone together in the same room was a novel occurrence.

It was Marianne who got everyone settled at the table outside in the garden for lunch, taking advantage of the excellent weather. There was so much to catch up on, Vennor didn't know what to ask first. Lunch passed in a haze of titbits. There were children to discuss: Cassian had a son named Collin Richard for Cassian's brother and for Vennor's father; Eaton had a stepdaughter, Sophie, who lit up his face whenever he spoke of her. There were projects to discuss, too: Eaton's mining schools, and Cassian's nearly completed Cornish pleasure garden. A lump formed in Vennor's throat when he surveyed the table, seeing physical proof of his friends' good fortune. He was happy for them, but envious, too.

'You've been reinventing the world with all of your reform legislation,' Cassian said during a lull in the conversation.

'*Father's* legislation,' Vennor corrected. 'I have managed to pass his projects, slowly but surely.'

Cassian slapped him on the shoulder. 'You are too

modest, Ven. You've done important work these past years. Your father would be proud. Now we have to get you home to Cornwall to work your magic there.'

Vennor gestured for the footmen to refill the wine glasses, the cold white going down impeccably with the chilled shrimp and poached salmon Cook had served for lunch. 'Is that what's behind the visit? You've all come to drag me home?' It was congenially said for all its boldness. Vennor hazarded a look at Marianne at the other end of the table. How much of a hand had she had in this part of the ambush as well? She met his eyes and gave a small shrug.

'It's been three years,' Eaton put in with equal congeniality and boldness. 'I imagine there are some folks who are hungry for a look at your face.' Like land stewards and tenants. Vennor knew exactly the people Eaton meant. But there were people here who needed him, like the anonymous woman on the docks. Who would help them if he left the city?

Sensing a change in the mood of the table, Marianne rose. 'Ladies, perhaps I can show off the rest of the house. We've just finished the ballroom. The chandelier is a treat.'

Vennor missed her the moment she was gone—missed her smile at the end of the table, missed the encouragement of her presence. He was too aware that all the male gazes at the table had followed her as she and the ladies departed the garden. Or maybe he was putting too much significance on that. Perhaps they'd only been watching their own wives. The doors shut, the women taken from view, and Inigo didn't hesitate to broach the subject. 'She's a natural here, Ven.' It was tastefully said as the footman brought a decanter forward for an afternoon brandy, but the implication was clear.

'Is that the way things are headed?' Inigo asked as Vennor passed the brandy to him. 'The place looks much better than the last time I was here.'

'The last time you were here, you were more interested in shooting at Manton's and avoiding thugs on Jermyn Street. I'm surprised you noticed anything.' Vennor took a swallow of his drink. He saw too late how things would look through Inigo's eyes—Marianne fixing up the house, Marianne hosting his luncheon with ease, but damned if he knew how Inigo knew that much.

'Marianne wrote to Rosenwyn and Cade and Rose had tea with Eliza up at the school,' Eaton put in, taking mercy on him at last. That explained it.

'What exactly did Marianne tell Rose?' Vennor tried to ask casually.

'That she was helping clean up the town house and that she hoped to talk you into the charity ball.' Eaton smiled. 'We all thought it was worth coming up to town and having a look. I think the ladies are expecting an announcement of some sort.'

'Then I think they will be disappointed.' Vennor was firm on this. No ball. No proposal—not from him anyway. 'I believe Viscount Hayes has offered for Marianne's hand.'

'And you've allowed it?' Cassian was blunt and quick in his reaction. He looked about the table. 'Fellows, I think we've come just in time.' To Vennor he said, 'You've got to be crazy. Marianne is perfect for you.'

What did one say to that? A brief silence descended on the table of friends, punctuated by bees in the nearby garden. It was Inigo's low tones, his words slow and measured, that broke in. 'Gents, he knows.' Another long pause and Vennor was acutely aware all eyes were on him, waiting for an explanation. Again, it was Inigo, with his deuced accurate intuition who spoke. 'How far has it gone, Ven? You might as well give us the details, since most of them were written all over both of your faces.'

Was it that obvious? Apparently so. Still, this was no one's business but his and Marianne's. Vennor rose from the table. 'I'm sorry, but a gentleman never tells. Let's join the ladies on their tour.' They accepted his refusal with good humour, but Inigo slid him a look that plainly indicated this was not over.

'I'll check out Viscount Hayes, just in case,' he murmured. 'He'll be at the Russian embassy's fête tonight.' As would most of the *ton*. Alexei Grigoriev's annual ball was highly attended, everyone eager to see the Russian acrobats and to eat the Russian desserts that populated his buffet tables. Damn, Vennor had forgotten about that. How would he manage to sneak himself and Marianne off to Blackwell if they were surrounded by people who would notice? The general crush would hardly miss two people, but Inigo would, especially after his refusal to discuss the arrangement this afternoon. It might have to be done anyway and Inigo's curiosity could go rot.

There had been absolutely no time to speak with Vennor before everyone left Newlyn House to change for the evening. Did his friends suspect anything between them? She rather thought Inigo did. He missed nothing. She'd been looking forward to sharing her good news with Vennor, but there'd been no chance to celebrate and the news was too private for the group. The editor at *Gentlemen's Weekly* had given her a whole page for the next instalment of her series on London's working poor. Her first chance to share the excitement was at the Russian embassy, and even then, manoeuvring to get Vennor alone had been something of a challenge.

'I have news!' she whispered under her breath as they made their way to a private spot in the mostly deserted hall, the guests all crowded into the ballroom to see the acrobats hanging from a trapeze suspended from the ceiling. Vennor was alert, his muscles tense beneath the sleeve of his evening jacket. 'The magazine has been receiving mail about my column and readers want more.'

'Marianne, that's wonderful.' Vennor smiled, but she sensed an air of distraction about him. His eyes glanced about the hall.

'Are you looking for someone?' She looked about, too, trying to deduce what had caught his attention.

Vennor took her by the arm, drawing her back into

an alcove, surprising her with a sudden kiss, fierce and hard. 'I've been wanting to do that all day.'

She wound her arms around his neck. If that was the reason for his distraction, she'd forgive him. 'Me, too. I hadn't realised how disruptive having your friends around would be.' She laughed gaily. She loved Eaton and Cassian and Inigo like brothers, but, like brothers, they could be annoying, too. 'I think Inigo suspects.'

'He definitely does.' Vennor's hands settled at her waist, his thumb idly drawing circles in the fabric at her hips. It wasn't just the kiss. It was something more, Marianne thought.

'Last night, when I...when the Vigilante went out, there was a note left on the post,' he said. 'It was buried beneath the broadsheets. There's a woman who's asked for help. She believes she is in danger. I need you to come out with me, Marianne.' He blew out a breath. 'I shouldn't even be asking, shouldn't even be thinking of exposing you to her company, but I think the Vigilante will intimidate her. She needs to talk to another woman. Will you come with me?'

'When?' Her mind was a riot of questions and elation. Vennor had *asked* her to come. He saw her as a partner in this. He *needed* her, as a lover, as a co-conspirator against crime. He wanted her involved in his life. The request touched her deep at her core.

'Tonight, as soon as we can sneak out of here.'

'Let's go now while everyone is ogling the acrobats.' Marianne slipped her hand into Vennor's and in that instant she knew she'd walk out into the unknown on a moment's notice with him any time he asked.

Chapter Eighteen

He should not have brought her here. Vennor regretted it immediately. Delilah's was hardly a place for a lady, as exhibited by the rather obvious display of a couple in flagrante delicto on a tatty divan in the parlour, the woman's head between the man's knees. He'd thought…well, it hardly mattered what he'd thought would happen, but it hadn't. Vennor, mask in place, steered Marianne away from the couple. He caught sight of Delilah in her customary red dress. She smiled at the sight of the Vigilante and came forward. 'Let me take you upstairs.' She frowned at Marianne. 'What is this?'

'Support, comfort,' he replied tersely, brooking no complaint from the madam. 'For the woman. It might be easier for her to talk with another female.'

Delilah ran a hand down his arm in overt invitation. 'Would you like some entertainment while they talk? Waiting can be tedious.' She was all solicitous concern.

Vennor removed her hand. 'No, thank you, you know I don't indulge.' He was quite aware that Delilah had set it as a personal challenge over the last several years to bed the Vigilante. She would have to remain disappointed.

She laughed, a deep throaty sound. 'When you are tired of playing the monk, you let me know. I find celibate men very erotic.' He was thankful he could not see Marianne's face within the folds of her cloak. She'd either be beet-red with embarrassment at the frank talk or she'd be shuddering with laughter. 'Here's Elise's room.' Delilah turned to him. 'You're in luck; it's a room with peepholes if you care to listen without being seen. There is a secret chamber here to the left.'

She opened a small door revealing a narrow space. There would be no room to fight, no way to escape if he was discovered, or ambushed by those who'd taken offence at his efforts. 'You will be safe, Vigilante.' Her voice was low and her touch, this time, reassuring. 'No one will know you're here. You will not be interrupted. I will not forget what you did for me. It is a debt that cannot be repaid, although I will always try.' She flashed him a surprisingly soft smile.

He slipped inside with a final nod to Marianne and the door shut behind him. Barring any security concerns, the room was ideal. He could hear Marianne's interview and be on hand in case anything happened. He found the peepholes and looked through them to see the woman in question sitting on the bed, nervously pleating her shift between her fingers and dart-ing glances at the door, her anxiety palpable even at a distance. Vennor settled in to watch, to wait—two things he was not extremely good at. He liked action; he liked being the Vigilante. He'd long ago acknowledged that being the Vigilante gave him control in a world that usually offered so little of it.

For a short time, and for a few souls, he could make the world a better place. He'd made life better for people like Delilah and Mrs Broadham who'd been at the mercy of insurance men. There was lingering hope in that, but more often his help was the help of the moment, like the young man on the docks the other night, attacked for his pay. Those efforts kept people safe, but they did not bring lasting change, and he was starting to see that. Those efforts were just another version of charity baskets. It had taken working with Marianne, talking to her about what he did here, to see the limitations of the Vigilante. Always, there'd been the limitation of being only one man. He'd seen that from the start. But there were other limitations as well. What would happen when he left the city?

The door to the other room opened and those thoughts had to be put aside as Marianne entered and was introduced by Delilah. The girl nodded and bobbed, more nerves on display. Whatever it was the girl wanted to say, she felt very certain it was dangerous information. That made Vennor all the more curious. Her note had been brief and lacking in details, as the notes usually were, but it had come from Delilah's so he'd responded. There was little trouble there these days, which had made the note stand out all the more.

The girl rose, but Marianne went to her and sat on the bed. 'No, please, don't move. We can talk right here.' Marianne was all reassurance as Delilah left the room. Marianne pushed back her hood, another gesture designed to put the girl at ease, but the girl, already slight and pale, paled further and leapt off the bed with a scream that had Vennor's hand going reflexively to his dagger. What was happening? He strained through the peepholes to see, but there was nothing amiss, only Marianne moving towards the girl, a hand outstretched in reassurance.

'Did he send you? Is this a test of my loyalty?' The girl was moving furtively around the room, trying to keep the table between her and Marianne as she edged towards the door. Dear heavens, she intended to make a run for it! Vennor tensed, prepared to dart into the hall if need be.

Marianne was working hard to put the girl at ease. 'Please, don't be afraid. The Vigilante sent me. I have your note.' Marianne's voice was soft and soothing. She reached into her pocket and pulled out the small sheet of paper. 'What's wrong?' Marianne reached a hand to her curls. 'Is it my hair? My gown?' The girl nodded. Marianne smiled kindly. 'Can you tell me why?' The girl shook her head, the mad desire to flee still in her eyes. 'Would you like to see the Vigilante?' Marianne offered softly. 'Would that be proof enough that you are safe?'

That was his cue. Vennor slipped out of the viewing room and into the chamber. Immediately, the girl's nerves lessened. 'Forgive me, I thought perhaps he'd found the note.' Her voice trembled and Vennor's anger rose that someone could strike such fear into another person. Whoever was tormenting this girl had done it well. Close up, he could see traces of rice powder on her skin. That explained the paleness. There was a fading mark at her throat, perhaps an indication that there were marks elsewhere. She clutched the neck of her shift to her, aware of his scrutiny or perhaps anticipating his questions. Scrutiny was common enough in her line of work. Questions less so, but Marianne was ready with hers.

'What was it about my hair that startled you?' Marianne took her by the hand and led her back to the bed, but the girl pulled away, making a gesture to wait as she went to retrieve something from behind the dressing screen.

'One of my customers makes me wear this.' She held up a rather luxurious long red wig, complete with waves and curls, a fair approximation of Marianne's own hair.

'Who is he?' If the sight of the wig had startled Marianne, she gave no sign of it. Vennor settled against the table, content to let Marianne work with the girl.

'I don't know. He never gives his name. I call him milord—it's what he prefers. Perhaps he's a lord in truth; he did mention once that he had to attend a ball.' A lord who liked to go slumming. A certain picture was starting to form in Vennor's mind. He knew the sort of men who indulged in such things, men who didn't want to be held accountable for their actions so they preyed on the weak.

The two women sat on the bed, the wig between them. 'How long has he been a customer?' Marianne's tone was gentle. One would think she discussed the careers of prostitutes on a daily basis given her ease with the subject matter. Vennor was impressed. She was exactly what the situation needed—a firm, gentle, but guiding hand. He would have been too impatient.

'Four years, since I started working here. I thought he was gone for good a couple of years ago, but he turned up last month.' It didn't sound as if his reappearance had pleased her. 'That's when he started asking me to wear the wig.' Vennor would bet money the man was a role player, a fantasiser. If he was slumming, then his fantasies ran deep and dark.

'Do you have any idea why he wants you to wear the wig? Does he like redheads?' Marianne probed carefully. Vennor hoped she didn't get more than she bargained for with the answer.

'I think there's a woman he aspires to have who has red hair, but she does not return his affections.' She twisted the bed sheets in her hands, apparently not used to having her opinion regarded with interest.

'Why do you think she doesn't return his affections?' Marianne asked, having quickly picked up on the conjecture. Conjecture wasn't evidence, but Vennor knew it was often useful to know what caused someone to think a certain way. Still, they would have to leave off with this line of interesting questioning and get to the real reason for the visit—the note. They couldn't linger here for long.

'He beats me because he can't beat her.' Her gaze slid to an item propped in the corner and Vennor saw Marianne's eyes go wide at the sight of the crop. 'I think she might be a real lady. I hope he doesn't win her. I hope she sees what he really is before it's too late for her. He comes here to hide, I know it. I've seen men like him before.' So had Vennor and they disgusted him. Men who exerted their power by exploiting those who could not fight back. He'd like to track this man down and give him a taste of his own medicine.

Vennor cleared his throat. 'I am sorry, miss. But we need to know about your note. What danger are you referring to?' Perhaps there would be something he could do for her personal situation later.

She took a moment, her face suddenly clearing with recognition. 'My client *is* the danger. Oh, not for myself, I understand the risks of my trade,' she rushed on. 'It's what he plans to do. He's asked me to find him men to do odd jobs. I don't know what the jobs are, but the men have to be discreet.' Vennor could imagine the type of tasks they'd be set to—perhaps following someone or threatening someone, something the man in question couldn't do on his own because he'd be recognised. 'He pays them very well, but on his last visit, he asked if the men might be up for something a little bloodier, a little more violent. That was when I sent the note.'

'Why did you decide to act then?' Marianne asked.

Vennor exchanged a look with Marianne. He understood what Marianne's question implied: what had prompted the girl to act now instead of earlier? It might be that she was trying to protect herself, wanting to set herself apart from being an accomplice now that the man's actions might have blood attached to them. He thought it was more than that, though. She was genuinely frightened.

'He's done it before. Right before he went away the first time, he recruited two men to kill someone.' She was starting to cry now, overcome by her situation. Marianne had an arm about her, her questions for the girl coming in a soft barrage, but there was a limit to what the girl knew. She did not know who the target had been or why. She'd not said anything because she had no proof, because there was no one to believe her, because she had no name, and then he was gone, vanished for two years.

Vennor shifted uneasily where he leaned against the table, clues starting to come together. So far he'd concentrated on the girl, on reading her body language for the truth, but he hadn't connected the pieces of her story. Perhaps he was reading too much into it because of his own perspective—two men, a murder, no trail to any suspects because the man who orchestrated it had fled.

'What does he look like?' Marianne passed the girl her handkerchief.

'Tall, blond, slender in build, but stronger than you

might think. He has blue eyes.' The girl shrugged in apology. 'I am sorry, it's not much to go on.'

'No discerning marks?' Marianne asked delicately. 'A scar? A freckle, a birthmark, um, somewhere?'

'Not that I've ever noticed.' The girl hiccupped.

Vennor shot a furtive look towards the door. The clock was running and he wanted Marianne safely away, he wanted to be alone with her and his thoughts before he jumped to any more rampant conclusions. 'We have to go, but we thank you for your information. If there's anything else that might be of use, please send word. I will be watching.'

'No! I can't.' The girl wrested free of Marianne and flung herself at him, grabbing him about the knees in supplication. 'I can't ever send word again. There's something else. This time, he threatened to kill me if I betrayed him.' Her eyes were wild now, the terror of that threat washing over her anew.

Vennor raised her to her feet. 'Then why did you?'

'I couldn't go to the police. They'd never believe me. It wouldn't be worth the risk to tell them. And if I ended up dead a week later, they wouldn't think anything of it. Whores die all the time. But you're different. You're above the law. You listen to people like me. If I end up dead, you will know why.'

No. Not on his watch. Vennor made a split second decision. He nodded to Marianne. 'Help her dress, help her pack. Have her downstairs in five minutes. I'll make the arrangements with Delilah. Five minutes, I mean it. We must hurry.' He'd take her to Mrs Broadham's for the night and in the morning she could take a coach out to one of his estates. There'd be a cottage there for her; she could take up a new life and a new name in the country, or wherever she chose, but she would *not* die here, not if he could help it.

Marianne watched the dark streets rattle past. Delilah had found them a hack. They'd left Elise at Mrs Broadham's with instructions for the morning coach and some money, but they were not going home, not going back to the Russian embassy's fête, not back to Mayfair. They were going to the Vigilante's lair, the little room in the old warehouse. She was glad of it. Her blood thrummed with the thrill of a good night's work. She couldn't have gone back to the party and pretended all was well. She wouldn't have fooled anyone, least of all Inigo who would have had every secret out of her in five minutes flat. She and Vennor needed time to be alone, to sift through the information they'd been given and to decide what to do about it.

Vennor was quiet until they reached the tiny room, but energy and tension rolled off him in waves big enough to drown out the silence. He knew something. What could he know? When it was all boiled down, their information made a rather weak tea, like Mrs Broadham's used leaves. A man who had killed before was planning to kill again. It was certainly something worthy of following up on, but it also had a needle-in-a-haystack quality about it. There was no name, no proof.

Vennor paced the room, a manic quality to him as she said as much. 'I wish we'd got more.' Marianne shook her head. 'I don't know how we begin to find such a man.'

Vennor halted, his blue eyes fierce flames in the lantern light. 'You're wrong there. We have enough to test my theory. I know who the man is, at least I think I do.' He pushed both hands through his hair, gripping his skull. 'I think there's a very good chance it could be Hayes.' He held up his hand to stall her protest. 'Hear me out. It is admittedly a new idea. It came to me tonight when Elise took such fright at the sight of your hair. She thought he'd sent you to her as a way of letting her know she was caught.'

Marianne sat down slowly on the bed. She did see and she didn't. 'You're basing this all on a wig. I'm not the only redhead in London.'

Vennor laid out his case like a barrister before the bar. 'No, but you've made it plain you do not return his favour and Hayes has just returned from two years abroad. The timing works and he meets her physical description.'

'As does much of the male population of London.' Marianne tried to wrap her mind around the idea. 'This is Viscount Hayes we're discussing, London's most spiritless bachelor, the very definition of lukewarm. He's perfectly boring, not a scandal to his name, or a vice. He's hardly the sort to...' She let her voice trail off. Vennor would fill in the omission. Not the sort to engage in the things that had been described in that room, things she hadn't realised people engaged in as practices of intimate play. Tonight had been eye-opening in several ways, some of which had repulsed her, but some of which had been quite titillating.

Vennor raised a blond brow. 'What do you know of Hayes's proclivities? A ballroom is just a stage of another sort where everyone is at their best.'

'He did kiss me once,' Marianne answered. 'It was hardly the stuff of dreams.'

Why had she not thought of that before? In a ballroom everyone wore masks. That certainly put a different slant on things. She'd always felt so safe in a ballroom, surrounded by people she knew. But did she really know them at all? She was still grappling with Hayes visiting a brothel for riding crop role play.

'He has to. Who would let their daughters marry him if anyone knew?' Certainly not her father, Marianne realised. He would have to be told and that would officially end any pretence towards an engagement. 'Hayes is supposed to be one of the good people, boring but good.'

'He hides it well,' Vennor murmured, his thoughts running far ahead of hers. What did he see that she'd missed?

'There's still the issue of murder. Not just once, but twice. Even if he has vices, I can't imagine him as a murderer.'

Vennor gave a harsh chuckle. 'It's always the quiet ones. Besides, it doesn't sound as though he actually did it. He hired people to do it for him and he's willing to hire someone to do it again.'

'Because he was unsuccessful the first time?' Marianne wasn't keeping up.

'No, because he was and now he wants to finish it.' Vennor's hands gripped the table, fingernails leaving marks.

'All right, I'll bite.' Marianne leaned forward. 'Who does he want to kill?'

'Me.'

Chapter Nineteen

'You?' Marianne was incredulous just as he'd been when he'd started putting the pieces together. Incredulity made it easy to discard what was right before his eyes. 'Do you think he'd kill someone over a courtship gone sour? I doubt I mean that much to him.' She worried her bottom lip, thinking. 'It just seems extreme, that's all.'

Vennor sat down beside her on the bed and reached for her hand, taking comfort from the ability to touch her. 'You mean that much to me.' They laughed together in the dim room and he felt a smile creep across his face despite the seriousness of the situation.

'We're different, Ven.' Marianne leaned her head against his shoulder. He liked the ease with which her body responded to his, sometimes sensually, but also with a casualness that bespoke long comfort. She laced her fingers through his in their old familiar gesture. 'I don't think anyone in the world will ever care for me the way you do, or see me the way you do.'

'Nor I you.' Vennor sighed. 'Inigo thinks you'd be the perfect Duchess for me.' What would she think of that? Did it ever occur to her that perhaps they ought to do something about the way they felt about each other? There were obstacles, of course, but what if he were free from his obligations? They were self-imposed, after all. What if he set aside his quest to find the killers? Or what if he had found them…? That was the thought driving his suppositions tonight, his willingness to explore the incredulity that Hayes might be hunting him. If it were Hayes, if he could put an end to the nightmare that had haunted him, what might be possible then? It seemed as if the whole world was on the verge of opening up.

'Inigo may think what he likes. He doesn't know everything. Perhaps he'd feel differently if he knew I mean to be a journalist; he'd be scandalised.' Marianne dismissed Inigo's comment. She shifted against him and his arm went around her in an automatic gesture. 'I am more interested, however, in why Hayes wants to kill you.' She yawned, a reminder of how late it had grown. 'Please explain.'

Yes. Back to work, back to the reason he'd dragged her up here instead of taking her home. He needed to try his hypothesis out on someone who would give it a fair hearing. And, he just plain *needed* her. He would be honest with himself about that. He had not wanted to share her with anyone just yet. 'Not meaning to bruise your ego, but I think it would have to be driven by more than just his ardour for you.' Vennor gave his thoughts time to assemble. 'If it is him, it wouldn't be the first time he's done it.'

He felt his body begin to shake with suppressed rage as he let the realisation he'd held at bay throughout the interview steal over him. 'After all, that would make him responsible for my parents' deaths.' He forced himself to choke out the last word. It had to be said.

'No! Oh, God. How could someone we *know* do such a thing?' Marianne's hand was at his back, stroking, soothing, even as she rocked with him, murmuring her own disbelief. Her horror would be different to his. She'd danced with the man, given him attention; Hayes had touched her, been in close proximity to her. Vennor shuddered with the knowledge of it. If he was right, never again would he let that man within a mile of Marianne. 'That's just it, though, Ven. How could he do it?'

'He didn't do it, exactly. He didn't hold the weapons. He sent others to do it.' He'd sent the hired men Elise had recommended without knowing what was intended. He felt Marianne cringe.

'To order murder is perhaps even more callous, to treat life so cavalierly as to dispose of it with the flick of a hand. It truly disgusts me.' Marianne met his gaze, her initial horror replaced by anger. 'It would disgust most people. So what would prompt him to want to destroy an entire family? And to want to do it badly enough to wait three years before finishing the job?'

'Revenge. Reward.' Those were Vennor's two immediate assumptions. They were what motivated most of the crimes he saw. In Hayes's case, the reward must be great indeed if he'd been willing to wait for it. How disappointed Hayes must have been when his thugs reported he'd not been with his parents that night. Another thought occurred. 'It would have been premeditated. He knew all three of us meant to attend the opera that night.'

'But then you didn't, forcing him to spend two years abroad, licking his wounds and celebrating only a partial victory.' Marianne's dark eyes moved in thought. 'Whatever he wants, he needs you out of the way, the dukedom out of the way. Killing your father wasn't enough to get it. What do you have? What do you control?'

'Cornwall, but only in part. The others control plenty of it, too.'

'But Richard Penlerick was the one everyone in the circle looked to,' Marianne whispered. 'Hayes would have seen him as the leader.' Yes, that was true, but Vennor could not imagine what Hayes would want with Cornwall. Hayes had lands and interests of his own. Unless he was wrong about that. They talked a little longer, going over possibilities, but making no significant headway. There was too much they didn't know yet. 'Inigo is looking into Hayes's background. He volunteered to do it this afternoon when I mentioned the man had proposed to you. Maybe we'll know something very soon. Inigo works fast.'

What if he was right and it was Hayes? How would he prove it? Or should he not worry about proving it and simply challenge Hayes to a duel of honour? That would be one way to decide things. Another way was always the Vigilante. As the Vigilante, he could choose to dispense whatever justice he chose. If he was right, he would have discharged his self-imposed obligation. But what if he was wrong? What if he'd forced these pieces to fit together because he was desperate for forward momentum? So desperate to have this resolved that he was seeing truths where they didn't exist? It would almost be worth it to be wrong, if it kept Marianne safe. If it was Hayes, the man was using Marianne for some nefarious purpose, his regard for her was non-existent and that put her at risk. A sour suitor was one thing, a man bent on revenge was quite another. One could be anticipated, the other could not be overestimated as to the lengths he would go, especially if he'd killed before, violently, brutally. Images of his parents swam before his eyes, bodies on a dark pavement, twisted and lifeless.

'Shhh, Ven. I can hear you thinking. There's nothing more we can do about Hayes tonight.' Marianne kissed his cheek, soft and alluring. This was not one of her casual touches. She moved over him, straddling his lap, her skirts rucked up about her thighs. She kissed him again, on the mouth this time, her hands a feather-light frame at his face. 'Perhaps I might take your mind off it. The brothel was instructive but brief. I might require some additional tutoring, but I think I got the gist of it.'

Her hips moved against his, and he felt himself rising in answer. This was where he had to be strong for both of them. 'Marianne, we should not risk it again. There are consequences.' He began to make the argument, wondering if he sounded as uncommitted to that position as he felt. He wanted nothing more than to roll her beneath him and take her, to let his body lose itself in the peace of her until it forgot Hayes and his treachery.

She gave him a coy look that surpassed even the most skilled of courtesans and he went from merely aroused to madly rampant. 'What I have in mind is quite safe, I assure you.' She kissed him one more time and slid to the floor between his thighs, her hands working his trousers loose. 'It looked rather enjoyable for both parties from what I saw at Delilah's.' Her eyes glistened dangerously as his member sprang free.

Vennor swallowed hard. She was teasing him. Surely she didn't mean to… Her hand grasped his shaft and he groaned. Yes, she did mean to. She circled him with her thumb and forefinger, her strokes slow and exploratory. He released a breath, letting himself relax into her touch. It was heavenly to be touched like this by Marianne. She glanced up from her provocative position, hair gathered over one shoulder, looking like an exotic Titian painting—*Eve Tempting Adam*, or something of that nature.

'You're enjoying this.' She gave a satisfied smile. She was enjoying this, too, Vennor noted. 'I like touching you.' Her hand came down his length, burying itself in the blond nest of hair at its base. 'You are hard where I am soft,' she murmured. Her other hand drew a line up his thigh. 'What else is in your nest, I wonder?'

Vennor gasped as her hand found his sac. She tested it, weighed it, before gently giving it an experimental squeeze that left him hoarse with the erotic pleasure of it. 'That's a very sensitive spot for a man,' he rasped, a little shiver taking him. This was starting to be a little less relaxing and a lot more stimulating.

She ran her hand back to the tip of him, her thumb stroking his head, finding the milky bead of moisture at its slit. She held his gaze and raised her thumb to her mouth and sucked. 'You're salty, Ven. Like the Cornish sea.'

Good Lord, he was going to spend himself right here, brought to climax by words and a licked thumb, so intense was his arousal. *I ought to do something*, came the last vestiges of reason from the depths of his mind, but they were no match for Marianne's seduction. Her gaze held his for a moment longer as she issued the single most provocative instruction a woman ever uttered to a man, 'Lie back.' Her hands gave him a gentle push and she bent to him, her mouth taking his length in full.

This was heaven with an edge, pleasure with a precipice, and she was driving him towards it with her hands at his thighs, bracing them apart, and her breath warm against his furred junction; little moans of delight escaped her as if she were savouring the finest of delicacies. That *he* was the finest delicacy was enough to drive him wild; add to that the wicked teasing of her mouth and he was a primed powder keg.

She licked up the length of him and he plunged his hands into the fiery depths of her hair, desperate for an anchor against the surging waves of his desire. At his tip, she sucked hard, her teeth nibbling in delicious nips that brought him close once more to the shore of release—no, not a shore, his pleasure-drenched mind argued. A crashing cataract. Soon, oh, very soon, his release would roar over the falls. The precipice was indeed nearing.

He felt his body tighten, the muscles of his thighs shuddering against the strain. His hands gripped her hair in warning, wanting to give her time to decide. Hands were all he had for words had long since failed him. He was reduced to groans and shivering exhalations of moaned pleasure. Marianne gave a final, long tug at his tip and rocked back on her heels, her hand closing about him. But it was the rapt expression on Marianne's face that held his attention as his body spent itself, exhausted at last. This had mesmerised her. *He* had mesmerised her. There was utter joy in that, in knowing that, for the moment, he'd been enough for her. He closed his eyes, letting that knowledge take him away.

He must have slept, but not for too long, he thought. When he awoke, Marianne was curled against his side, warm and soft; his trousers were still undone, his member relaxed, his mind still in a state of sated peace. She moved against him, awake and in tune to his own wakefulness. He threaded his fingers through her hair, combing through the curls. 'I haven't thanked you for tonight, for coming with me.' His voice had almost returned to normal. 'You knew all the right questions to ask; you got her to open up.'

She traced an idle circle around the aureole of his left nipple. 'We make a good team. Think what we could accomplish here.' She smiled.

'I have been thinking about it,' Vennor ventured carefully. These thoughts were somewhat new-formed. 'We've talked before how a charity basket doesn't bring lasting change, just sustenance for the short-term. I've been thinking that the Vigilante is a little of both sustenance and change, but not enough of the latter.' He played with her curls, lifting them and dropping them in a rhythmic fashion. 'When I cleared out the insurance men, I effected change. I made it possible for people to earn their livings. But when I stop a mugging, I only make a difference for that person in that moment. There's no long-term change from that. Even with the insurance men, what happens if I leave? They will come back and the change will be erased. The change has to be something more than the Vigilante's physical presence.' It made sense when he spoke it out loud. He could feel Marianne nodding against his chest as he continued, his words bringing ideas to life.

'I was thinking of doing something here in the East Docks like Eaton and Eliza did with their mining schools. If it works, we could try it in Seven Dials. Education is the place to start when addressing poverty. The more I think about it the more convinced

I am. How can a person change their circumstances without skills? They can't.'

Marianne was fully awake now. She raised herself up on an arm and peered at him. 'Schools? Here? What a wonderful idea. M.R. Mannering will write about them. I can do stories about the children's successes. We can advertise apprentices looking for work.'

'I was thinking about schools not just for children.' Vennor offered this idea more tentatively. It had not been done before to his knowledge. 'I want to educate adults, people like Elise. Night schools for adults where they can learn to read and write.'

'Oh, Vennor, what a splendid idea! They can learn after work.' Marianne's support warmed him, encouraged him.

'What else is percolating in that busy mind of yours?' She snuggled close and he felt in that moment that he could conquer the world.

'Just the schools for now.' He chuckled and then sighed. 'We have to go back soon, Marianne.' He didn't want to, though. He wanted to stay in this room, with her and his ideas, for ever. Here they were safe. Once they left this room, he'd have to contend with the possibility that a murderer hunted him, that he was on the brink of bringing his parents' killer to justice and that, if his suspicions were correct, Marianne was in danger, too.

'Marianne?' He jostled her out of a little doze. 'Do you still carry your knife?'

'Yes,' she murmured.

'Good.' He hoped she wouldn't need to use it. If the need arose, he would protect her with all at his disposal. He would surround her with his friends, with the authority of his title, the power of the Vigilante, with his very life if need be. He would not fail her as he'd failed his parents.

Chapter Twenty

Inigo had not failed to impress. He arrived in time for breakfast, a dossier beside his plate as he tucked into sausage and eggs. 'The food here tastes better than last time.' He shovelled up a forkful of eggs.

Vennor grinned at his old friend. Whenever Inigo was in town, they'd made a habit of taking breakfast together at Newlyn House. Having him here now made it seem as if no time at all had passed since he'd seen his friend. 'Perhaps you're less distracted. Marriage suits you. You're certainly happier than the last time you were in town.' Vennor winked. 'Although I am surprised your wife lets you out of her sight.' The love between Audevere and Inigo was a near palpable thing.

Inigo laughed. 'It's the other way around, I assure you.' It was humorously said, but Inigo had nearly lost Audevere to a bullet wound shortly before they wed. There was likely quite a lot of truth to that statement. Inigo was ferociously protective of his wife.

Inigo made an expansive gesture to incorporate the breakfast room. 'The house *does* look good. It's alive again, as are you, my friend. I am happy to see it,' he said in all sincerity. 'For your sake, I would like that happiness to continue. Is there any chance of that?'

Vennor shook his head with a disbelieving chuckle. 'Are we talking about me and the house or about something else?' He knew Inigo too well to be inveigled into discussing his private life as small talk on their way to the larger issue of whatever was in that dossier.

'You're getting sharp in your old age, Ven. You're on to me. Or perhaps my skills are getting rusty.' Inigo took a swallow of coffee. 'My wife instructed me not to come home without all the details. So, let me rephrase my question more bluntly. What the hell is going on between you and Marianne Treleven? Perhaps yesterday at lunch was not the ideal time to ask, but we all sensed it. I feared if I lit a match at lunch there might have been an explosion at the table.' No, Inigo's skills were not getting rusty. They were sharper than ever. His strong suit was seeing through the words to what went unsaid.

'There can be nothing between us until the matter of my parents' murders is settled. I cannot marry with that hanging over my head.' There were other reasons as well, such as Marianne's desire for a career, but he had to protect her privacy even among friends.

Inigo nodded, but was not fooled. 'But if it were settled? Or if you gave it up? Would there be something? The gazes passing between you yesterday were, frankly, smouldering. Whenever you weren't looking at her, she was looking at you. I don't have to tell you that kind of curiosity can be dangerous.'

'No, you don't.' Vennor snapped. They were well past curiosity, but Inigo didn't need to know that.

'I am sure I don't.' Inigo gave him a long, penetrating stare. 'The two of you have transcended that curiosity, is my guess.' Vennor said nothing, letting Inigo decide what came next. 'The gentleman will neither confirm nor deny the question. That means only one thing.' He let out a low whistle. 'You've made love to her.' The statement was followed by a long exhalation. 'Dear God, Vennor, do you know what you've done?'

Oh, yes. The feel of her mouth on him was still quite fresh in his mind. He was shockingly clear on what he'd done. He'd gone and fallen in love with Marianne Treleven, the one woman in the entire *ton* who had no interest in marrying him, a woman who might even now be carrying his child.

'Hell, Vennor,' Inigo swore. 'You have to marry her. The Trelevens are our friends. Sir Jock and Lady Sarah have trusted us with their daughters for years—'

'I know,' Vennor cut him off, quiet and stern. 'I don't need a lecture. Do you think I didn't contemplate any of that? This was not undertaken lightly. I did not seek it out, it just happened. One night we were friends. The next, I looked at her and realised I could lose her and all that our friendship had meant over the years and it was a slippery slope from there.' He could *still* lose her. Making love to her had not secured her; it had only thrown his feelings into sharp, unmistakable relief.

'I can see how it happened.' Inigo played with his fork. 'You were celibate for almost three years, weren't you? There's no shame in celibacy, but let's be clear, it can play with your mind, drive you wild. And there's Marianne playing house at Newlyn, picking out wallpaper, filling vases with flowers, tossing those red curls and that magical smile of hers your way, along with a healthy dose of nostalgia, no doubt. She's a piece of your past—a piece of your happier past—all conveniently beautiful and grown up. Now you're sneaking out of Russian embassy parties for some quieter venue. It would tempt any man, Vennor.'

Inigo had paid attention last night. He'd been afraid of that. 'Who else noticed?' Vennor sighed.

'Just me.' Inigo gave a wry grin. 'Everyone else was too potted on Grigoriev's vodka and *vatrushka*.'

'Just for the record, I hate how you do that, Inigo.' Vennor refilled his coffee. 'You just strip a man bare, don't you?'

Inigo's smile widened. 'I've been accused of that before.' He leaned forward, his palms flat on the table. 'Well, why not? Why not Marianne?' He kept his voice low. 'She's been out for three years, she's seasoned, an Incomparable, and she can handle being an instant duchess. You've known her and her family your entire life. There's something to be said for that, for having history. You're not the sort of man who wants a blank slate for a wife, anyway.' He picked up the dossier. 'There's just Hayes's proposal to get out of the way and there might be some help for you in that.' Inigo conveniently ignored the issue of his quest to avenge his parents' murders, but then again, Inigo had never endorsed the quest to begin with. He'd be glad to see him set it aside.

'Look inside.' Inigo passed the folder to him. 'The squeaky clean Viscount Hayes is not as bland as he lets on, certainly not with his finances, which are quite the inferno. He's one step away from being consumed. I'm not sure how he thought to keep that from Sir Jock when they sat down to discuss settlements. It wouldn't have slipped by me at any rate, even if he had sneaked by Sir Jock. Perhaps he was hoping Sir Jock would be dazzled by one of his girls marrying a title.'

Vennor nodded, listening to Inigo's summary as he scanned the pages. Hayes was struggling financially. 'He's hidden it with loans from non-traditional sources, that's how he's done it. There's the one loan from Coutt's—that's nothing worrisome. But then there are these.' He passed the pages back to Inigo. 'If Sir Jock didn't know to look for them, he'd not be aware of them.' 'These' were a list of moneylenders from less savoury parts of the city where interest rates were exorbitant and the price of life was cheap. 'He's in hock up to his neck.'

'That was my assessment as well. Which leads to other discussions.' Inigo set the dossier aside. 'I asked myself, how did it get that bad? The viscountcy had always seemed solid, so Father and I did some digging yesterday afternoon at White's.' He grinned.

Vennor knew what kind of digging that would have been: probing the social memory of the *ton* over fine brandy. 'Seems like a series of bad investments over two generations accounts for the state of Hayes's finances, failures on his grandfather's part and on his father's part.' That made sense. Financial disaster didn't usually strike deep coffers all at once.

'What I don't understand, though, is why he wants to wed Marianne.' Inigo knit his dark brows. 'I went over her dowry with Sir Jock when she first came out. It's respectable, but she's no heiress with the type of funds Hayes needs. With his title he could have aimed for Amelia Helmsley or Leah St. John. I've been asking myself: what does Marianne have that he needs?'

'Me.' Vennor gave Inigo a moment to digest that. It would be the first of many things Inigo would have to grasp in order to accept his case. 'There are things I learned last night that lead me to believe Hayes is behind the murder of my parents.'

'You think he means to go after you next,' Inigo summarised calmly when Vennor finished laying out his theory. Vennor took it as a good sign that Inigo wasn't laughing his head off. Then again, it was part of the code of the Cornish Dukes that one supported the others without question. Inigo nodded, pondering the information. 'What's the connection to Marianne other than the petty revenge of a thwarted suitor? It doesn't fit. Murder is not petty revenge and he was after her well before you were manifesting serious interest.'

Vennor splayed his hands on the table, the breakfast dishes long since cleared. 'We have to figure that out. Why did he want my parents dead in the first place? What had they ever done to him? Other than the situation with Marianne, what have *I* ever done to him? What does Marianne offer him that makes her valuable? How does any of this tie into his financial problems? If we knew that, then everything would make sense, or we'd know I was barking mad.' That was always a possibility, especially when he iterated the missing pieces. It had sounded so convincing when he'd laid out his case; the timeline of Hayes's absence from England, the information from Elise about hiring thugs. But he could drive a carriage through the remaining holes. He needed to close those holes and fast. 'Money talks, Inigo. We just need to listen to what it's saying.' From what the Vigilante saw in the slums, money—or the lack of it—was indeed the root of all evil. He'd wager it was behind Hayes's story as well.

Inigo nodded. 'I'll start enquiring into the investments and see if there's a trend.' He handed the dossier to Vennor. 'This doesn't solve the mystery of your parents, but it will give Sir Jock the leverage to disengage Hayes. Go save your damsel, Ven. I will see you tonight at Treleven House for Marianne's birthday.'

'Damn, I'd nearly forgotten!' Vennor swore. In all the craziness of the last two days, it had completely slipped his mind. Possibly because it was just three days before another less joyous anniversary. He could think of plenty of presents he'd like to give her, none of which could be unwrapped in front of an audience. It looked as though he had some shopping to do this afternoon. Marianne loved a good present.

'You could give her a ring,' Inigo suggested as they walked to the door. 'Her friends and parents will be there and Hayes will be routed by then.' He knowingly tapped the dossier in Vennor's hand. 'I can't think of a better setting for a proposal.'

Vennor gave a neutral nod. 'I'm not certain she's ready and her sisters aren't here. I'm sure she'd want that.' He didn't want to place her in an awkward spot. How could she refuse in front of family and friends? They'd not discussed marriage again and he wasn't sure her position had changed.

'You've taken her to bed. A certain amount of choice has been ceded.' At the door, Inigo gave him a questioning look. '*She's* not ready or *you're* not ready?' Vennor didn't like the implication that he wasn't prepared to do his duty.

Vennor met his stare evenly. 'Maybe neither of us is ready.' He held up the dossier, not wanting to part on a sour note. 'Thank you for this. You are a true friend. I will put it to good use.' He could at least free her from Hayes, socially, without her incurring any scandal. Hayes would want to keep his disappointment quiet in order to keep the reasons for Marianne's refusal from being exposed. There would be no shame in rejecting an insolvent suitor. Hayes would be at a disadvantage if his situation was known. But even as he prepared to go to Treleven House and enlighten Sir Jock, Vennor worried it wouldn't be enough. What would a jilted, enraged Hayes do? Was he helping Marianne's cause or bringing her closer to danger?

Damn it! Hayes threw a glass against the wall of his study, hard enough for it to shatter. Then he threw another and another until the carpet was littered with glass shards. He'd never been so humiliated in his life as he was right now. Sir Jock Treleven had broken off negotiations regarding the betrothal.

He'd called in person to deliver the news, as if that made it better. To have that piddling baronet explain to him how his finances were inappropriately arrayed for marriage, that there was significant concern over the source of his many loans! As if he himself wasn't concerned? As if he didn't know any of this? Sir Jock would prefer he not contact or communicate with his daughter in any way. He was to keep his distance and Sir Jock would not bring this difficulty to light. He was to keep his pride in exchange for Sir Jock's discretion.

He'd argued, of course; there was too much at stake for him to let Marianne go easily and because it was expected. He'd just been to Treleven House professing his proposal to be the result of a whirlwind courtship, that he was a man swept up in his ardour for Miss Treleven. He'd argued that this was the work of a jealous suitor looking to make trouble in order to smooth his own way. Who had told Sir Jock these tales? Where had he found his information?

Sir Jock had simply risen, taken the file and said, 'From a man for whom I have the utmost respect.'

There was clearly no room for creating doubt. But Hayes could guess who the man was. Who in Sir Jock's circle would care enough to thwart his suit? If it wasn't Vennor Penlerick, then it was one of the supercilious Cornish Dukes who'd been prompted to it by him.

Well, what he couldn't take by legal means, perhaps he could take by force. There was more than one way to wed a bride. He'd rather not have to resort to that, but needs must when the devil drives. He only needed to get near her, which might be a bit trickier now that he'd been asked to keep his distance. But there were ways around that, too, and Vennor Penlerick would be dead just as soon as an opportunity presented itself.

Chapter Twenty-One

He waited for the right opportunity to give Marianne her present. Vennor firmly believed that gifts were a private matter between the giver and the receiver. He was also well aware that there was an air of expectancy hovering about the small party tonight. The understanding with Hayes had been broken, which was all to the good, but Vennor knew there was a sense of loss there, too. Now there was no viscount in waiting for Marianne. But perhaps there was a duke and a friend who might take his place? He read that message in Penrose's soft smile, and Eliza's knowing gaze. The same was mirrored, somewhat smugly, in Inigo's stare as it sought him out in the crowd. Vennor could tolerate that from his friends. They were eager to see him wed, to embrace the happiness they had found. Harder to tolerate was the speculation from the Trelevens.

Sir Jock had been grateful for the information this afternoon, but there'd been a long moment when the interview had finished where Sir Jock had looked at him expectantly from behind his desk as if all this had been in prelude to something more. Only there'd been nothing more. Vennor had excused himself on the premise of shopping for Marianne's gift. Tonight, that same expectancy rolled off Sarah Treleven in waves.

Vennor finally managed to manoeuvre Marianne into the gardens after dinner, although he was cognisant everyone was watching. They might as well just press their faces to the glass for all the subtlety they'd discarded. It was all the privacy he was going to get. At least no one could hear them. Marianne looked fetching tonight in a green dinner gown, tiny gold bobs dancing at her ears, her spirits high.

'Birthdays suit you,' Vennor complimented.

'You suit me.' She gave him a wide, unguarded smile. 'Father told me what you did this afternoon. Thank you. You've made it possible for me to refuse Hayes without scandal. I'd kiss you for it, but I fear everyone would see.'

'I'll put that kiss on account then for another time,' Vennor joked before turning serious. Her comment was at the heart of the matter that lay between them. 'I wish we didn't have to hide, especially from our friends. We are lying to them.' He nodded towards the glass windows of the drawing room. 'They're expecting a proposal tonight. Inigo was quite blunt about the evening's perfect conditions. I told him it was not what we wanted. Was I right to do so?' Did she still feel that marriage and her writing were incompatible?

Her touch was light on his sleeve. 'You have criminals to catch. My journalistic opportunities are just starting to develop. Being a duchess is the greatest gilded cage of all, Ven.'

'Maybe you're looking at it all wrong. Maybe being a duchess is the greatest freedom. You can do what you want, you can redefine the rules, be a leader, set new trends instead of kowtowing to tradition.' He covered her hand with his. 'You wouldn't be just anyone's duchess, Marianne. You'd be mine. I like to think that makes a difference.' He felt Marianne's hand tense beneath his.

'Is this a hypothetical proposal?' Marianne raised an auburn brow. 'I thought we were decided, Ven. You don't owe me anything. I did not make love with you in order to trap you.'

'Is that a hypothetical refusal?' Vennor let her hand go.

'No, it's just a question. Why now? We had our terms defined between us, Ven. What's changed?' Marianne's eyes were searching his face for answers.

'I have,' Vennor answered bluntly. 'These last weeks with you, I have come alive again. I don't have everything worked out yet, but I feel a sense of purpose I didn't have before. You helped me see that perhaps it was always there, just unrefined.' He was going to establish schools for children and night schools for adults. He was going to fight poverty.

'What about your parents' killers?' Marianne prompted.

'That may soon be resolved, but even so, perhaps you were right when you argued I needn't make that quest and marriage mutually exclusive. Perhaps that was just an excuse to cover up for not having a purpose for myself.' He'd made that quest his purpose instead, trying to fill that vacuum; he saw that now.

'And the Vigilante? Is he to be set aside?'

'I don't know. I haven't got that far yet. Perhaps in time he may not be needed. For now, he may still have a part to play. But does that matter, Marianne?' He smiled briefly. 'I thought you rather liked the Vigilante.'

She smiled, too. 'I do like him. He's a good kisser.'

Vennor sighed. 'But his kisses aren't enough, are they? Your position hasn't changed.' He'd hoped her reservations about marriage would change once the potential husband changed. 'I won't push you.' How long, though, did she think they could slink off without being caught or brought to account for it? He reached into his coat pocket and drew out a small, square black box tied neatly with a length of pale blue ribbon. 'Your present,' he said as he offered her a half-bow.

'I thought the Hayes dossier was my present.' Marianne took the little box with surprised delight. 'You didn't have to, Ven. The dossier would have been gift enough.' She untied the ribbon and lifted the lid, exclaiming over the hair clasps seated on black velvet inside. Diamond brilliants twinkled in their nests. 'Oh, they're lovely.' *She* was lovely. He'd give her diamonds every day if it meant he could watch her face glow which such appreciation.

He reached into his pocket for an envelope. 'This

goes with the hair clasps.' He watched her face as she opened the envelope, pulling out two tickets, her eyes scanning them, her brow knitting. 'I want you to wear the hair clasps to the opera on Friday night and join me in my box,' Vennor explained. 'Everyone is invited. It will be quite the party.' He stopped himself. He was starting to ramble.

Marianne's gaze moved slowly from the tickets to him. 'Are you sure? This is the anniversary of...' She couldn't bring herself to say it.

'Of their deaths. Yes. I know. I picked the day deliberately,' Vennor confessed. 'I meant it when I said you made me feel alive again. It's time to start living.' He'd been doing penance for years now. Living was something else entirely.

'Society will take note,' Marianne cautioned. He thought he sensed a note of regret in the warning. Did she resent the subsequent deluge of debutantes that would follow? She needn't. He knew what he wanted and he hadn't given up on persuading her yet.

'That's what I am hoping for. Perhaps M.R. Mannering might even make an early mention of it. I hear he has a column due tomorrow.' Vennor tucked her arm through his. 'Shall we go in and disappoint your guests?'

They would all blame him, of course. If there was no proposal, they would lay the failure at his feet. But it was one small way in which he could protect Marianne. He would happily take the blame.

'Ven, they will not be disappointed. It's not the announcement they're expecting, but they will be glad to hear about the opera.' He could have kissed her for it if not for the knowledge that eight pairs of eyes were surreptitiously watching from the windows.

He was mostly right about the reaction to the opera invitation. His friends were supportive and suspicious, although they'd held off on voicing their suspicions until drinks at White's on Wednesday. Inigo was late, but Eaton and Cassian were more than able to carry on the interrogation without him.

'You've definitely made a splash with the opera. M.R. Mannering's even covered it in his column.' Eaton slapped the magazine down on the table, page folded back to the news. 'Word travels fast when a reclusive duke comes out of seclusion.'

'I heard tickets have sold out and people are selling them on the streets for exorbitant prices.' Cassian took a seat and called for brandies before fixing him with a stare. 'It will be a circus, everyone gaping and gossiping. I can't say it will be pleasant, Ven. Have you thought this through?'

Eaton answered for him. 'Of course he has, Cass.' Eaton's whisky eyes were on him. 'This is more than announcing his return. He's drawing Hayes out.' Vennor and Inigo had briefed them fully on the Hayes situation in the hopes that they might be able to probe their own sources for information regarding the origins of Hayes's financial problems. They'd all spent the last two days looking for that particular needle in the *ton*'s haystack. Eaton's eyes were steady on him, seeing too much. 'He's setting himself up as live bait.'

Cassian rubbed at his upper lip. 'I think that's risky, Vennor.'

'It may not be risky at all. We currently don't have any motive as to why Hayes would be after me, only suspicions. It can't be Marianne, although he'll be angry over that. But if he's after me, he was mad at the Penlericks long before this. We have no link to that scenario, just a man who is broke and desperate at this point,' Vennor reminded Cassian. 'Besides, you will all be there to guard my back.' He was putting on quite the show for the *ton*. He hoped it paid off and that Hayes would expose himself.

A flurry of activity at the door drew their attention. Inigo had arrived. He divested himself of his coat and walked purposefully towards their table with long, eager strides. Vennor felt a bolt of excitement shoot through him. Inigo had found something. He tried to read his friend's face as he settled in the remaining chair. Eaton offered him a glass, but Inigo waved it away. He definitely knew something. Vennor's gut clenched.

'Gentlemen, I may have the answers we seek,' he began in low tones, his pale blue eyes moving carefully around the room to see that they weren't overheard, but the club was still quiet. They were safe. 'It appears a series of bad investments are at the source of Hayes's financial woes.' Inigo held up a hand. 'Now, before you say that's not news, look at this: they start with Hayes's grandfather, the third Viscount. Right after he married, he began investing in infrastructure projects. They should have been sound investments and they might have been if they'd come about. But they didn't.'

Inigo spread out a map. 'He was part of a group who wanted to build a road here.' He tapped a spot on the map showing the north of Penzance and Porth Karrek. 'But the road ended up south of Penzance, making use of Newlyn Harbour instead.'

Vennor nodded, listening carefully as Inigo traced the accumulation of failed ventures. Roads. Mines. Investments that had not lived up to their potential. A pattern began to form. Newlyn had gained when the Hayes viscountcy had foundered. The road south of Penzance had benefited the mines transporting ore to a harbour for shipping, while mines north of Penzance had to spend more time and money transporting their ore to its final destination which cut into profit margins.

'You mentioned that the investments started after the grandfather married. Who did he marry?' Vennor was unaware that the family had any natural interest in Cornish environs. The Hayes family seat was in neighbouring Devonshire.

Inigo grinned, a satisfied cat indeed. 'I'm glad you asked. The grandfather married an earl's youngest daughter whose name is not important. What is important, however, is who he didn't marry: Miss Evangeline Warnick.'

Vennor gave Inigo a sharp look. '*My* grandmother?'

'Yes, apparently, the third Viscount Hayes was jilted in love. Like grandfather like grandson it seems in this case,' Inigo added drily.

Vennor voiced the scenario forming in his mind. 'You're suggesting there was a grudge? That the third Viscount Hayes made a series of investments in the hopes of deliberately thwarting my grandfather's successes.' It made sense, competing for the right to build a road that would direct traffic to certain harbours and enhance the income of one region over another.

'Hayes's father carried on the legacy and now Hayes himself seems to be continuing the game,' Inigo concluded. 'Look at the last investment. Audevere found this among her father's papers. Hayes had invested in Brenley's ill-fated road.' Inigo shot an apologetic look at Cassian. 'The same one Collin invested in.'

'The same one,' Vennor confirmed for them. 'There were others that my father's legislation blocked because of how many families its construction would dispossess.' He let out a low whistle. 'No wonder he hates the Penlericks.' Vennor could see how the history and the grudge had grown apace over time. How the thwarted Hayes family had vilified the successes of the Penlericks and held them responsible for the financial and matrimonial woes that had befallen them. Hatred was an effective poison. 'But murder? What does that accomplish?' Vennor asked. Now that they had established motive, they needed to connect it to the action. 'Our next question is this: is financial hardship enough to prompt murder?'

'Hayes was close to his grandfather,' Cassian supplied. 'I didn't think much of the information at the time, but one of my father's friends mentioned it when we asked. We are talking about three generations holding a grudge and spiralling circumstances. Who knows what that might prompt, especially if Hayes didn't have to be the one holding the weapon.'

'But what does revenge achieve? It can't bring back the money; it can't change the past,' Vennor argued. As much he'd like closure and answers about his parents' deaths, he was not willing to grasp at straws no matter how tempting it was.

'Allow me to play the cynic,' Inigo put in and they all chuckled, despite the weighty matter. Inigo was always the cynic, but it helped relieve the growing tension. 'Perhaps Hayes is looking to the future. Eliminate the Penlericks and, forgive me, but how hard would that be? There were only the two males, you and your father, until you marry and have a son. Once he was rid of you and had a well-placed Cornish bride by his side such as Marianne, he'd be poised to fill the vacuum left by the Penlericks.'

'That might be your darkest hypothesis yet.' Vennor frowned. 'It wouldn't work though. There'd be no vacuum. There would still be the rest of you.'

Cassian stiffened beside him. 'Perhaps he wouldn't stop with you. Perhaps he has longer-ranging plans for his sons and their sons. Perhaps he means to wipe out the Cornish Dukes, one house at a time.'

'Whoa, I think that might be a bit drastic.' Inigo held up a hand. 'Not that I don't see your point. But that takes a certain unstable genius to pull off.'

'The same kind of unstable genius that might take the opportunity to finish what he started at the opera three years ago,' Vennor put in. What Cassian described was indeed drastic, but he knew better than anyone how deceitful and manipulative Hayes was. He'd seen what the man had done to Elise, all the while pretending to the *ton* to be the most regular of gentlemen while courting Marianne. His stomach shifted at the thought. Hayes had nearly got away with that.

Inigo gathered up the papers and folded his map. The club was starting to fill with late-afternoon members. Not that it mattered. They could decide nothing more, do nothing more until the opera. Vennor raised his glass. 'Here's to Friday night, gentlemen, and the end of the chase.' He hoped it would be the end of it; he wished the culprit was Hayes and he wished the man would expose himself in the trap Vennor was setting for him.

The group broke up, but Eaton stayed behind, worry etched on his face. 'You understand that Friday night might come and go without Hayes making a move, whether he is guilty or not.'

'Yes.' Vennor let out a breath. He'd told Marianne that he wanted to start living again. That meant living with successes and failures, the past and the future. 'Eaton, I am coming to accept that I may never catch the killers, those who'd actually held the weapons that ended my parents' lives. In fact, it seems unlikely I will. But I might catch the man who ordered it.' Either way, he had to find a way forward.

'I hope for your sake we catch the bastard.' Eaton leaned forward with a comforting hand on his knee.

'But for my sake, I'd rather have my friend safe and happy.' He waited a moment before going on. 'I was in your position not so long ago, thinking that I wasn't entitled to happiness because I wasn't a complete man. But the love of a good woman showed me I was wrong. Eliza couldn't give me happiness. No one can do that. But she helped me find my own happiness, my own completeness.'

Vennor looked up, startled at his friend's words. He'd never heard Eaton talk that way before, Eaton who was the nominal leader of the group, who'd been his rock during the funeral. Nothing seemed to faze Eaton. He took care of people and he always knew what to do. Vennor would not have guessed this self-assured man had carried such doubt within him. 'I didn't know,' he said.

Eaton smiled and shook his head. 'That's the whole point with men like us, isn't it, Ven? No one guesses. We don't want them to. Sometimes, we don't even guess ourselves because we wear our masks too well. Then someone comes along who can look into our souls and we're never the same again. We're better.' He sighed. 'I know Inigo has been pushing hard on the subject of Marianne. I don't want to repeat that. But don't let her get away. She sees you, Ven. That's the most priceless gift you can have in a wife.'

Vennor swallowed, emotion threatening. 'I know. I just need her to see that, too. She has other ideas about her life. She thinks marriage is a dead end.'

Eaton chuckled. 'I've experienced that as well.

Eliza thought the same thing. Perhaps I should send her to talk with Marianne?'

'Well, if you think it would do any good…' Vennor gave a half-smile '… I'm open to suggestions. It's ironic really; I was the one who should have married first and you should have married last, if at all, and now our positions are reversed.'

'Just for now. She'll come around,' Eaton offered hopefully as they finished off the last of the brandy.

Chapter Twenty-Two

Tonight was the night! Excitement ran through him as Hayes stuck a pin in his cravat. It was one of his favourites—a round blue topaz, the stone of loyalty. It had been a gift from his grandfather when he completed university. Hayes tugged at his jacket one last time and straightened his shoulders with a final look in the mirror. He'd dismissed his valet, wanting these last moments to himself, a private celebration of sorts.

After a string of bad luck, things were finally starting to go right. Tonight, he would fulfil his pledge to his grandfather to eradicate the Penlericks. They'd driven his grandfather and then his father into early graves, but not without cost to themselves. Their avarice would be the end of their line. They would be done to death by their own greed. Which just went to prove it was hard to keep a good man like himself, a man with direction and purpose, down. Never mind that his whore had fled in the night, never mind that his marriage proposal had been refused, his desperate finances exposed by his enemy. Those were merely obstacles set up to test him. He'd survived. More than that, he'd not let those obstacles beat him down.

He slid a sharp knife into a secret sheath inside his coat. He likely wouldn't need it—his men would take care of the violence—but one must always be prepared for any eventuality. It was time for the opera, but the real show would happen afterwards and he would have a front-row seat for it all. Afterwards, he'd have Marianne all to himself. He would bring her to heel in short order, make her pay for her father's refusal and for her own treachery. No wife of his would ever cuckold him. He would be damn sure her sons were his. She would regret the day she'd chosen Vennor Penlerick over him. He would show her what a real man could do and in turn she would give him abject obedience. The curtain was about to rise on the Age of the House of Hayes.

Tonight was the night! Marianne turned a circle before the long mirror in her bedchamber, laughing in delight at how the skirts belled out at the motion. The dress was new, ordered at the beginning of the Season, but never worn. She'd pulled it out of its box this morning for pressing.

'You look delightful.' The feminine voice at the door startled her and Marianne blushed, having been caught in a moment of giddiness.

'Eliza, I didn't know you were coming over.' Marianne hugged the other woman. 'You look beautiful. Green becomes you.'

'Eaton's downstairs. We thought you might like to ride over with us and your parents can follow.' Eliza sat down on the bed. 'What an exciting night this is—Vennor returning to the opera house, with you beside him.' She gave a light laugh. 'The men think everyone will spend the evening watching Vennor, but my money is on you.'

'Me?' Marianne fastened a strand of pearls about her neck and checked her appearance in the dressing table mirror. 'People have had all Season to look at me.' She watched Eliza in the mirror; Eaton's wife had something on her mind.

'I think you underestimate the *ton*'s appetite for speculation.' Eliza met her gaze in the reflection. 'Vennor has danced with you for two years, has only shown up whenever you're present, and now he's back at the opera house with you by his side, in his box. The gossips will have you engaged by morning.'

Marianne's hand stalled on the pearls at her throat. Was that what was behind Vennor's sudden desire to return to the opera house? Did he want to push towards a proposal? He'd intimated rather plainly on her birthday that his thoughts in that regard had changed. Despite his acceptance of her answer, her answer *had* disappointed him. 'I think it's rather sudden to be discussing marriage,' Marianne offered vaguely, not sure what Eliza was hinting at.

'Sudden? You've been friends for years.' Eliza seemed to have arrived ready for a little debate. That put Marianne on alert. 'Would it be so bad to marry him? A girl could do worse than to wed her best friend.' Eliza smiled benignly, but the seed had been planted. Marianne could extend that—a girl could do worse than to wed her lover, to wed a man who saw her as she was, a man who embraced her ambitions, who included her in his own life's purposes, who entrusted her with his secrets, a man who would be true all the days of his life.

Eliza's gaze did not waver and Marianne saw a glimpse of the renowned tenacity that had won Eliza a reputation in the boardrooms of men. She did not back down. 'I see I've struck a chord with you. You and I have not had a chance to talk much, but I was once like you, resistant to giving a man control over my life. After my first marriage, and watching my mother's marriages, I felt that control and freedom were the most important things I could have, Marianne. I did everything I could to protect that freedom. I made money, I hoarded money, I guarded my mines so that no one could ever take away that freedom. In doing so, I nearly missed something that was much more valuable: the love of a good man. Eaton was not intimidated by me or my missions. I don't pretend to know what you think you might have to give up, but I cannot imagine Vennor asking you to do that.'

No, he wouldn't ask it of her. Hadn't he promised her she could set new trends? She could keep writing. She would work with him side by side with his new school venture, publishing stories about his efforts, about *their* efforts. Doubt came to Marianne for the first time. Had she been wrong to put off Vennor's suit, hypothetical as it was? Why did she continue to resist? At the moment it was hard to remember. 'There are things I want to do that would be scandalous. I cannot bring shame to him and yet those things are important to me; they're like breathing to me. I will not give them up.'

Eliza nodded, letting the vagueness of 'those things' go unchallenged. 'I run a mining corporation. I am the daughter of a commoner, a mere businessman. I also once worried about bringing scandal to Eaton. Once I figured out that I loved him, I tried to convince myself I couldn't have him. I was wrong. Scandal is nothing in the face of love. But to give up love for the sake of saving face? That would be by far the greater tragedy.'

'Why are you telling me this?' Marianne turned from the mirror, facing Eliza directly.

Eliza crossed the room and took her hands. 'Vennor loves you and you love him. I can see it on your faces when you look at each other, when you look *for* each other in a crowded room.' Eliza paused. 'My dear girl, I almost left it until it was too late to tell Eaton I loved him. He nearly died for me. I would not want you to make that same mistake. When you love someone you should tell them. Right away. The people who find love in this world are the lucky ones.'

Marianne nodded, her throat thick with emotion. She'd spent the last month convincing Vennor to live and she'd not done nearly enough of that herself. Living meant taking risks, testing assumptions. And she hadn't, not where Vennor was concerned. She'd clung doggedly to her old standard, her old way of thinking about marriage even when Vennor had shown her a new way to think of it; marriage to him could be whatever she made it. She squeezed Eliza's hands. 'Thank you for being bold enough to tell me, to help me see what's right in front of me.'

She loved Vennor. Her heart had known it long before this. She needn't be afraid of it. She needed to embrace it. She needed to tell him and she would, tonight, after the opera and his triumphant return.

The return of the Duke made for a noisy lobby at the opera house. There was a crush of people, everyone jostling for a glimpse of the Duke of Newlyn. Vennor gave them a show, with Marianne on his arm, dressed gorgeously in her trademark white silk, her striking red hair done up in careful ringlets held in place by his birthday gift. His considerable entourage followed him up the opera house staircase: the Earl of Tintagel, Viscount Trevethow and the Marquess of Lynford, with their elegantly gowned wives. They were followed by their fathers, the Duke of Boscastle, the Duke of Hayle, the Duke of Bute and their Duchesses. He needed their strength. It had taken all of his strength to face the opera house tonight, to come to a building that had become a monument to his own guilt, his own sense of failure.

Marianne squeezed his arm. 'You're here now and your father would be proud of you. Your mother, too.' She fairly glowed tonight, as if some secret candle had been lit inside her. He felt like the luckiest man in London to have her beside him. But looking at the faces of his friends, he knew they'd argue the point, thinking themselves worthy candidates of the moniker, too.

They made a happy party in the box. Champagne corks were popped and the curtain closed behind them, cutting off onlookers from peering in from the saloon. It was only partial privacy, Vennor knew. The rest of the audience looked on from their own boxes and through opera glasses from the floor. They could not escape scrutiny entirely nor did he want to. Being noticed was part of the plan. Was Hayes here? Was he even now watching their box?

The lights dimmed, warning everyone the performance was about to begin. He helped Marianne to her seat and sat beside her, her hand firmly in his. *Let them look, let them all look*, he thought. *Marianne is mine.* A bubble of joy welled up in him at the fierceness of the thought. She was his. Tonight, he was one step closer to claiming her in truth, one step closer to facing his own demons so that he could offer her a whole man, a man who knew himself, a man with purpose, the man his father had wanted him to be. Only then could he give her the most precious words of all, *I love you*, because he could love himself.

The lights went down. Marianne leaned against him and whispered in his ear, 'I have something to tell you. Tonight, afterwards.'

'Good,' he whispered back, 'then I have something to look forward to.'

* * *

If they hadn't been surrounded by friends and family, Vennor would have been tempted to steal her away and tease her secret out of her right then and there, but there was no question of that tonight. Perhaps another time. He spent the first act dreaming of ways to seduce Marianne at the opera. He spent the intermission regretting his choice to stay. It was as bad as he'd expected it to be, their box flooded with well-wishers who wanted to let him know how nice it was to see him, and oh, did he know they had a daughter, a niece, a cousin?

'It reminds me of the funeral,' Vennor remarked drily to Eaton as they ushered the last of the guests out of the box. 'Everyone politely pushing their female relations at me.'

Eaton slapped him on the shoulder with a laugh. 'Another good reason to put all of them out of their misery and yours, too.'

The joviality faded during the second act. Vennor's own performance for the evening was entering a new stage as well. He'd made his presence known; he'd announced to the *ton* that he was officially back—and to Marianne as well. He hoped she understood that while tonight fulfilled many functions, one of them was for her. He hoped she knew that he'd done this for her, because of her. She'd brought him back. But now it was time to focus on what came afterwards, to be on alert for Hayes—or more precisely, Hayes's minions. He did not expect trouble from Hayes directly.

* * *

The final curtain came down, the audience applauded and began the process of migrating to the street. Vennor exchanged a look with his friends. It was time to be on their guard. If anything did happen, they had strict instructions to get Marianne away and see to the safety of the others. Vennor tucked Marianne's hand through his arm, keeping her close as they journeyed down the crowded stairs. They'd nearly made it to the doors when he realised the crush of people had separated them from the rest of their party. He looked back to see Cassian well behind them, but there was no question of swimming back upstream to join them. Cassian gave a wave indicating he saw them and Vennor relaxed. The others would catch up with them soon enough.

Outside, the cool air was welcome after the heat of bodies inside. Marianne was talking excitedly about the performance when the covert assault came. A strong hand took him from behind. At first, he thought it was Cassian simply letting him know they'd caught up. But the heavy prod of hard metal into his side disabused him of the idea. Bracketed on either side by two men, they were ushered into the alley. He couldn't fight for fear of endangering Marianne further. Did the man on her side hold a gun as well? He could only hope Cassian had noticed and was following even now.

'What is this? I have money,' Vennor barked, hoping by some mad quirk that these men were actually thugs bent on simple robbery. But thugs didn't have guns. Guns were a rich man's weapon. They'd been given these weapons for an express purpose. He swallowed hard. Marianne's hand was tight around his arm and it was the only sign that she was afraid, that she understood this was not a robbery. This was history repeating itself. He needed to keep the men talking, needed to get one of them away from Marianne, needed to keep Marianne behind him to protect her. He'd not intended for her to be involved. She was supposed to be safely away by now.

The alley went through on both ends, but at that moment the far end looked blocked by something. A carriage? A dray making an evening delivery?

'Ah, quite the party we're having here.' A figure emerged from behind a stack of pallets, dressed darkly, meant to blend into the night, but Vennor recognised the voice and the glimmer of blond hair.

'Hayes,' Vennor breathed out, forcing himself to calmness. It would be three to one if he could get Marianne away. He could handle those odds. The Vigilante was experienced at being outnumbered.

'Bring the girl here.' Hayes gestured to the man holding Marianne.

'She stays with me,' Vennor growled dangerously, but Hayes was not deterred.

'Your authority is useless here, Newlyn, as was your father's. You cannot enforce your orders. There is a gun at your side and at hers. I'd prefer just to shoot you, but she is safe enough for the moment. I have plans for her.'

The man holding Marianne tugged at her, but

Marianne didn't let go. She held his arm with all her strength, as if she knew that to separate them was to doom him. She kicked the man in the shins and he gave a gratifying groan, but didn't release his grip.

'Miss Treleven, do you really want us to shoot the Duke?' Hayes drawled, putting an end to the scuffle. 'You decide. You fight and we'll end him now. You come to me and we'll see how this plays out.'

'Go, Marianne.' Vennor grimaced, hating the thought of releasing her, of putting her in Hayes's power, but he needed to play for time, time for Cassian and the others to find them and for an opportunity to fight that wouldn't endanger Marianne.

'You looked so pretty tonight, my dear.' Hayes grabbed for Marianne's arm and roughly pulled her to him. 'Keep a gun on that one at all times,' he instructed his man. 'That's your job now that the girl is delivered.'

'Does this scene look familiar to you at all, Newlyn? It should. This is how your parents died. This is how you will die. You will die knowing that Marianne is mine. I claim her in trade for the bride your grandfather stole from mine. You can die imagining how I will put my sons in her and make a dynasty that will exceed anything the piddling Penlericks could establish.' Marianne began to struggle; it wasn't in her nature to accept defeat.

'Quiet! You don't know how to listen. I will have him shot on your behalf if you aren't still. Do you not understand? You are mine now.' Hayes struck her hard across the face. She went to her knees, stunned from the force of the blow.

Fury rose in Vennor and he grabbed for his captor's hand in a lightning move that turned the gun away him, firing into the ground, loud but harmless. They both went to the ground, wrestling hard as Vennor struggled towards Marianne. The other gunman couldn't fire without risk of hitting his comrade which meant that Vennor had some relative safety at the moment, if he could just reach Marianne.

Hayes had her up on her feet and was dragging her, stumbling and falling, down the alley to the blocked end. He meant to take her away! Rage fuelled Vennor. He was nearly free of his captor when the other man leapt to action, wielding his pistol like a club. Vennor tried to duck as he ran. He stumbled, missing a dodge, the butt of the pistol coming down hard on his skull.

Consuming darkness clawed at him as he fell, his one thought in the seconds before he hit the ground was to grab the man's arm, to bring him down with him, to force him to fire the pistol at him, or in the air, it didn't matter. The sound would bring help. Not for him—it would likely be too late—but for Marianne. Cassian and the others had to be near. The shot would bring help. His fist closed around the man's hand, fighting for the trigger with all that remained in him before the darkness came.

Chapter Twenty-Three

A shot exploded in the alley and Marianne screamed for fear of what it meant. 'Vennor!' She twisted frantically to look behind her as Hayes thrust her wriggling and squirming into the waiting carriage. Vennor was down, unmoving on the ground. She went for Hayes's face, nails raking his jaw, her feet kicking out for his shins, his legs, whatever she could reach. 'You've killed him!' Her cheek still stung from where he'd hit her, her arm sore from rough handling, but none of it seemed to matter. Vennor was dead in the alley. She had to get to him, had to help him, as if she alone could bring him back.

'You little hellcat!' Hayes shackled her wrists in one hand and looped a length of rope over them, pulling the loop tight and fastening it to a grip. 'Yes, he's dead and about time,' he sneered. 'Your golden boy is more tarnished than you know. Soon enough, you'll be thanking me for saving you from him.' He seemed to soften for a moment. 'You are restrained for your own good, you know. As soon as you've paid for your betrayal, I'll let you free.'

He reached out a hand and gently stroked the red mark on her face. Marianne stiffened at the touch, her eyes wary and alert. What sort of game was this? What did he want from her? What could she give him in order to create an opportunity for escape? 'I know...' his voice was deceptively soft like his touch. '...it's too soon for you. But you'll see. We have a brilliant future ahead of us. We'll be the toast of Cornish society.'

The coach was moving through the dark streets. To a destination in town? To a place outside town? Perhaps he would tell her if she could draw him out by showing interest. Marianne managed a tremulous smile, forcing back her sobs and her fear that Vennor was dead in the alley. Vennor would not want her to give up. Vennor would want her to fight, not just for her freedom, but to see his quest achieved. She'd interviewed enough people to know when they *wanted* to talk. If ever there was a man who wanted to tell his story, it was Hayes. She was a reporter. She could do this. Vennor had believed in her.

Marianne settled in as best she could with bound hands and began the most important interview she'd ever conducted. With luck, the others would find her and, when they did, she'd have a full confession. 'What did the Duke of Newlyn do to you?'

'Not the Duke, the Duke*s*, plural. They've engaged in a conspiracy passed from father to son to ruin the Hayes viscountcy.'

Sometimes madness was expressed in rational thought, laid out sanely as if presented by the best of barristers in a court of law. That was what was happening here. Marianne listened carefully, committing every word to memory even as she ached for free hands and a tablet to write upon. Vennor's grandfather had apparently stolen Hayes's grandfather's true love and then systematically set out to financially ruin the viscountcy. She could not show horror or disbelief. She reminded herself that a good reporter was neutral and showed no bias no matter their personal tendencies. The storytellers were not to be judged.

She coaxed details from him instead of arguing against the alternative understandings he presented. The Penlericks were not destroyers of the social fabric, but builders of it, weavers of it. But there would be no convincing Hayes of that. 'We didn't want it to come to murder, but I swore an oath to my grandfather. I would finish what my father could not.' Marianne listened in morbid fascination as he outlined the fatal night three years ago. 'I hired two men to ambush the Penlericks after the opera. It went well enough, except that Vennor Penlerick wasn't there. Survivors are a dangerous nuisance. They want answers and they are doggedly determined to have them, especially when they have resources. There was little chance of Penlerick finding anything of use. I personally saw to it that the thugs vanished shortly after the crime so there was no chance for them to rat me out. Then I left for the Continent on a Grand

Tour until I felt it was safe enough to come back.' He smiled smugly, obviously proud of his planning. He'd tied up his loose ends.

Almost. Marianne thought. There was the prostitute, Elise. He'd thought she wouldn't talk, out of desire for money and fear of him. He'd underestimated her. Of course he had. She was a woman. He whipped women. He hit women. Even with her, a woman he pretended to admire, he had not discussed marriage with her first but had gone straight to her father to settle the matter of her life between two men. Seeing him now, listening to him now, it was a wonder she'd missed the malicious evil in him. But neither she nor society had been looking for it. Elegant clothes, good manners, a strict adherence to etiquette with ballrooms for backdrops had effectively disguised the monster within. They all had only seen what they wanted to see.

She drew a shaky breath. Vennor had died to reveal the madness. Dying to reveal it or just dead because of it? There was a very large difference. Her breath caught on the idea. *Had he known?* Was that why he'd been adamant about the opera? Dear God, if that were true... Implications spread like ripples on a pond. Had he uncovered the connections between Hayes's finances and the Penlericks with the dossier? If so, he'd known it was Hayes who was responsible and he'd set himself up as live bait, to draw him out. He'd known how irresistible the lure would be to a desperate, angry, vengeful Hayes: the date, the time, the place, the man. They'd both had a chance of completing their own redemption stories tonight. Now one of them lay dead, dependent on others to complete his.

I will, Vennor. Marianne promised silently.

'Where are we going?' Marianne ventured once he completed his tale. She strained to see out of the window, but her bonds didn't allow more than a glimpse into the darkness. She thought, however, that they were still in town.

He grinned. 'Somewhere we can start our future together.'

She froze at the insinuation. She'd been fixated on getting his story, on holding her grief at bay over Vennor, oddly comforted by the knowledge that she had time because Hayes did not mean to kill her—he needed her for the completion of his bloody fantasy—so she had not given much thought to the immediacy of her own situation beyond looking for an opportunity to escape. Hayes's next words were a chilling reminder that she had her own exigency to look to.

'I mean to have an heir with you as soon as possible.' There was a gleam in his eye that captured her attention. 'But we must make sure you're not carrying Penlerick's child. You've been led into wickedness with him and we must drive that wickedness out, purge you of his touch. I have taken Penlerick leavings long enough. Certainly you can understand a husband's desire for surety, my dear? What is a little discomfort against that?' His words made her skin crawl and her pulse race with a panic she had to hold back. 'Ah, here we are. It's a place called Delilah's and she knows all about handling unwanted babies. It's quite safe.'

He could not possibly know the boon he'd just handed her. Marianne kept a straight face as a little flicker of hope jumped for the first time since she'd been pushed into the alley. If she could manage to get a word to one of the others, they would come. She simply had to stall long enough for them to reach her. 'You should untie me.' She nodded towards her bound hands. 'No one would ever believe a man would bind his fiancée.'

Or bring her to a brothel on the East Docks, but Marianne wasn't going to mention that. She needed to be here. It was the best chance she had of rescue or, if opportunity arose, to escape on her own. She began to think: if she could get free, she'd go to Mrs Broadham's.

Delilah spared her the briefest of sharp looks as she escorted them upstairs to a room Marianne knew well—the empty room left behind by Elise's own escape last week. She pretended not to recognise it, but Hayes acted as if he had great familiarity. 'This will do fine, for the night,' Hayes pressed money into the madam's hand. 'There is another matter of some delicacy my fiancée and I need help with. I would like to discuss it with you and make arrangements downstairs after I see her settled.'

Delilah's gaze moved between them. 'Yes, please come to my office,' she told Hayes before her gaze landed on Marianne for a moment. 'We are very busy tonight. It's a Friday. Men have full pockets. It may take us some time to accommodate you, but we will do our best.' Marianne understood. She knew what Delilah meant to do. It was well-intended but futile. Delilah would send out her hulking doormen to search the streets for the Vigilante, never knowing those efforts would be in vain because the Vigilante would not be found. He would never come again to answer the call of the downtrodden. The Vigilante was dead. Marianne swayed on her feet, the events of the evening suddenly too much, her hope too little to overcome the facts and the grief pressing against her, begging to be let out. Would Hayes catch her if she fell? She stumbled towards the bed and felt someone catch her beneath the arms—Delilah, she thought. She was eased down on the sheets. Her courage was spent and Vennor was dead, and she had been pushed to the limits of her strength. She'd not told him she loved him. Now it didn't matter. Others would catch Hayes. Vennor's quest would be completed. She didn't want to wake up again. Nothing mattered because *Vennor was dead.*

Marianne was gone.

Vennor struggled towards consciousness, his mind a riot of thought and pain.

He had to get up, had to go after her. He had to move. Why couldn't he move? Hayes had Marianne. Hayes had killed his parents. Hayes meant to marry Marianne, to put her beyond his reach. Hayes didn't mean for him to live. Hayes thought he was already dead.

The thoughts raced ahead of the pain, a jumbled wave of ideas crashing into one another, but one thought was clear.

'Marianne.'

Was that croak his voice?

'We're here, Ven. Don't move. Stay still.' It was Eaton's voice that answered, not Marianne's. He struggled, but someone held him firm. 'I mean it, Ven. Don't move.' Eaton's tone was firm. He was giving orders. 'Help me sit him up, gently, now.' He was propped up in strong arms—Eaton's, he guessed. He forced his eyes open; the world swam and he managed it into stillness by focusing on one specific spot, a brick wall in the darkness. Sweet heavens, where were they? 'Get a blanket,' Eaton barked and instantly one was produced. The warmth felt good, he realised. Whatever he was lying on was wet. The street? No, the alley. He was lying in the alley. It was coming back to him in more orderly fashion now: the ambush, the guns; Marianne ripped away from him, Hayes hitting her, his own temper exploding at the act; Marianne dragged off, his own futile charge, then the pistol butt. Ah, that damned pistol butt was the cause of his pain.

He moaned and reached a hand out to grip Eaton's arm. 'Where's Marianne? Did you get her?'

'No, not yet.' That was Inigo. He bent down beside him. 'I have men looking. We will find her.'

'Let me up,' he groaned and tried to push against Eaton's restraint.

'No.' Eaton insisted. 'You have a head injury. We

don't know how severe. I've sent for a doctor. You are not moving until we know for sure.' He heard Eaton's voice shift. He was talking over his head. 'This is why we weren't going to tell him about Marianne right away,' Eaton was scolding Inigo. 'Do you want him to stand up and die?'

'He's entitled to the truth,' Inigo argued. Vennor could tell from the silence that followed that Eaton disagreed. He took advantage of the moment to lever himself up a little further.

'Tell me what happened, tell me everything. How long have I been out?' He hoped not long. Marianne could be anywhere. Every moment they didn't know, every moment they lingered, expanded the radius of where Hayes might go.

'You were out for twenty minutes, maybe. The longest twenty minutes of my life, I might add.' Eaton let out a breath. 'We heard the shot. We'd just come out of the opera house. Cassian was looking around and he knew something was wrong, but we couldn't find you. Then we heard the second shot and we ran towards it. You were down and Marianne was gone. We thought you were dead, Vennor.' There was an unmistakable tremble in Eaton's voice. 'You were so still.'

'The men, there were two of them plus Hayes. Hayes ran with Marianne but the other two, where are they? What happened to them?' His mind was starting to exert itself beyond the need to find Marianne.

'We caught them. Cassian and I ran them down.' Inigo gave a latent growl in recollection. 'A good boot to the neck does wonder for confessions. They were happy to confess to what they'd been hired to do, although they didn't name, *couldn't name*, Hayes specifically.'

Eaton made a gesture. 'The doctor is here.' A black-coated man knelt beside him, gingerly moving his head, his hands running over his skull. Vennor winced.

The doctor smiled apologetically and held a set of fingers in front of his face. 'Very good. You'll have a lump for a bit and your head will hurt, but no real damage. You were lucky. An inch to the left and it could have been serious.'

Vennor grunted and struggled to his feet, steadying himself on Inigo's arm. 'Good, then we can be off.' Somehow he would find the strength to go forward. Marianne was out there with Hayes. She was not safe.

Eaton and Inigo exchanged looks. 'We will be off. Let us be your legs and your eyes, Ven. You need to be at home, resting. You can run headquarters.'

Vennor dusted at his ruined evening trousers. 'I will not sit at home while Marianne is in danger. *I* put her in danger and *I* will be the one to get her out of it.' The sound of hooves clattering on cobblestones interrupted what would have become a quarrel. The sea of people who'd gathered to gape and which had been held at bay through a combined effort from Bute and Hayle and Boscastle, parted before a broad-shouldered man leading four horses, two in each hand. Vennor squinted, his vision clearing. 'Cassian!'

Cassian tossed a set of reins to Inigo and Eaton. 'Can he ride?' he asked Eaton.

'Of course I can ride,' Vennor answered for himself.

'Then let's go; my man brought word. Hayes is in the East Docks.'

The four men swung up on their mounts, wheeling them around, Vennor ignoring the pain in his head. He brought his horse up alongside Cassian's. 'How does your man know?'

'Marianne sent word via the madam of the brothel he's at.' Cassian grimaced. 'A place called Delilah's? I can't say I know it.'

'I do.' Vennor kicked his horse forward, relief and trepidation sending his head to throbbing. Delilah would know something was wrong if Marianne showed up in Hayes's possession. Marianne had been smart to send word to Cassian. Then the reason for that occurred to him. His last memory was of her screaming his name. She'd heard the shot; she'd watched him fall. She was assuming he could not come for her. She had every reason to think he'd died in the alley.

Vennor took the lead, urging his horse on as fast as he dared, navigating slippery cobblestones on dark narrow streets, the others falling in behind in single file. His mind was filled with worry for Marianne, with images of what Hayes might do to her. The man's threats had been plain enough to leave nothing to the imagination. Vennor would kill Hayes if he defiled the woman he loved in any way. *Loved.* He *loved* Marianne. He'd not told her, not in words at any rate. He should have. It might have served as some comfort to her in whatever situation she found herself in now. She would be devastated and determined not to show it and, oh, so desperate to fight. Hayes would like that. It would give him excuses to harm her.

Please don't hurt her, he begged silently. *Hold on, Marianne. I am coming.*

He was coming?

It occurred to him that Hayes quite likely thought him dead. Hayes would not be expecting Vennor Penlerick. The scandal would be all over London by morning if two peers brawled in a whorehouse. There would be legal justice to be served and anything could happen on the way to trial. Hayes had killed his parents. Hayes had kidnapped Marianne. The legal system was too good for him, the process too tenuous. A peer could be acquitted of any number of crimes. His father had always disagreed with that level of immunity. All men should be equal before the law, but they weren't. Hayes was counting on that. What he wasn't counting on was the Vigilante, a man who understood how it was possible to serve justice beyond the law.

They sped through the streets, windows opening, people spilling out of taverns to watch the four deadly horsemen pass. Vennor felt for the mask in his pocket. This would be the last ride of the Vigilante. If he could save Marianne, if he could see justice done to Hayes, he would give up the Vigilante for good. It was the kind of promise a desperate man made, but Vennor knew he'd give up even the dukedom itself to save her.

Chapter Twenty-Four

She couldn't save him. Vennor was dead. It was the first thing that came to her on waking. It seemed as if it had been the last and only thought she was capable of summoning. Marianne felt her mind force her towards complete consciousness. She fought it; she didn't want it. She didn't want to wake to a world devoid of Vennor. That world was brutish and cold, a world without hope, a world where Hayes held her in his power. Someone was pushing a glass to her lips. She turned her head away. Water splashed on her chin and dribbled down her neck. Something was wrong.

Marianne tried to raise a hand and couldn't. She struggled, her mind suddenly registering the reason for it. She was tied. To the bed. She shifted again, there was something else wrong. She felt…lighter, somehow. There was no rustle of silk or petticoats. Panic rose. There was nothing for it. She had to wake; she had to take charge of the situation, although thinking she could take charge of anything while bound hand and foot was laughable. What control could she manage? Still, she had to try. For Vennor's sake, she told herself. He would not want her to give up.

'Good girl, you're awake.' A soft feminine voice was at her ear. She had to turn her head to see the source. Delilah. She craned her head trying to see if Hayes was in the room.

'He's downstairs, having a drink on the house,' Delilah whispered, divining her thoughts. 'May I assume you are in some danger from him? Who can I send word to? Shall I send for the Vigilante?'

Tears formed and spilled, sobs choking her. 'The Vigilante is dead. Send word to Viscount Trevethow.' Marianne thought rapidly. 'He will be at the opera house if you act fast enough.'

'I am sorry. He was a good man.' Delilah put a hand on her shoulder. 'I cannot untie you. But I will protect you as best I can until Trevethow can get here.' She went to the door, cracking it open to speak in low tones to the guard posted outside. Then she returned to the bedside. 'Word has been sent.' She cleared her throat and sat down. 'I am supposed to be ascertaining whether you're with child. I will tell Hayes whatever you like. I owe him nothing. He cost me a good girl when Elise left.' Her voice softened. '*Are* you with child?'

'No, I don't believe so.' The truth was, she didn't know. She'd not given it any thought. She and Vennor had only made complete love the once. Another wave of sorrow swept her. They would never lie together again, never lie on the low bed at the warehouse whispering their secrets, confessing their hearts, exploring one another's bodies.

There was anger in her sorrow, anger at herself for holding back, for thinking there was something more important than Vennor, for thinking that she could not have both Vennor and her career. Now, there was only her career. She would print Hayes's confession. She would expose him for the vengeful madman he was, even if it meant scandal for herself. She simply did not care. Hayes had destroyed two men when he'd killed Vennor: the Duke of Newlyn and the Vigilante, two men who had done so much good for so many people. How callously their light had been snuffed out. Tears ran down her face and she was helpless to wipe them away. She didn't want to be weak. How fast would Cassian get here?

Perhaps Delilah understood her need for some modicum of privacy. The madam rose and gave her what privacy she could. 'Your dress is on the chair. You're in your shift. I insisted there was no need for anything else to be removed,' Delilah offered after a while.

'Thank you,' Marianne whispered. But there was a limit to what the madam could do for her.

'Soon, Hayes will finish his drink and come upstairs,' Delilah said. 'What would you like me to tell him? If I tell him you're with child, he'll want it removed. I've a potion I can give you that will convince him it's been done. It's not pleasant, but it will buy you time. He won't force himself on you until he's sure.'

Marianne saw where the madam's logic was headed. If she was not with child, Hayes would make demands of her, immediately, perhaps before Cassian could arrive. And if she was with child, or became with child, how would she ever know if the child was Vennor's? But she could not selfishly risk the potion if there was a chance she might carry Vennor's child. The enormity of that swept her. Might she carry the last piece of him? She had a fierce, futile urge to touch her stomach. The next Duke of Newlyn. A son. It would mean Hayes would be thwarted even as he sought to seize victory. 'Is there another choice? I cannot win either way,' Marianne pleaded, her eyes meeting Delilah's.

The madam shook her head as a knock pounded on the door. Hayes entered, making it clear a knock was not a request for permission to enter, but an announcement that he had arrived. 'How is my blushing bride?' He stripped off his cravat and flung it aside before going to work on his cufflinks. 'Do not mind the bonds, my dear, we needed to make sure you did no harm to yourself when you awoke from your faint.' He shot a cheery look at Delilah. 'What is our verdict?'

Delilah shot her a look. 'There is no child, milord. We have no need of any further interventions.'

He rubbed his hands together. 'Then you may leave us. My bride-to-be and I have business.'

Marianne stiffened. She was reluctant to see Delilah leave, but how could the woman stay? To make it appear Delilah was a friend would be to rouse Hayes's suspicions. She took comfort in knowing Delilah would be downstairs, on the watch for help.

The door shut behind her and Hayes narrowed his gaze. 'We have just a last bit of unpleasantness between us, my dear, and then in the morning we can seek out a man of the cloth. I should probably look into getting that ridiculous law changed that says no one can marry at night.' They might have been talking about the news of the day for all the casualness his tone evinced. The bed took his weight. 'At least it will give the girls here a chance to launder your dress for the ceremony.'

His hand rested, hot and heavy, on her flat stomach, the heat of him penetrating the thin fabric of her shift. She fought back panic. There was no reason to be afraid. Cassian would come long before then. There would be no ceremony, no forced wedding. This time tomorrow, she'd be home and she could cry all she wanted. But not now. Now was for surviving, for lasting until help came. He pulled up her shift and she shut her eyes, his hand splayed at her naked mons, fingers digging into the nest of hair there. 'By Jove, you're the colour of fire here, too. I'd suspected...hoped you would be,' Hayes breathed.

She didn't dare cringe, didn't dare show any sign of emotion for fear of provoking him. She shut her eyes tight, trying to put her mind away somewhere else. It didn't matter what he did to her. It didn't. His weight shifted. He reached for the bonds holding her hands. 'We'll loosen them just a bit. I want you on your stomach.' He manhandled her into position, his efforts rough. 'I know you've betrayed me with Penlerick. You've been to his bed and you need to pay for that; you need to be purged of that feminine sorcery. It's not decent in the wife of a viscount.' Marianne bit into the pillow and waited for the blow to come. She would not scream for him. She would not.

He would not fail her. Vennor dismounted, pleased that his legs held. Fury had sustained him thus far. The others followed suit and prepared to enter. But Vennor held up a hand. 'I go in alone. Someone needs to watch the back entrance and the front in case anything goes wrong.' Nothing would go wrong, he promised himself. Hayes thought he was dead. The man was not reckoning on anyone finding them and he was without allies, although he probably didn't realise it. Hayes would think his money had bought the loyalty of the whorehouse. He would be wrong.

Vennor pulled out his mask and tied it on, getting an arch-browed look from Inigo as dawning crossed his friend's face. 'I'll explain later,' Vennor murmured.

Inigo nodded. 'I'm counting on that.'

Vennor stepped inside. The place was busy even for a Friday, but Delilah waited by the stairs, her face lighting with pale surprise. 'I heard you were dead.'

'Not yet. Upstairs I presume?' Vennor was already taking the steps two at a time. The door was locked. He did not wait for Delilah's master key. He kicked the door in with enough force to break it off its hinges. 'Hayes! Get off her, you filthy swine!' He crossed the room in two strides, grabbing Hayes by the collar and dragging him from Marianne, his mind registering her dishabille, the ropes, 'You will not lay a hand on her!' Thank goodness it appeared he'd arrived in time before Hayes had harmed her. The man was the basest of creatures to use a woman against her will in such a fashion. Rage possessed him in full. He threw the surprised Hayes against the wall, watching him bounce before he came at him with his fists. The strike at his jaw was for Marianne, the blow to his stomach was for his mother, the second blow for his father, and every blow after that for everything that been stolen from him.

Hayes wheezed, gasping for air on his knees as he begged for mercy. 'This isn't your fight, Vigilante. The girl is just a whore. We were playing. I paid her fair.'

'She is no whore. That is the daughter of Sir Jock Treleven.' She was other things, too: the woman he loved, his future wife, the future mother of his children, the sum of his world. But he could say none of that without giving away his identity. Let Hayes think the Vigilante had come for him. The Vigilante knew no law. Hayes should be very afraid. He'd wish Vennor Penlerick had come in his stead, that he hadn't left him for dead in an alley.

'There is no mercy today.' Vennor drew his blade and advanced. 'I take your life in trade for the lives of those who cannot claim their own justice against you.'

'No!' A cry from the bed stopped him. 'Don't do it. You don't want his blood on your hands.' Marianne was struggling, slipping one hand free and then another. She sat up, her hair dishevelled, her face tear-stained. 'You are not a murderer, not a monster like him,' she pleaded as she came to him. She was pale, her body trembling with shock and perhaps doubt. Her gaze studied him and he saw her thoughts, that perhaps it was one of the others who had come in his place, that somehow they'd known his secret.

'This man has committed crimes that deserve to be paid for with his life.'

'Then let the courts decide it,' Marianne begged.

'You, who have suffered at his hands, desire mercy for him?' he growled, his fury at war with his better self. He wanted this man dead. Here. Now. No one in this place would ask any questions. No one would think to connect Vennor Penlerick to the murder.

Marianne's hand was at his arm. 'No, not mercy for him. Mercy for you. You do not want this on your soul.' Mercy for him. She would sacrifice her own vengeance for a man's peace. He would honour that.

Vennor sheathed the knife and collared Hayes, pushing him down the stairs, announcing to the crowd that had gathered below, 'We will take him to the watch and he will stand trial for the Penlerick murders. His men have confessed to last night's attack.' He caught sight of Eaton at the door. 'And we have documents that support the rest.'

Eaton opened the door and Vennor manhandled Hayes outside, aware of Marianne behind him. 'Eaton, a cloak for the lady, please.' The moment's distraction, the brief instruction, was enough to give

Hayes an opening, perhaps inspired by a realisation of how dire his circumstances were. Hayes shoved an elbow into Vennor's stomach, pulling himself free and dashing off into the night. Vennor doubled over and swore, hands on his knees. Marianne was at his side, worried. He shook off her hand. The man was not going to get away, not now when he was so close to ending this.

Vennor righted himself and gave chase through the streets, down to the docks, his legs pumping, his head throbbing. It was entirely possible Hayes might simply outrun him, but the Vigilante knew the docks far better than a half-crazed man running for his life. Vennor cornered him on a length of pier and chased him to the end of it, where nothing waited but dark water. 'Give up, Hayes. It's over. Come back with me and stand trial.' The Vigilante held out his hand. 'You won't get past me and I have a blade. I won't hesitate this time.'

'I know you,' Hayes panted, looking at him queerly, his gaze riveted on the mask. 'But it can't be. Vennor Penlerick is dead. I had him shot tonight. I saw him go down.' He was rambling out loud, unaware that he was damning himself in the process.

'Restless souls with unfinished business often walk the earth before departing,' Vennor growled, taking a step closer. He was nearly there. He could almost grab him, so paralysed by fear had Hayes become.

Hayes paled at the thought. Vennor reached out to take him, but Hayes let out a wail, 'No, you won't take me alive!' He stepped back and was gone in a splash, the dark waters closing over his head as he sank. Left to his own devices, he would not survive the current.

Vennor pulled at his boots. Damn the man for thinking he could elude him. Damn the man for making him go in after him, to save him, to bring him to justice. Footsteps pounded on the wooden pier behind him. Marianne grabbed his arm. 'No, let him go, Ven. I won't risk losing you twice in one night.' Then she was in his arms, sobbing openly, undone by the surprise of finding him alive. 'Don't you ever die on me again and don't you ever keep a secret from me again. You didn't tell me you were the bait tonight.'

Her fists pounded on his chest. He grappled for them, holding them still against his beating heart. 'I'm all right. I'm alive.' Then he took her face between his hands, tipping it up to meet his gaze. 'And you, Marianne? Are you all right? Has he harmed you? You must tell me the truth; whatever happened, it wasn't your fault.'

'I'm fine, just a bit bruised. Nothing more.' She gasped and gave a breathy laugh. 'We're both a bit battered, but we're both here.' Then she started to shake, her words coming out in a rush. 'I love you, Ven. Eliza was right. I should not have waited to tell you. When you fell tonight, I thought I'd lost the chance for ever.'

'I'm alive. We're alive, Marianne.' What a glorious thing it was, too, to be alive, to be standing on the pier while the dawn broke above them. He held her close. 'I love you, too. I meant to tell you tonight once I felt I could claim it, once I could offer you a whole man who'd dealt with the demons of his past.'

She looked up at him from the shelter of his arms. 'And can you? Offer me a whole man?'

'Yes, I can. Do you want him?'

A soft smile took her face. 'Yes. Always. More than anything, although it's taken me far too long to realise it.' She turned her face into his hand, kissing his palm where it cupped her jaw. 'You're bleeding.' She reached for the hand. 'Your knuckles.' She gave him a rueful smile. 'You have blood on your hands, after all, despite my best efforts to keep you from it.' She kissed his palm. 'I was afraid you were going to pummel him to death in that room. I'd never seen such fury unleashed. I didn't want his blood on your hands. It would have haunted you. Revenge is never worth it.'

He held her gaze steady. 'No, revenge isn't, but you are. When I saw what he'd done to you, what he was doing to you…' His voice broke with emotion restrained no more. 'This isn't blood on my hands, Marianne, it is love. A man must always be willing to fight for what he cherishes and a woman must let him.' He reached up and took off the mask with a smile. 'Besides, it was the Vigilante's hands.' He wiped at his knuckles with the silk mask and passed it to her. It was time to make good on his promise. 'Would you like to do the honours?'

'Are you sure?' Marianne took the mask cautiously.

'It's time to let him go. The Duke of Newlyn and his new Duchess can carry on his work here.' He was the Duke in truth now, no longer afraid to step into his father's shoes or walk in his own.

'The Vigilante saved me,' Marianne prevaricated.

'The Vigilante saved us both,' he amended.

'Are you sure he has to go?' Marianne asked.

'Yes, I'm sure.'

'Then we'll do it together.' She took his hand and together they cast the mask into the water.

He kissed her hard then, sweeping her up into his arms and carrying her home—or as close to home as he could get tonight. Tomorrow there would be a formal proposal to offer, an acceptance to celebrate, a wedding to plan, explanations to make and the rest of his life to begin. But for tonight, it would be just the two of them in the little room in the warehouse, on a low bed wrapped in each other's arms, celebrating the joys of a second chance.

Epilogue

July 31, 1826

Joy had come to Mayfair. The doors of Newlyn House were thrown wide open, garlands of summer flowers festooned the door frames and the staircase leading up to the ballroom where dancing would begin as soon as the handsome Duke of Newlyn and his new bride, the radiant Marianne Treleven, the Season's leading Incomparable, finished with their receiving line. That line stretched out into the street on a warm London summer night and sounds of laughter could be heard several streets away.

Vennor stood beside Marianne, still smiling despite the length of the day. They'd been wed in the morning at St George's amid all the pomp that befitted a duke's marriage. Later, he would not remember much of that pomp or the decorations. He would rely on Marianne to recount it thoroughly though in M.R. Mannering's next column. But he would remember the sight of the church doors opening and Marianne stepping through, dressed in her signature white, pearls at her neck, the bouquet of red and white roses he'd sent over that morning in her hands, her smile wide, her dark eyes dewy with a gaze that was just for him.

The world had faded for him when Sir Jock Treleven had put his daughter's hand in his and he had lifted back her veil. There was only her. His lover, his best friend, his wife. His future. She'd cried when he'd slipped his mother's wedding ring on her finger and she kissed him with all the passion of her soul when they'd been pronounced man and wife.

There'd been the carriage ride through Mayfair and the tossing of pennies, and the drive through the East Docks where they'd cut the ribbon on the old Penlerick warehouse, declaring it the site of their new school. He'd felt his father's approving presence there in that moment. This was what purpose felt like. This was what loving felt like. People would have a second chance with their school.

The wedding ball had been Marianne's idea, a resurrection of the Penlerick Charity Ball on its old day, another second chance of sorts. He thought it was a marvellous idea. It had not been easy to get it done. There'd only been a month between the proposal and the wedding. But Eliza, Audevere, Penrose and Marianne had been a collective force of nature, organising the wedding and the ball to perfection while the men had watched in amazement.

'Is it time to dance yet?' Vennor turned to Marianne as they greeted the last guest. He swung her about, feeling energised despite the demands of the day. 'Dancing with you is one step closer to my wedding night.' He kissed her, not caring who saw. People would have to get used to seeing such displays from him. He meant to love his wife every day of his life.

She moved against him, her skirts indecently close to his trousers, her smile hiding nothing. 'I can hardly wait. The ball had seemed like such a good idea at the time, but now I wonder if it was. We might already be in bed otherwise,' she whispered mischievously. 'I can think of nothing but how I want to undress you, to stare at you in the candlelight and feed you strawberries in bed.'

'Hmmm. Great minds think alike.' Vennor nipped at her ear. 'I was imagining the same, only I think mine involved drinking champagne from your navel.' He pulled her into an alcove and drew the curtain around them. 'I have a gift for you. Perhaps I should give it to you now, since we will be busy later tonight.' He gave her a wicked grin and pulled an envelope from inside his coat.

'What is this?' She unfolded the paper and scanned it. 'It looks like a deed.' She read it and he delighted in watching her mouth make an O of surprise. 'You've bought the magazine?'

'Yes. M.R. Mannering can write whatever he or *she* pleases, whenever it pleases her. Perhaps I can even persuade the Duchess of Newlyn to lend a hand as editor-in-chief.'

'Oh, Vennor!' She threw her arms about his neck,

laughing loudly enough to make people beyond the curtain wonder what they were up to. Vennor didn't care. At last, after three years of being lost, he was found. Marianne was the beacon that had shown him the way home.

The orchestra was finished tuning up. He took Marianne's hand and kissed it. 'Shall we, my Duchess?'

They led out the first waltz, Marianne radiant in his arms. 'They're here, you know.' Marianne smiled up at him as he swept her into the opening steps. 'Your mother, your father. They are happy for you. The people we love are never far from us.'

Vennor smiled warmly and gestured for the Cornish Dukes to join them. The Dukes, their duchesses, their heirs with their wives, took to the floor with them and Vennor's heart was full as his friends sailed by, filled with their own joy. What a summer it had been! What a future it was going to be. Tomorrow he and Marianne would depart for their wedding trip to the ducal properties, with promises for all of them to reunite in Cornwall in late autumn. There would be babies to hold and visits to be made, and the way Marianne was looking at him right now as he swept her through the turn, they might just have an announcement of their own to make. He hoped so. He could hardly wait to be a father, a husband, a man of worth, as all the Cornish Dukes were.

* * * * *

If you enjoyed this story, be sure to read the first three books in The Cornish Dukes miniseries by Bronwyn Scott

The Secrets of Lord Lynford
The Passions of Lord Trevethow
The Temptations of Lord Tintagel